I
KNOW
WHO
YOU
WERE

I
KNOW
WHO
YOU
WERE

N.K. CURRAN

CONSTABLE

CONSTABLE

First published in Great Britain in 2023 by Constable

1 3 5 7 9 10 8 6 4 2

Copyright © Steven Savile, 2023

The moral right of the author has been asserted.

A CIP catalogue record for this book is available from the British Library.

ISBN: 978-1-40871-724-0

Typeset in Adobe Caslon Pro by Initial Typesetting Services, Edinburgh
Printed and bound in Great Britain by Clays Ltd, Elcograf S.p.A.

Papers used by Constable are from well-managed forests
and other responsible sources.

Constable
An imprint of
Little, Brown Book Group
Carmelite House
50 Victoria Embankment
London EC4Y 0DZ

An Hachette UK Company
www.hachette.co.uk

www.littlebrown.co.uk

*This one is for the survivors of that
Stamford Green School Trip.*

Into the wilds all those years ago . . .

Now

I gagged on a mouthful of brackish water.

The rain came down, tears of damnation from a blackhearted sky.

I stumbled deeper into the water.

On the bank, somewhere behind me, she howled at me, her words losing all shape beneath the wild wind. I wasn't listening. I didn't care. I had to get to them.

The storm had robbed the day of its last few hours, and the night threatened to rob me of everything I loved.

I ran until I couldn't run, stumbled until I couldn't stumble, and still I kept on going, plunging forward as a streak of lightning split the sky. Those blinding electric-blue forks froze the world around me. All the ugliness of it was trapped in the those tines, the stark angles and the contrast of deep shadow that gathered around the monster and the woman I loved, too far away to save.

I sank deeper into the water, fear flooding through my senses until the only thing I felt was cold. And still I kicked and swam and dragged myself on, deeper into the lake, still so far from the other side.

The rain lashed at the bleak landscape, hiding so much of it from me.

Shouting and sirens were muffled beneath the storm.

I swallowed water with every step I took.

I had to get there, to them, to the other side.

1

That was all I could think. The be all, the end all. I had to get to the other side.

I fought the water to haul myself forward, every step or stroke one little victory as my clothes tried to drag me under.

The water was up over my chest, in my face. The reek was rancid in my nostrils. The rain hammered at me, churning up the filth of the lake, getting in my eyes as I forced myself to half-stumble, half-swim on, always forwards, always deeper, until there was nothing beneath my feet to kick off from and I had no choice but to claw at the water, swimming for the thick reeds in the distance.

Searchlights overhead.

The chop of rotor blades cutting through the storm.

Even with the lake water clogging my ears, the noise was a tormented chorus.

I twisted my face to the side, trying to gulp down a breath and spit out the algae that clung to my lips before my mouth went back under the water.

I had no control over the next few minutes of my life, and with every desperate stroke I felt my strength being stolen away.

Every second hurt, but I wasn't going to let the lake beat me. I arched my back, like a salmon rising out of the water, blinking back the bitter sting of the rain as I struggled desperately to focus on where they'd been, Morven and the monster.

I saw him.

Not her.

He stared at me through the rain. His hands were under the water. The surface churned as though piranha were in a feeding frenzy around his legs. A slow smile crept across the face I'd come to hate, made more haunting by the searchlight as it found him again.

Sirens howled above the wind.

I heard them now. And I heard screaming.

I pulled the gun out of the waistband of my jeans. It was heavy in my hand; heavier than it had any right to be, as though the bullets inside it were already weighed down by the life they were destined to take.

Poppy was on his back, clawing at his face. Fighting for her life. My life.

In the madness of it all I heard voices crying out my name.

God, I was shaking.

Adrenaline flooded through my body.

Tremors shivered the length of my arm as I raised the gun.

My breath hitched in my throat.

My head swam.

I pulled the trigger . . .

LAST WEEK

ONE

I can't imagine having to make my entire life up.

Think about it.

The sheer amount of energy it would take is mind blowing.

We're this patchwork of life lived – all these random experiences that simply happen to us and around us. They dent us and shape us and eventually we become this person at the end of it. I'm not just talking about the big stuff either, the divorces and the broken hearts as well as the broken bones, or the whole nurture versus nature argument and how we're all products of our environment.

It's the stupid stuff that ends up defining who we are.

Like the fact I put the maple syrup on my plate before I put the pancakes down. It's a nothing detail, but I always do it the same way. I do it because I've always done it.

Then there's the stuff of our souls. I still listen to bands no one remembers because this girl that fourteen-year-old me was hopelessly in love with loved them. 'Love is a Wonderful Colour' is right up there at the top of my favourite songs with 'Love Will Tear Us Apart', just because she played them for me once and said they were the most beautiful songs she'd ever heard. She was over-the-top enthusiastic about everything, and it all came out of her in a breathless rush. Funny though, I can't remember much more about her than the fact she loved a couple of songs I've carried with me through my life. I couldn't draw a picture of her to save my life. The one in my mind is a cobbled together montage of false memories and people I've fancied in the years since that somehow distilled to put a face to this perfect childhood crush that couldn't possibly be real.

Then there's Vicky, who sat cross-legged on the floor, earnestly telling me why some other singer was the greatest vocalist of our age just a few months before she killed herself and guaranteed I can never listen to his voice without crying my eyes out.

I remember rushing out onto the dance floor as the first notes of R.E.M.'s 'The One I Love' came through the speakers, and how I was absolutely in love with this curly haired blond, Julie, who broke my heart by sleeping with my best friend, and for all the pain that came with that, I can't remember her surname.

But there's no getting away from how they chipped a bit off the shape of my soul and left me closer to being me than I was before I met them.

And then there's the physical reminders we carry, like the inch-long scar above my left eye where Sasha slammed the door when we were fooling about and I ran right into the sharp edge and split my head wide open to howls of laughter from her; or the two-inch-long ridge of gristle on my arse where I fell out of that tree and the memories that were attached to that little humiliation, the team of student nurses watching fourteen-year-old me with my jeans and pants around my ankles, bent over as the doc practiced her macramé on my tender parts.

Let's be honest, this stuff's not even scratching the surface.

It's not stuff I ever have to *think* about, it's just there.

Like being nine years old and sitting on a street corner breaking my heart because dad had just said he was going away and I might never see him again.

The idea of trying to dream it all up like some immense

forty-nine-year-long fiction of *me* is exhausting, now try to imagine keeping it up, living the made-up life day after day after day without getting caught in the lie, that's the real twisted genius of it.

I really don't know how the stranger lying beside me in bed that morning had pulled it off for the best part of the sixteen years we'd been together, but she had.

TWO

Morven rolled over, up onto one elbow and smiled that smile that always got me.

I'm a lucky man. I'm more in love with her today than I've ever been, and I wake up every morning safe in the knowledge that I'm going to be even more in love tomorrow and tomorrow and tomorrow.

She's a morning person. I'm not. I tend to sit up well into the night knowing I should just drag my arse up to bed but unwilling to actually do it. I pretend it's about creativity, and these hours somehow being more sacred, in tune with the rhythms of the universe. It's all so much bullshit and we both know it, but she never calls me out on my need to sit up and watch crap TV shows in the name of research. Come morning I'm bleary eyed and shuffle around the place like an extra from The Walking Dead. Not Morven, she's one of those monsters who leaps out from beneath the covers in a single bound, like some shiny happy superhero.

That smile, though. . .

If you'd have asked me at that moment, I would have told you I was lying beside the one person in the world I knew better than myself. It's funny how a single day can make a liar out of the best of us.

She kissed me good morning, the lingering spices of last night's jalfrezi on her tongue, and ran her finger through the tangle of my hair, nails dragging lightly across my scalp.

It was all just normal life. There was nothing remarkable about it. Nothing that said this would be the last time. I don't know if I would have savoured it more if I'd known that, if I would have tried to burn the sensation of her touch into my skin or the taste of her sweat onto my tongue, committing every inch of her skin to a Braille memory, or if I would have taken it for granted anyway, because I'm basically an idiot? Probably the latter, if I'm being honest. I don't want to admit how many things I've promised myself at the time I'd never forget that are long since consigned to the dustiest corners of my mind, while I can quote you the lyrics of every Postcard or Kitchenware record verbatim. It's just the way I am.

The kiss became another, and that second kiss became a third, as Morven persevered dragging me out of my coma with her lips. I make a pretty lousy Sleeping Beauty, but she was 100 per cent committed to her role as handsome prince so there was no way I was sleeping the day away.

The clock radio perked up, the deejay deciding I was the 'Only Living Boy in New Cross' which felt about right, all things considered, as Morven guided me inside and for a few minutes longer life was normal.

God, I miss normal.

After, while she showered, I went down to make breakfast. We have never been the kind of partners who climb into the shower together, but more often than not we'd leave love notes for each other in the glass for the steam to reveal, sometimes hours, sometimes a day later. It was a nice little relationship shorthand. Something we'd done for years.

First things first, I put some noise on. The deejay had given way to Traffic and Weather. I shuffled around, fixing the coffee first. It's all very ritualistic. Every morning it's exactly the same, milk from the fridge into the centrifugal frother, power up the espresso machine, empty the drip tray, grind the fresh beans and then use the three-minute lag while the milk warms and froths to sort out the muesli and fresh berries compote and drown it in Skyr, this Icelandic yoghurt that tastes nothing like yoghurt. Little rituals.

Morven came down, dragging Popsicle with her. Poppy takes after me. She has this thing where she refuses to get out of bed, so Morven ends up dressing her while she's still in her pit, one foot at a time, sock, sock then underwear, then skirt as the school uniform materialises around her tiny frame, and all the while she's still under the blankets. It's a skill. Once she's up, that's a different story. Then it's Hurricane Pops and heaven help anyone caught up in her storm.

We're not the most talkative family over breakfast, but unlike my own dad I've never been the kind of parent who hides behind the sports page and grunts a few sounds in answer to the yammering of his offspring. 'So, what have you got this morning?'

'Double Maths and English,' which sounded nightmarish until you realised it was basically another way of saying guided play, because luckily for Pops she was still a few years away from the nightmare of algebra and quads, and the notion of the Oxford comma was every bit as mythical as Puff the Magic Dragon.

'But that means you have gym this afternoon, right?' I said, proving that I paid attention now and then. 'So, it's not *all* bad.'

Poppy looked at me like I'd just threatened to torture her teddy bear.

Morven just shook her head and refilled my coffee cup.

Sometimes I felt like a rose between two thorns.

'How about you?' I asked Morven, earning a shake of the head and look that proved I didn't pay anywhere near enough attention while I was busy patting myself on the back for remembering gym was on the timetable. Ah the swings and roundabouts of a cluttered mind. I offered a wry smile. If in doubt, try and cute it out.

'Are you going to remember to feed yourself without me around?'

'Ah.'

'Yeah, *ah*. You remember now?'

'Of course. Fancy three-day corporate retreat, outward bounds, hiking, zip wires and trust exercises in the New Forest. All very Bear Grylls while me and madam here pine over the mum-shaped hole in our lives.'

'That's the one. I'll try not to enjoy myself *too* much.'

'Okay, so, what do we want mum to bring us back from her trip?'

Poppy wrinkled her nose up, like it was a trick question. That was another thing she got from Morven, this incredible sincerity and seriousness in the way she looked at the world. Most kids would have been bouncing in their chair firing off a stream of bright shiny things as they leapt to mind, but not my little ray of sunshine. I could almost see the cogs grinding away as she tried to decide what she could live without as opposed to what she really wanted.

'Go finish getting ready for school while you think about it,' I suggested, which sent her racing off up the stairs to stuff her duffle bag full of whatever mysteries nine-year-old girls needed to survive the school day.

Morven kissed me on the top of the head, then reached around my neck to run her fingers across my chest. 'Can you do the school run this morning?'

'I'm wise to your ways, woman,' I grinned, reaching up to close my hands over hers.

Little gestures of intimacy. Those are the things I remember most. Those are the things that cut the deepest.

'I'm sure you are, but I've got to pack. *Someone* kept me busy this morning.'

'I think that was entirely your fault, not that I'm complaining.'

'You'll miss me when I'm gone.'

Oh, how true.

I kissed her palm. 'Fear not, I'll get madam to school on time.'

THREE

We live in a narrow house in Shoreditch. It always amused me to call it that, given the fact that's an old nickname for a coffin. But it was true, at least from the front. The three of us could stand, arms outstretched, fingertip to fingertip, and reach across the entire width of the red brick façade. I love this part of London. It's a riot of colour. Nearly every wall around us is a work of art. There's a stork on one building, and evil eyes and lightning bolts on another, but Poppy's favourite is the giant panda head that dominates a black wall beside a message urging us to adore and endure each other, which, given the state of the world feels fairly prophetic.

I was always more fascinated by the train carriages threatening to plunge off the roof of the next building along, but that's me.

The endless creativity is inspiring.

Plus, everything smells so good in the morning. There's a small bakery that fills the air with the cinnamon, chocolate and vanilla, and a coffee roastery that is like a hit of pure caffeine as you walk beneath its high windows. The place has changed a lot in the ten years we've been living here. It isn't so much that it has gentrified as it has become this bohemian paradise in the heart of London, filled with brasseries and rooftop restaurants, artisan confectioners and microbreweries.

Poppy skipped along beside me, her little hand in mine.

We'd never intended for her to be an only child, but we were what they rather horrifically termed geriatric parents – even accounting for me being a couple of years older than her – and after two miscarriages in the two years after she was born, we reached the unspoken conclusion that Penny and Alice and our ideal world of three little girls filling the new house with laughter and life wasn't to be and we stopped trying. It wasn't a conscious thing, not at first at least. It had just been easier not to try than to deal with the ache of it, the fact that we were in bits, so we kept telling ourselves that even though all the bits weren't there we could put together the ones we had and make a good life for the three of us.

I walked her all the way to the school gates, ruffled her hair and marvelled at the fact she could race away across the playground without looking back once. Her home room teacher saw me and waved. I offered a nod in return. There were dozens of other parents up and down the street going through their own little rituals.

One of the joys of being a freelancer is not being tied to a desk. I decided I was going to do a couple of hours in this nice little café around the corner from the school and start in on my third cup of coffee of the day while I borrowed some free WiFi to research the piece I was playing with. Walking through the door I was rewarded with smiles from the pushchair mafia and took up one of the free tables near the window. I prefer the window seats. I like to watch the world go by while I pretend to work. It helps me to feel connected to the world.

'Hello stranger,' Maggie, the owner, said from behind the counter.

'Hey Maggs, how are you this fine morning?'

'Can't complain,' she told me in that rich Jamaican accent of hers as she busied about measuring out the Blue Mountain beans to grind. There were more than a dozen different bags on the shelf above the grinder, each one originating from some slope on the Blue Mountains, each one claiming to deliver the authentic flavour of Jamaican coffee.

12

She didn't bother asking me what I wanted because the order was the same every day. One day, I swore, I'd surprise her and mix it up, but not today. She came over with the latte and one of her thick homemade coconut Totos – though she pronounced it toeto, conjuring an extra vowel in there somehow. It was a simple cake of molasses and coconut but tasted exactly how I imagined island life would.

The aromas of Jamaican spices were infused into her skin like culinary perfume.

I took the laptop out of my bag and set it up on the small reclaimed-wood table. Part of it had been a railway sleeper in another life. The laptop chimed as I took my wireless ear buds and reading glasses out of my bag.

Ear buds in, the pushchair mafia disappeared into the background as Apple Music predicted my needs and wants for another day in the word mines, kicking it off with something random from the playlist. I'm big on playlists based on my mood, I've got work ones, walking ones, late-night-chill ones, all carefully curated to hit the right spot.

I hate being between projects. It's this weird limbo where I'm never sure what comes next. It needs to be more than just a good idea. The last one, a deep dive into the manipulations of social media on our children and the rise of teen suicide, had been picked up by Channel Four, which meant we'd get to eat for another six months. But there's the whole 'you're only as good as your last failure' aspect to it all; that dread-infused panic that this time the idea won't be good enough, or hard-hitting enough, or thought-provoking enough for anyone to give a shit about it and actually want to part with cold hard cash for.

I ended up wasting three hours getting nowhere, just copying and pasting reference images and article links into my notes and listening to a lot of Scottish '80s Indie Pop while I drank a fourth and fifth coffee of the day, taking me up to lunch. Music is important to me. I'm one of those people who measures out the key moments of my life by tune and can remember what song was playing when I lost my virginity, when I broke my elbow, when I first stumped up the nerve to ask Morven out, and so many other sliding doors moments of my life. It's why I tend to be fairly aware of the soundtrack of my life. The more obscure the better. I interviewed a guy from one of these bands a few years back, asking him if he'd ever been tempted to get in on the reunion circuit thing and cash in on the nostalgia boom. He'd just looked at me and laughed saying, 'Could you imagine the stench of failure on the tour bus?' I kind of liked that, the way something that felt fundamentally important to me could be nothing more than a bitter reminder of their failures to someone else.

I figured I'd walk home to the empty house and try and work out what we were going to do without Morven to keep us both in line. Okay, I'll admit it, I love these daddy daughter days where we get to pretend the world revolves around us.

FOUR

Morven had left her phone on the kitchen counter, still plugged into the wall.

I shook my head. Sometimes, I swear, that woman would forget her head if it wasn't screwed on. I figured I'd give her a few hours to get settled in, then call the hotel and give her some stick about it.

In the meantime, I put my laptop on charge, taking her phone out of the socket, and woke Siri up and got her to carry on working her way through the playlist as I made myself busy around the kitchen. I like to cook. I had ever since my dad had died six years ago. I'd been struggling and Morven had suggested I needed to find something I could just lose myself in. It was pretty good advice. Sometimes we just need a place to hide. I'd tried collecting old vinyl records, meaning there were about two thousand of them taking up wall space. For a while it had been more like an addiction than a hobby, and every bit as hard to quit as the cigarettes were after those two weeks back when I was fourteen.

There was something about cooking that was cathartic. I got to lose myself in the precision of the recipes, the exacting timings and trying to decipher the chemistry of flavours. And it worked, to a degree. We ate better, and after six months the grief was less all-consuming.

I ended up making three days' worth of meals to a soundtrack of my youth. I put them in the freezer before I went to check the details of the hotel that Morven had pinned up on the fridge door.

I hushed Siri and called through.

The receptionist picked up on the third ring, all bright and breezy. She was having a good day and she really hoped her infectious enthusiasm could spread down the phone. 'Hi,' I said, nowhere near her level of perky. 'Could you put me through to Morven Kerr's room? It's her husband, Alex.'

'One moment, Mister Kerr.' I heard the flutter of keys, followed by, 'I'm sorry, sir, Mrs. Kerr hasn't checked in yet.' I checked the time. It was maybe two hours from our place to the New Forest. Three with traffic jams. She should have been in her room before lunch.

Two hours late wasn't anything to panic about.

Even so, I've got that creative brain which immediately hurtles off into the dark places. I was imagining the worst, a multiple car pile-up on the M3, mass fatalities south of Basingstoke. It was always the same. My mind went dark. I know why it happens. I can rationalise it. It's ingrained. One a.m., aged nineteen, someone came knocking on my dorm room door. I dragged myself out of bed and went down to the communal phone. I was shaking. I remember that. One a.m. phone calls are never good. Ever. But this one . . . my mum was in tears. She couldn't get any words out. My dad took the receiver off her. He wasn't much better. But he managed to tell me that my older brother Matt had been killed in an accident. He'd been coming home from Uni in Nottingham for Christmas. A long-distance lorry driver had fallen asleep at the wheel – only for a second or two, but long enough to go through the line of orange cones dividing the lanes of traffic around the roadworks, and straight into Matt's crappy little Fiesta. They told us he hadn't suffered, but I've never believed that. A spur of metal had torn free and lanced clean through his spine and out the other side. There had to be seconds . . . minutes even . . . when he felt his life bleeding out across the cheap seat fabric . . . so yeah, my mind always went there. Without fail. Scars.

'Are you sure?'

'It would appear several of her party are already checked in, but she's yet to join us, I'm afraid.'

'Okay, thanks. Could you let her know she's left her phone at home, but that doesn't mean Poppy's going to let her get away without saying goodnight come bedtime, no matter what damage your obstacle course does.'

'I'll make sure to pass that on,' she said, amused.

I went back to thinking about ways to keep food on the table and distract myself from worrying, then wandered back to make sure I was waiting outside the school gates when Poppy came skipping out less than thirty seconds after the bell had rung out across the playground. I don't know how she did it, but it was the same every day; she'd come racing across the spongy tarmac net-ball court, trailing her backpack behind her, and hurl herself into my arms like she hadn't seen me for a month. We spun around, her legs flying out behind her as she giggled, and then I plonked her down on the ground again and we set off back to the house, Poppy skipping, me trudging. Thinking. And hating myself for it.

I knew something was wrong before I set foot inside the door.

FIVE

There was glass scattered across the welcome mat, and a little way down the hall, half a brick.

'Stay there,' I told Poppy, my hand across her chest.

My mind raced. It's London. Shit happens. Bricks get put through windows, walls get graffitied, cars get torched. It didn't have to mean anything more than that. But it was the second time it had happened to us in less than a month. My skin crawled as the glass crunched underfoot. I could still smell the lingering fragrances of the food, like a ghost that had remained long beyond its last breath, unable to let go. I crouched down beside the half-brick. There was a powdered white corner, but otherwise nothing remarkable about it. A prank. Probably. I mean, not a funny one. But not targeted violence. Even so, I closed my fingers around it, and walked from room to room, ready to use it like a cosh if I had to.

Everything was just as I'd left it.

There is nothing stranger than walking through your own house dreading that you're not alone in there. That old chestnut about your heart hammering? It was as though it had stolen a pneumatic drill and was splitting a way out through my ribs.

I double-checked upstairs before I let Poppy into the house.

We bolted the door behind us. 'Go and change out of your uniform, kiddo,' I told her. 'I've got to call someone to fix the window.'

For once there were no smart-arse comments. She sprinted up the stairs two at a time and slammed her door behind her, Hurricane Poppy in full force.

I still had the guy we'd used the last time in my recent call list, so I hit redial and fifteen minutes later he was pulling up outside in a canary yellow van, panes of glass strapped to the side.

'We're going to have to stop meeting like this, people will talk.'

'Yup, becoming a bit of a habit, this,' he joked along with me, and set about unloading.

I left him to work on the window.

Poppy still hadn't come down, but that was fine. She had a TV in her room, and enough stuff up there to keep her distracted through the end of civilisation as we know it.

I checked the phone to make sure I hadn't missed any calls from Morven and decided to give the hotel another shot.

'I'm sorry, she still hasn't checked in,' the same receptionist said, less perky this time. I think she was getting as worried as I was, but she had a rational explanation. 'I'm sure she's just gone to join in with the afternoon's activities and will come back to get the room key later. Lots of guests end up doing that if they're running late.'

Of course that was what she'd do.

'Can you get her to call me as soon as she checks in?'

'Of course. And if I see any of her party, I'll be sure to pass the message you're trying to get in touch.'

'Thanks, I really appreciate this.'

'No problem.'

She hung up after telling me to have a nice afternoon and not to worry.

But of course I was going to worry.

I checked Morven's phone. As the screen woke the message, *I know who you were* appeared in the little green message bubble over Poppy's grinning face. There was chocolate fudge sauce smeared across her smile. Normally it melted my heart. This time I couldn't see past the words.

I know who you were.

What the hell was that supposed to mean?

I didn't recognise the number that had sent it, and without Morven's face I couldn't get beyond the lock-screen to see if there was anything beneath the opening line. It wasn't like I could hack into the thing. I'm not a technophobe. I use this stuff every day, and have an interest, but there's a difference between an interest and the skills it demands to really know how all of this stuff works, and more importantly how to crack it.

The glazier called through that he was done and asked where I wanted the broken glass. It had only taken him ten minutes to pin in the new pane and seal it. 'I'll clean up, don't worry,' I assured him, coming to the door with a dustpan and brush in my hands.

'I'll go get the card reader from the van,' he said, and was back on the doorstep before I had got off my hands and knees, holding out the card reader. A tap on the screen and five keystrokes and my bank account was a couple of hundred quid lighter. Technology.

I thanked him and locked up.

It still wasn't four o'clock. Poppy would be engrossed in her cartoons. I wasn't about to try Morven's hotel again. They'd block my number if I kept harassing the poor woman on the desk, so I decided to go for the next least sane option and hit the internet, looking for traffic and accident reports between Shoreditch and the New Forest. I'm not too far gone to admit that way lies madness. It didn't stop me. I scrolled through crash reports dating back months, and in some cases years, trying to find anything happening right there and then. I wasn't 100 per cent sure what route she would have taken, so, using Google Maps I tried a few of the alternatives and noticed that they'd got a little icon that indicated delays so held the cursor over them one after the other, bringing up the details. Technology. This kind of thing was unthinkable when I was a kid.

I put Morven's name in the search bar and brought up a bunch of hits that had nothing to do with her. Morven was one of the few people I knew who hadn't bought into the whole social media thing. She didn't have a Facebook page, no Instagram, no Twitter. She didn't use TikTok or Snapchat. I used to tease her about it, right up until the time I started researching the teen suicide documentary and began to see the damage we were doing to our kids, feeding them with this obsessive need to become internet famous. I wasn't surprised that I couldn't find anything. She was an anomaly in this day and age. I mean, when the urge hits to look up an ex or go and try to find an old school friend, there's always something. No one is truly invisible unless they are dead, and even then, you come across obituaries, memorials, memories and social media posts all about being seen to mourn in public. I wasted half an hour going round in circles, and then, out of curiosity, did something I'd never done:

I put her maiden name into the search engine.

SIX

Morven Muir.

It wasn't like I expected to find anything interesting. It was a pretty weird name though, not generic, so maybe it would turn up a few hits that had nothing to do with anyone famous who shared either of her names. I tried refining the search with stuff like her school, her university, other stuff we'd talked about over the years. I mean, she was the one person in this world whose life I knew inside out.

And I still couldn't find her.

Not even a mention on someone else's online diary.

It was starting to freak me out.

Half an hour became an hour, and our little Popsicle came stomping down the stairs ready to be fed, so I set stuff aside, while she laid the table and I warmed up the food.

While we were eating, I had an idea. I'd been thinking about how much easier it would have been if that old website Friends Reunited had still been around, because that used to have class lists for different schools and school years, so all you had to do was visit the school's page and you could search by year and class lists, find the names of classmates and teachers and often links to reminiscences that told their own stories.

But just because a website was dead didn't mean you couldn't dig through it. That was one of the secrets of the internet, nothing truly disappears. Not really. There are places like the Wayback Machine that cache everything that has ever been put out there. The trick is knowing where to look. And how.

While we were doing the dishes, me washing, Poppy wiping, I started to think about where, exactly, I wanted to look. It was all displacement activity, obviously. If I didn't have something to occupy my mind, I'd only end up worrying. And if I ended up worrying, I'd spiral, which wasn't going to do anyone any good.

It wasn't like it was going to do anything apart from satisfy my curiosity to see photos of her at school. I'd heard stories, of course. It was all very St Trinians. A convent in Edinburgh that had closed down a few years back when the nuns got too old to run it. There were plenty of photos online, loads with links to Facebook profiles with the girls in them all grown up now and prefacing each with a variant of the 'Oh my God, can you remember when. . .?' caption. I didn't recognise any of the names from Morven's stories but given the thousands of girls who had gone through those cast iron gates to be broken by the nuns it didn't mean they weren't there, only that I'd barely scratched the surface. As with every story I researched, it came down to the same thing, going deeper.

So, I dug.

The Wayback Machine didn't help as much as I might have hoped, beyond offering a few names I could scour social media for, that would have been around Morven's age.

I didn't see her on any of the class lists, and in another half an hour of searching, her grinning face didn't turn up once in any of the old black and whites and grainy Kodak scans I managed to find.

'Your mum's a ghost,' I told Poppy, but she had much more interesting things to do than listen to me.

The landline rang. No one ever used the landline. I'm not even sure why we still had it. Probably for the cold callers.

Smiling, I pushed back the chair and went to answer.

'Hey you,' I said, expecting to hear Morven laughing in my ear at the ridiculousness of it all.

'Is that Alex?' It was a man's voice. I knew I should have recognised it, but I was blanking on a name.

I couldn't keep the edge of worry from creeping into my voice as I said, 'Yep.'

'It's Jace,' Jace. Of course. Jason Nolan. Morven's line manager.

'Hey Jace, dare I ask what you've done with my wife?'

'I was about to ask you the same thing, mate.' He was a Northerner. Everyone was his mate. 'She didn't turn up at the event today. No one has heard from her all day.'

'Please tell me you're fucking with me.'

'Sorry.'

I looked over at Poppy and saw her smiling up at me from where she was colouring cross-legged on the floor in front of the fire. I needed to stay calm for her sake, keep my voice nice and normal and not freak the fuck out. 'Okay, thanks for letting me know. I'll try a few friends.'

'Hope you track her down soon.'

'Me too,' I killed the call, and put the landline back in the cradle on the wall.

'Who was that?'

'A friend of mum's from work,' I said, not exactly lying.

'Oh,' she said. Nothing more curious than that. I said a silent thank you to whichever god watched over stay-at-home dads and let her get back to her colouring book.

I kept thinking about that message I'd seen on Morven's phone: *I know who you were.*

I checked it again.

There were no new messages, no missed calls.

'I've got to go and do a bit a work for a few minutes. Will you be okay down here?'

'Aren't I always?' Poppy said, grinning up at me.

'Okay, try not to burn the house down while I'm upstairs.'

'That's my evil twin, not me.'

'Ah, right, well keep twinny under control then.'

'Will do.'

I went up to my study, which was a grand name for the box room. Books were piled floor to ceiling. There were posters of some of my favourite movies on the walls, including *Duck Soup* and *Diary of a Lost Girl*, not that you could see any of them for the mess. The desk was cluttered with research materials, most of it useless. I hardly ever worked in here. I couldn't tell you why. I powered up the main computer and started searching for ways to get into an iPhone without knowing the passcode. It didn't take long to find a bunch of alternatives that offered less than legal ways to circumvent the security, but before I paid for any of them, I went out to the landing and shouted down to Poppy, 'Do you know the code for mum's phone?'

'My birthday,' she shouted back.

Of course.

Meaningful numbers. No matter how intelligent we might be, we almost always pick significant numbers.

I tapped in the six digits and was rewarded with the home screen. The first thing I did was check the *I know who you were* message to see if there was any more to it. There was. That same message had been arriving at the same time every day for the last week. The further I scrolled back, the more threatening those five words began to feel.

I couldn't understand why Morven hadn't mentioned the texts.

I jotted down the number, but a reverse-directory look-up online offered nothing, likewise the couple of open-source intelligence tools drew a blank, suggesting the number was a fake.

One of the things I'd learned doing that teen suicide documentary was how easy it was to get disposable phone numbers online, using burner phone apps. There were even listings in the app store. It made sense, as a single woman you'd want to protect your phone number on dating sites and places like eBay, so being able to create these fake numbers at a touch of a button that disappeared when you wanted them to disappear was a godsend. But they played a massive part in online bullying too, and in a handful of cases had driven the recipients to suicide while shielding the identity of their tormentors.

One thing I remembered was that these fake numbers often began with the same double-digit code. I double checked it, confirming my suspicions that these mails were from a disposable account.

The police had more sophisticated checks they could do, but even so, if the person behind the threats was smart, they were looking for a needle in a digital haystack.

I was resisting making the call I knew I had to make, but could only hold off for so long.

I dialled and waited for the emergency services operator to ask me what service I required. I knew there was no point going into any detail with her, so I simply said, 'Police. Missing Persons.'

She told me to stay on the line as she put me through to the Missing Persons Unit.

I explained the situation to an officer, who told me, 'I'm going to need you to do a few things for me, Alex. First, I want you to go through the house, make sure Morven hasn't left you any sort of note or clue that might help us work out where she is. Make sure there isn't a voicemail or email.' I was nodding along. 'Then I want you to call around family and friends, make sure she isn't with them. Can you do that for me?'

'Sure.'

'Some people find it useful to use a notebook to write down everything they've done, step by step, including everyone they contact, who they can't get through to. It can help to break things down into manageable tasks.'

'Do I need to call the hospitals?'

'No, it's fine. We will take care of that side of things. I'm going to take some details from you, then I'll send a couple of officers round to go through things with you.'

The next couple of minutes were filled with the kind of numb dread that for most of my adult life I've worried was waiting around the next happy corner. I gave the officer a description of Morven, height, hair, eye colour, anything I could think of in terms of distinctive features or distinguishing marks that might help identify her. I knew one key word was missing from that sentence: *body*. That might help to identify her body.

'This last question is going to be hard, but I need you to be honest with me, Alex. Do you know if Morven was suffering any sort of depression, or if she's ever considered suicide?'

I said 'No,' far too quickly for her liking.

'I know it's not nice to think about, but we really do need to know if she's at risk of self-harm. If there's been anything out of the ordinary or suspicious—'

'There is something . . . I don't know how relevant it is, but I found a message on her phone. It doesn't seem like much. All it says is: *I know who you were.* But she's been sent the same message several times over the last week or so.'

'So, you think she's being harassed?'

'I'm not sure what to think. If you'd asked me when I kissed her goodbye this morning, I would have told you we have a perfect life. I mean, I know there's no such thing, but . . .' I trailed off.

'Okay, this is good, Alex. Now, I want you to make that list and start going through those calls.' She kept saying my name, reinforcing the link like a hostage negotiator. 'The officers will be with you shortly. I know it's easier said than done but try not to worry. The truth is most people are back home within 48 hours.'

But those weren't the ones I was worrying about. I was more concerned with the few who didn't make it back.

SEVEN

It wasn't exactly Santa stuff, but I made a list and checked it twice before I made a single call.

I started out with family, then friends, which was so much harder because in so many ways we led separate lives. It wasn't like when we were fresh out of Uni and had this group we went clubbing with, or that group we hung out with on Sunday afternoons for barbecues in the park, or a few years later when it had become Mummy and Me friends and those old drinking friends had slipped back to acquaintances. We didn't have an address book, either. We had contacts lists in our phones and friends lists on social media – well at least I did. But friends that were just hers? It's not that she didn't have friends, more that she didn't keep them. I remembered a flatmate back when we were first dating, but for the life of me, now I needed to remember her name, I couldn't. There was the friend from that Uni reunion, whose face I could remember, and maybe that she'd been called Jenn, or Wrenn . . . something like that. The problem was, we'd grown older, and those friendships had faded to Christmas cards and then promises that we had to stay in touch, and then, ultimately, silence and a few distant memories. I wasn't good at this. Under pressure, other husbands would have been able to rattle off a list of twenty important people in their partner's lives; me, I could name everyone she worked with, and that was about it. And that freaked me the fuck out.

I transcribed the list of names from Morven's contacts. There were dozens I didn't recognise, but she never deleted any of them, so I'm pretty sure the guy who fixed our blocked drains nine years ago was in there right alongside the vicar who'd married us and the midwife who'd come to visit in those first few months post-Poppy-arrival. I didn't bother writing those names down. Then there were the workmates, but, of course, they were all at the retreat doing their team building. Thing is, I knew she hadn't gone to any of these people. And she didn't have anything back home to go to. Her life was here, with us.

I ended up with a list of forty names, more for the benefit of the Missing Persons liaison than out of any hope that one of them might offer up anything remotely useful. Then I started thinking about the difficult question – had she been feeling depressed or suicidal? Were there signs I'd missed? I mean, there weren't. She wasn't lying in bed late or complaining about feeling tired or down. No fatigue or exhaustion. She slept like the damned. There were no real changes in temperament, no shouting at Poppy when she dug her heels in. She was just Morven.

But once that possibility was inside my head it took root, festering, infecting every thought I had until I was picturing her having pulled over at the side of the road and walking to the middle of a suspension bridge before she clambered up onto the rails and stepped off the side into nothing. I even wrote the words Suspension Bridge on the list like they were a real possibility before I scratched a thick black line through them, scrubbing them out. There wasn't even a suspension bridge between Shoreditch and the New Forest. I hated my brain.

The doorbell sent Poppy tearing through the hallway in a mad rush to be first to answer the door.

I set my pen aside and went to show my face.

Two officers, plain clothed. One male, the other female. Judging by the body language the woman was in charge. Her partner seemed to defer to her, expecting her to be the one to lead in with the introductions. That could purely have been down to the psychology of the situation, the female officer taking the lead on a missing woman, the male on a missing man. 'Alex?' She asked, seeing me. I'm glad she hadn't led with Mr Kerr, though I couldn't have told you exactly why, beyond the fact that most days Mr Kerr still felt like my father, even though it was six years since he had gone. Maybe it was about stepping up and taking his place in the mortality line. 'I'm Detective Sergeant Ellie Underwood. This is my partner, Detective Constable Josh Morris. Is it okay if we come in?'

'Of course.'

I led them through to the lounge, offering them a seat and a coffee at the same time. Ellie declined, but Josh nodded his thanks, adding, 'Milk and two sugars would be grand.' So, I put the grinder to work, knowing I was doing this stupid distraction stuff to stop myself from having to face the reality of the next few minutes just a little longer.

They were happy to let me do it.

I guess that was all part of managing me. The last thing anyone needed was the husband going off the deep end. It wouldn't help them, and it certainly wouldn't help me in their eyes, and soon enough that was going to become important. I knew that, even if I didn't want to think about it. They always look at the husband. I don't even know what the figures are for domestic abuse, only that they are right to look there more times than not.

I put the coffees on the table but didn't touch mine. I'd already had more than was healthy.

'Okay, Alex, obviously we've got all the stuff you told the officer when you called in, but how about you talk us through it?' Ellie suggested. Calm. Easy. Affable. 'And don't worry, we're not looking to trip you up. Josh isn't going to leap up in a second and yell *ah ha!* if there's a discrepancy in the story,' her smile was gentle. She was good at this. Calm. Looking across the table at her I could feel the compassion and the sense that if we stuck together, we'd come through just fine even if she wasn't about to make any such promises. I'd watched enough TV to know you never promised what you couldn't be absolutely sure you could deliver. 'It's just helpful if we hear it for ourselves, helps us get a feel for your situation and for who Morven is as a person. If we get to know her through your eyes, maybe we can work out what's happened. It's all about getting her home.'

I nodded. 'I'm not sure how much help I'm going to be, but I'll try. It's just . . .' I raised a hand to the side of my head, miming my confusion. Ellie nodded sympathetically.

'Anything different about today?' Her colleague asked. 'Anything strike you as out of the ordinary? Was Morven acting strangely?'

'No, no and no,' I said, shaking my head. 'I feel like I'm being so difficult, but you've got to understand, we're just boring people. Pretty normal, I guess. We've got our routines, like everyone else. Most of ours revolve around Poppy, taking her to school picking her up from school, taking her to ballet, picking her up from ballet, after school classes, dropping her off at friends' houses . . . you know what it's like . . . She's nine. She takes up a lot of life.'

Ellie nodded along. More shared empathy. It couldn't be easy, walking into a stranger's house at the worst moment in his life and not making him feel like he was under suspicion while trying to get him to open up. 'And today?'

'More of the same. I did the school run because Morven had to pack. She had some work thing, a team building weekend at one of those trendy corporate retreats in the New Forest.'

'You have the details?'

'On the kitchen counter with the list of numbers I was asked to put together.'

Ellie nodded again. 'That's great. You have no idea how helpful that will be. What car was she driving?'

'I already told—' I stopped myself, took a deep breath. Apologised. 'Sorry.' I shook my head. 'She's got the Golf. We've only got the one car.'

Ellie confirmed the registration with me. 'So, you said your goodbyes, took Poppy to school, and that was the last time you saw your wife?' No matter how gently Josh tried to say it, or dance around the missing word he left off the end of the question, my mind was more than happy to fill in the blank: *alive*.

I nodded again. I was starting to feel like one of those bobble-heads.

'When did you realise something was wrong?'

'I didn't. Not really. I went to the café to do some work for a few hours, then came home to do some cooking, setting me and Popsicle up for the weekend. That was when I realised she'd left her phone.'

'Does she do that a lot?'

'No. Not really. I mean, she's not scatter-brained, she's the glue that keeps the family together. But you need to know Morven. Sometimes it feels like she's wilfully living in a world that stopped existing twenty years ago, you know? I tease her for it, but I love her for it, too. She's not on social media, she's not snapping hundreds of photos of her lunch for Instagram or sharing bullshit inspirational quotes on Twitter. As far as she's concerned the phone's a tool for her convenience. So, she can reach us if she needs to. Not really the other way around.' Again, Ellie nodded along like it made perfect sense that a modern mother had no interest in the ways the world might bully her daughter into eating disorders, body dysmorphia or any of a thousand other torments. Okay, that was me projecting, given everything I'd seen during the process of putting the last couple of documentaries together. Maybe that was why it made perfect sense to me she wouldn't want to let that into our home?

'Okay, so you found her phone? What then?'

'I called through to the retreat, ready to tease her mercilessly, you know the kind of stuff, forgetting her head if it wasn't screwed on, only the receptionist said she hadn't arrived yet.'

'And this was?'

'Early afternoon, just after lunch, One-ish, I guess. I didn't think much of it, I mean there are a hundred reasons why she might be late getting there. She might have stopped off for food somewhere, taken a detour for whatever reason, got stuck in traffic or had to go back to the office first before she followed the others down. But you know how it is, you can't help thinking maybe there's been an accident, maybe something's happened.'

More nodding. 'It's only natural,' Ellie agreed. 'But it's counterproductive. What I can tell you now, and hopefully it will put your mind at ease, is that there have been no reports of major accidents along the route, and there's no one matching Morven's description in any of the hospitals.'

'That's something,' I said.

'It is,' she agreed. 'I want you to understand I have to ask this, Alex, I wouldn't be doing my job if I didn't. I'm not trying to be antagonistic or upset you, but is it possible she could be having an affair?'

Right up until that second it hadn't crossed my mind Morven could be cheating on us – because it would be us, not just me, it would be cheating on her family, and that wasn't Morven. It just wasn't.

I shook my head. I was about to say I would know, but how many other people thought that only to realise just how accomplished a liar they went to bed with every night? 'She's not screwing around behind my back,' I said, a little more vehemently than I'd intended. 'And before you ask how I can be sure, we're one of those annoying families, we spend every free minute together, doing stuff. Last weekend we went to the aquarium, we walked along the Thames and pointed out the different birds and told stories about the buildings. Then it was burgers and a visit to the Natural History Museum before we went to the movies. It's like that every weekend, we're in one of the museums, or visiting some market or just doing something together. It sounds stupid, but there just isn't time . . .' which sounded weak as far as rationalisations went, but it was the truth. There weren't enough hours in the day for a second relationship, or the energy to hide it, even if it was only a fuck every now and then on the side.

Ellie nodded. 'That's good. Is it okay if Josh has a look around, see if there's anything you might have missed? A note that's fallen behind the nightstand or something?'

'Knock yourself out.'

'Great, and while I'm thinking about it, we're going to need a recent photograph, and if you remember what she was wearing this morning, that would be helpful?'

'Sure, I've got about two thousand on my phone,' I promised. 'I'll text a couple over to you before you go.' I tried to remember what she'd been wearing when she came down for breakfast this morning. 'Clothes . . . I think jeans, this autumn rust jumper, like dying leaves, probably her New Balance given they were going to be messing about in the woods. I don't know what coat she took; she has about a hundred to choose from, but I can go through them, maybe one will stand out as missing.'

'That would be very helpful, Alex. I appreciate this can't be easy. It's not like you woke up this morning thinking I need to imprint this stuff on my brain.'

'No kidding.'

'Is she on any medication? Insulin? Anything like that? Any health issues we need to be aware of?'

I shook my head again. She made a note.

'And she wasn't depressed? No trouble at work? Nothing that could be weighing down on her?'

'Not that I know of,' I said. I resisted the temptation to add, but how can we know what's really going on inside someone else's head? That kind of thinking wasn't helpful. 'Like I said, it's all pretty normal. Nothing leaps out. But there was the message on the phone.'

That had her interest. She shifted in her seat, leaning forward, engaged. 'She was being threatened?'

I didn't say anything. Instead, I unlocked Morven's phone before handing it across to her.

Ellie Underwood scrolled through the message senders, fixing on the last one.

'I know who you were?'

I nodded.

'She got the same message half a dozen times in the last week. Once a day, every day, like clockwork. So, you tell me, is that a threat?'

'Sure looks like one,' Ellie agreed. 'It's enough of a coincidence to be a concern in the light of her disappearance. But let's not get ahead of ourselves. More often than not there's a perfectly rational explanation for something like this. Could she have gone to visit parents or friends along the way?'

'No,' I said. 'We're all the family she's got. Both of her parents are gone. Her dad died before we met. Her mum nearly ten years back. No brothers or sisters. Her friends are our friends.'

'Okay, what I'm going to need you to do is think about any meaningful places she might have gone, places that are important to her, or to both of you, and make me a list.' I didn't need to ask why. It was a process of elimination, if she hadn't had an accident, then she'd run, and if she'd run it made sense to check places she was likely to run to.

Running to?

Running from?

'I feel like I should be out there looking . . . doing something useful.'

'Trust me, Alex, you are exactly where you need to be, and you're doing everything you need to be doing.

There was a third alternative, of course; maybe she hadn't run at all, maybe she'd been taken.

EIGHT

Josh returned from his search, informing us, 'Passport's still here,' which was another thing that it had never occurred to me to even check. Why would it? She hadn't left me. This whole thing was turning my head inside out. I just felt so . . . helpless.

Even so, there was a momentary sense of relief that followed the confirmation Morven's passport was still in the drawer. It lasted right up until the second chime of the doorbell.

Ellie looked at me. 'Expecting anyone?'

I shook my head. 'Nope, and it's a bit late for Jehovah's,' I said, trying to be funny. I was already on my feet like Pavlov's dog answering its summons. I padded out to the door, thinking about the brick and the broken glass. I needed to tell them about that. It added to the seriousness of the threat.

I saw the silhouette of two figures, one taller and bulkier than the other, and assumed my joke had been on the money and a couple of God-botherers had chosen a bad time to come door-stepping with their Watchtowers. My atheist-sharpened excuses already on my lips, I opened the door on a man and a ghost.

'Hello, Alex,' the ghost said, like it wasn't nearly a decade since we'd sat across the table from each other in the little beachside café with the gulls trying to make off with scone crumbs while we talked about nothing and pretended to get to know each other. 'How are you?'

She was older, but she wore it well, making it hard to put an age on her. Ten years older than the last time I'd seen her, meaning she had to be getting on for seventy. That bit I could add up.

I shook my head; it was an involuntary reaction at this stage.

My whole world had stopped making sense.

How could Morven's dead mother be on the doorstep?

'Not as well as you, Nora, all things considered.'

The man with Nora was taller than me, hair close cropped, salt in his beard, neatly trimmed, with a boxer's nose and an uneven eyebrow that left him looking permanently confused as to why life kept beating him up. He had hard skin, like he lived out on wild Scottish islands where he was battered relentlessly by the north wind.

'Can we come in?'

'What's going on? I mean . . . seriously? What the fuck is going on? We buried you . . .'

'It's best if we do this inside, Alex. Please,' Nora said.

'Mr Kerr? I'm Malcolm Mason, I used to work with Nora in the Protected Persons Unit before she retired.'

My head was spinning.

I stepped aside to allow the ghost and the guy through, pointing towards the lounge. 'We're in there.' I closed the door behind them but didn't immediately follow. My entire life was spiralling out of control. I leaned back against the door trying to wrap my head around those three not-so-little words: *Protected Persons Unit*.

Morven disappeared.

Nora back from the dead?

A bunch of cops in my front room?

What the Holy hell was going on?

'Who is it?' Poppy called from the top of the stairs. I looked up to see her peering down at me.

I had no answers to give her.

'Just work,' I lied, glad that she was too young to remember what her grandma looked like. That was a conversation I wasn't ready to have. 'Go back to your room, kiddo.'

She nodded, satisfied that everything was fine. And why wouldn't it be, she was nine and her parents were immortal. Admittedly not as immortal as her gran. I almost laughed at the absurdity of that – slightly mad, hysterical laughter. That wouldn't have been good.

Blowing out my cheeks, I went back through to the doorway into the lounge. For once I fervently wished psychologists weren't full of shit and that doorway theory really was something, and by stepping through I could just forget everything that was inside my head right now. But there was no mental reset. I looked around the room at the faces looking back at me.

'Okay, does someone want to put me out of my misery?' I said, trying and failing to sound like I wasn't going out of my mind. 'I don't care who. Just one of you? Nora? Help me understand what the ever-loving fuck is going on. Please. I'm begging you.'

'I'll take this, if you don't mind?' Mason looked at the others but didn't wait for anyone to object to his taking charge. He repeated his introductions from the doorway, this time to Ellie Underwood and her partner, Josh. 'Malcolm Mason, Protective Persons Unit. I worked with Nora for several years. Alex, you should sit,' Mason said, which wasn't a good sign.

I looked at Ellie, wanting her to say something, but she looked as confused as I felt when I told her, 'This is Nora, Morven's mother.'

'But you said she was dead?'

I sat, literally right on the edge of the seat, clasped my hands and leaned forward, feeling myself begin to rock slightly as I waited for someone to put me out of my misery like I'd asked.

'Yeah . . . she was, or at least I thought she was. But I don't know much of anything, it seems.'

'Nora Flynn,' the older woman introduced herself to the room. 'I'm sorry to do this to you, Alex,' she said. 'Believe me. The last thing any of us wanted was this conversation, but all things considered, I know Morven better than anyone else having been her case worker since she was thirteen. Malcolm thought it was best I come in.'

'So, you're *not* her mother?' It was Josh, asking the question I'd already worked out the answer to.

Protected Persons Unit. Case worker. That pointed one way and only one way. I could see that Ellie and her partner were every bit as confused as to how quickly their missing persons case had escalated in a couple of minutes.

'No,' Nora confirmed.

'She's dead, isn't she?'

'We don't know that,' Malcolm Mason said, which was nowhere near as supportive as he'd intended it to be.

I closed my eyes, but I couldn't keep them closed and shut out the world, no matter how much I wanted to.

'We need to bring everyone up to speed or this could get very confusing if people just start asking random questions,' Mason continued. 'Nora, can you take it from here?'

'I don't know how much Morven has told you about her past,' Nora spoke to me, but she might as well have been speaking to the room. As she leaned forward a slice of grey hair fell across her eyes. She brushed it back with a hand. There were a couple of liver spots on the back. I was seeing this hyper-real version of the world, all of the minutiae blown up to the size of a cow. I started bouncing my toe off the floor, *tap tap tap*, in frantic Morse code, no doubt saying the *dead don't die* or *save her soul if you can't save mine*. 'The last time I spoke with her,' Nora continued, 'she'd told me she intended to tell you, that was why we met at the beach that day. She wanted you to know everything, but I cautioned her against it. I know you'd been together a long time, and it wasn't about proving your love or me not trusting you, honestly. I like you Alex, I always have, and Morven deserved to be happy. Maybe I was being selfish when I told her not to tell you, but I didn't want things to change, and the truth is they might have. The problem is, once the truth is out there, it can't be put back in the bottle. And if something happened between you and you knew who she was, she'd need to rebuild her life somewhere else, as someone else, all over again. I didn't think that was fair on her.'

'You're going to have to help me out here, Nora. I'm lost and everything you're saying is so . . . I don't know . . . I need something . . . Christ, I'm still trying to wrap my head around the fact you're here, not dead.'

'Retired,' she corrected, looking at me. Scratch that, looking *into* me, like she was trying to judge just how much she could tell me. 'And given everything we'd been through together, Morven's grief that day was absolutely real. It was like a death, which meant she could sell it. I've got clearance to tell you this much: when she was eighteen your wife was given a new identity – Morven Muir – and was subsequently relocated.' There was something in the way she said those words, *subsequently relocated*, that on any other day I would have picked up on. Not today. Not half out of my mind with worry. 'She got a new start, somewhere no one knew her, and where she wouldn't run the risk of being recognised by anyone from her old life. Everything about who she had been before that was sealed. The girl she had been effectively ceased to be. Including links to family. From that point on, I was all she had until she fell in love with you.'

I wanted to argue, to protest that she would have told me, but that we were here, going through this, was living proof that she wouldn't. I caught my gaze drifting towards one of the photos on the mantle, a family shot of me, Morven and Poppy, huddled up on the pebbles with wind-assisted Flock of Seagulls haircuts. I loved that photo. We just looked so bloody happy in it, us three against the world. Our little army of three.

I looked at Ellie Underwood for help here, then her partner, but could see they knew no more than I did.

41

'So . . . she's not Morven?'

She was. Of course she was. I'm rubbish at a lot of things, but my general comprehension of the English language is pretty good. Suddenly the whole social media aversion made a very different kind of sense. It wasn't that she didn't want to see stuff, it was that she couldn't risk someone from her past life seeing something and recognising her.

I couldn't begin to imagine how that must have felt, to live life looking over your shoulder all the time, permanently on edge, on the look out, dreading the moment someone called out your dead name in the street. No matter how much time had passed, there was still plenty about her that wouldn't have changed from when she was eighteen, not least her bone structure and her eyes, even if she'd aged.

My heart ached for her, but there was this weird feeling that I didn't know my wife at all – or at least that part of her. I thought of all the times we'd talked about stuff, the stupid stuff of life, and realised she'd been telling a made-up version of hers, and that was hard to wrap my head around. I mean, half a lifetime ago she'd suddenly become someone new and left the old her behind. How the hell did you do something like that? We're the sum of our parts. We're made up of our memories and experiences. And she'd lied about the foundation of hers. I knew she didn't like to talk about her childhood, or her family, but this took it to a whole other level.

The thing is, I was in shock. I hadn't even got to the part when I started to ask: *why*. That would come, it just wasn't my first instinct. I was too busy licking my own imagined wounds to worry beyond them. In retrospect, I should have caught the fact that Nora said she'd been with her since she was thirteen, not eighteen. That meant there were five years in there between whatever happened and the name change.

'She is.' Nora said. 'Of course she is. She's still your wife,

Alex. She's still Poppy's mum. She's everything you know she is. That's what we do here, we give people new lives. We give them a chance at being normal. You are her normal. Obviously, there are a number of protocols in place to ensure her new identity isn't compromised, but there's always a risk, even with someone like Morven.'

'Is she in some sort of witness protection?' I stopped clasping my hands and caught myself scratching at my chin. It was something I did when I was thinking. A tick. 'You're not going to tell me she testified against some Scottish mob boss or something, and that's why you are worried she's in trouble?'

'You're right, I'm not going to tell you that. Unfortunately, right now, I'm not at liberty to discuss specifics around her old identity,' Nora said. 'Not without her permission.'

'But you just told me she wanted me to know,' I looked to Mason. He was in charge here, so surely he could tell me more? He looked back, sympathetic but stony faced.

'That was then, Alex. And I said it was a bad idea. It's still a bad idea, but what I *can* tell you is why we're here.' I nodded, needing to know. Even one answer I could wrap my head around was better than nothing. 'As you'd expect, we have her name on a watchlist. We have people monitoring potential threat levels around her new life, watching social media platforms and the like to ensure no one is digging around in her past and linking it to her present. Of course, the more time passes, the more those protocols are downgraded until they are just there, working away silently in the background, unseen and un-thought about.'

I was nodding along like it all made perfect sense that my wife was the subject of this kind of surveillance.

'It means that we know when people start pushing at the edges of her new identity, internet searches, things like that.'

'That was me,' I said, putting two and two together. 'I was worried. She hadn't turned up at a work thing. I was thinking the worst. I'm guessing you know about my life, if you vetted me back then . . . you know what happened.'

Nora nodded sympathetically. 'We know.'

Mason said, 'And we know you filed a Missing Persons report, which is what brought the response team here,' a slight tilt of the head towards Ellie and Josh. 'That was flagged up to Protected Persons. It set all sorts of alarm bells ringing and wheels in motion, as you can imagine.'

Something occurred to me then, and I so desperately wanted it to be wrong. 'You wouldn't be telling me any of this if you didn't think she was at risk. You're worried.'

'Of course we are, Alex,' Mason said. 'This isn't a normal missing persons case, Morven is vulnerable. There's an instinctive fear that the worst-case scenario is in play here for us until we can make contact with her. As I'm sure you've already been told, there are no reports of accidents, and no one matching her description has been admitted into any hospital in any of the southern counties.'

'I know who you were,' I said then, reaching for Morven's phone. It made sense. 'She received the same text message half a dozen times in the last week. Once a day. Every day. I was just going through it with Ellie and Josh when you arrived. I know who you were. That's what it said. Not who you are. Were.' I unlocked the phone and handed it over for him to see the row of green bubbles all saying the same thing, their time stamps a day apart. 'That's not all of it. I came home tonight to find a brick through the window. It's linked, isn't it? She's in trouble.'

No one rushed to contradict me.

'That's our fear, yes. The thing is, she knows to reach out to us if she thinks her identity has been compromised. We have contingencies in place to relocate her and start again, a whole new life. She hasn't done that. She's been living like this for a long time, we need to trust her and not get ahead of ourselves even if our every instinct is to panic.' I nodded.

'In terms of what happens now,' Ellie said, looking to Mason for confirmation, 'Nothing's really changed, we still need to go through that list of significant places and people. They're our best option right now if she's turned to someone for help.'

'We're creatures of habit,' Josh agreed. 'We take comfort in the familiar, even when we're in the grip of fight or flight instincts.'

'They're right,' Mason agreed. 'Right now, you're our best hope of finding her, because you know her.'

'I'm going to stay here with you tonight,' Nora said. 'We're going to need to talk, think, remember. Okay?'

I nodded yet again, but I was looking at Ellie Underwood and her partner. 'This changes everything, doesn't it?'

'Absolutely. As of this second Morven is priority one. We'll find her, Alex. But I need you to understand we will have to treat this as a possible abduction. That doesn't mean we think she's been taken, but until we know different that's how we have to think. We'll liaise with the PPU. We'll have people hit the ground along the route to the New Forest, we'll scrub the ANPR footage along the road,' she caught my confusion. 'Automatic number plate recognition.' It was used to check for speeding, logging the license plates. It also meant they could map out a route any particular car took, assuming there were ANPR cameras in place along the way. It would give us breadcrumbs to follow through the woods. 'The thing is, it's old-fashioned police work that solves stuff like this more often than not, Alex. Feet on the street. We're going to need that photo so we can canvas the service stations. There are people who drive these routes regularly. Someone will have seen something. We'll bring her home.'

'If she wants to be found,' I said, thinking about the fact she'd left her phone behind. It wasn't some momentary forgetfulness. Morven had chosen to leave it behind because she knew it could be used to find her. 'What about credit cards? If she's running, she'll have to use them, won't she? To pay for a bed. Food.'

45

'Absolutely. We'll run all of that stuff. It's rare there's ever a single revelation that screams *look here, here's the answer you're looking for.* It's all about putting the pieces together to build a bigger picture,' Ellie assured me. Mason nodded his agreement. It was somehow reassuring to know they were both coming at it from the same angle. 'This is what we do. I want you to make me a promise, Alex. I want you to promise me you won't do anything stupid. I don't want to be worrying about you driving around the streets at night, falling asleep at the wheel and ending up dead in a ditch somewhere. Okay? I know every nerve and fibre is going to rail against sitting still and doing nothing, but right now nothing is the very best thing you can do. Look after your little girl. Be here. This is going to be our base of operations. And before you shake your head, remember, it's where Morven will look for *you*. We'll arrange for a Family Liaison Officer to come here. They'll help guide you through all of this and answer any questions you might have. Anything they don't know, they'll find out. I promise you.'

Before Mason, Ellie and Josh left, I said, 'I've got a question, but you're not going to be able to answer it.'

'Ask it anyway.'

'Who is she? I mean who am I married to?'

NINE

The next few hours were a blur of fruitless phone calls. I worked my way down the list, all the while trying to think of places, like the photograph of us all in the front room, where we'd been happy, where there might be an anchor or something to draw her there if she needed to run. I kept turning up blanks. I wanted to scream at Nora, who had stayed, that she knew better than me where Morven would run, because she really knew her, but that was just me being churlish, so I bit my tongue.

No one had seen her.

She hadn't been in touch.

I wracked my brain for more significant places and kept coming up with utterly insignificant ones.

It didn't take long to realise how small our lives really were. By the time I'd reached the bottom of the list, using Nora's mobile to keep mine and the main land line free, I'd run out of ways to ask if the voice on the other end of the line knew where my wife was without sounding broken, sure she was lying dead in a ditch somewhere along the motorway, accident report or no accident report. It was killing me.

The Family Liaison Officer, Olivia, turned up just after midnight. It's a terrifying thing, the doorbell going after midnight. It can never be the bearer of glad tidings at that time of night. It's a death call. A tragedy call. Its grief walked up to your door demanding to be let inside.

She came in, took her coat off and did the most British thing ever, putting the kettle on while I went up to check on Poppy again. She was flat out. That girl of mine could sleep through anything. I'd gone up earlier to tuck her in and explained away the presence of everyone downstairs as a meeting about my new film. Poppy just rolled with it, gave me a sleepy kiss and closed her eyes again. As an excuse, it would last for a little while, but she was a curious kid, she'd be eavesdropping soon enough, trying to work out what we were talking about, so it wouldn't last forever.

Forever.

A shiver chased down the ladder of my spine at the thought of going through all of this again tomorrow, the day after and the day after.

I padded back downstairs to join Olivia in the kitchen.

It was such an innocuous gesture. A nice cuppa made everything a little better.

I guess that was the baseline for building a relationship of trust. I took the offered cup but didn't drink it. Morven was the tea drinker in the family.

Olivia sat at the table across from us and walked me through her role.

I didn't catch her surname at the door when she'd introduced herself, it had been something Portuguese or Spanish maybe, but I was guessing based on her complexion and we'd already reached the point where I was too embarrassed to ask her to repeat it. I needn't have worried. She gave me a card with her details on it – Olivia Mendes – and impressed just how important it was for me to call her if I thought of anything. I put the card in my wallet.

I'd assumed her role would primarily be to walk me through the coming days, and make sure I knew what support was available for us, as well as acting as a single point of contact between the Protected Persons Unit, Missing Persons and the rest of the search, but long before the tea was cold in the cup, I'd reassessed

48

that. What felt like getting-to-know-you questions were her building a profile of who Morven was, and who we were as a family. She was good. Likeable, like Ellie Underwood. But the last thing I wanted to do was sit around talking about happy memories. Nora was right to worry about me – I was itching to be out there doing something. Searching.

I'd sorted out a bunch of recent photographs for Ellie and given them Morven's phone to take away and run tests on – I assume looking for more threats, but also looking at the GPS tracker in the fitness app and other stuff that could help build up a more complete picture of her last week and everything that had happened since the first 'I know who you were' arrived.

When it was obvious nothing else was going to happen for a while, Nora told me to try and get some sleep. Trying entailed lying in bed staring up at the ceiling and watching the shadows from the trees outside box each other on the canvas of white paint. It didn't take long for them to become more than shadows, developing a Rorschach quality that became deeply uncomfortable as the minutes stretched on with nothing but those shadow-shapes and my fears to occupy my mind.

I heard a phone ring in the middle of the night, answered after one signal.

I lay there in the dark, trying to listen and hearing nothing beyond the muted mumble of words.

I gave up and got out of bed, pulled on a pair of jeans and tee-shirt and headed downstairs.

Oliva didn't seem surprised to see me.

'I heard the phone?'

'They've found Morven's car.' *But not her.* That was the inference. It took the wind out of my sails, a proper gut punch. If she wasn't in the car, where was she? 'It's been abandoned a few miles from the Fleet Service Station on the M3.'

Abandoned.

Fleet was just south of Farnborough. She'd barely made it outside of London.

Before I could ask, Olivia said, 'There's no sign of her.'

I was reaching for my jumper from the back of the chair and putting it on before she could ask what I was thinking. Truth was, I wasn't thinking. If Morven was out there, alone, on foot, she needed me.

'Were there any signs of struggle?'

My mind was racing.

'Not that I'm aware.'

Which would mean Morven willingly ditched the car at the side of the road and what . . . walked the four hours to Basingstoke, or an hour and a half back to Farnborough, maybe less either way depending upon where she'd ditched the car. Someone would have seen her walking along the hard shoulder. They'd remember a woman alone, on foot. It was the kind of thing that stuck in the mind, even if they didn't see her face. There were backroads, of course, and footpaths, so that didn't necessarily hold true, but I clung to it as a moment of hope.

'So, what happens now?' It was a good question, but of course I already had my own answer for it. In my own version of now, I sorted out shoes and socks, grabbed my coat and got myself down to Fleet. My FLO's version was a bit different, but her expectations that she was dealing with a rational man in the middle of this crisis were at best optimistic.

'On foot, she can't have got far. We'll circulate Morven's description around hotels and hostels in the area, as well as refuges and shelters.' That caught me off guard.

'Refuges, like battered wives' refuges?' I barely caught myself before I said something I'd regret. I knew the statistics, but only because I'd seen Mel B on TV talking about the decade of abuse she'd suffered. One woman lost her life every four days to a male abuser. One woman every four days was killed by the only person she had to turn to. It was horrific. But knowing the statistics and how the isolation worked was very different to feeling like she considered me a part of them. That 'not all men' instinct rose up sharply, I'm not proud of it, but I bit it down. It was a dumb self-defence mechanism at the best of times. I was already looking around for socks, but of course they were back upstairs, and I wasn't thinking straight in my haste to get out of there.

'It's not a judgment on you, Alex,' Olivia said, as though reading my mind. Not that it would have been difficult to guess what I was thinking. 'It's about where she might turn for help. Refuges are one place that take a woman in in the middle of the night, no questions asked, no need for a name, no one asking who or what she's running from. They exist purely to keep women safe while the world around them is anything but.' It made sense, but that didn't stop me from hating it. 'It's also the one place you can't go looking for her, because the door will be slammed in your face, and that's just the way it is.'

I nodded. It made sense.

'There will be officers studying ANPR cameras trying to follow her on foot, assuming she stayed on the road. It's a laborious process, hours and hours of watching footage, looking for that blink-and-you-miss-it second when there's a pedestrian in the shot. And that's assuming she stayed on foot and didn't get picked up by another driver. If she did, then it's a case of trying to isolate that car and work backwards from the registration to the owner, then making contact to find out where they dropped her, what they talked about along the way, and anything else that might give us an idea of where she's going and why.

'It's important to remember there's a person involved, and that she's following certain motivations. If we can work out what they are that's going to help hugely in the long run. I know it feels hopeless, but finding her car abandoned isn't necessarily a bad thing. It's given us a place to start looking.'

I nodded, and without saying much of anything went back upstairs. I rifled my sock drawer, brushed my teeth, and ran my fingers through my hair in the mirror, before I went through to Poppy's room. I watched her sleeping for a minute, jealous of her ability to sleep through anything, then leaned over the bed and kissed her on the forehead, lips so light she barely stirred, then went downstairs.

I stuffed my feet into an old pair of Reeboks and grabbed my leather jacket, not thinking much beyond getting to Fleet.

Olivia caught me before I was out the door, 'I'm not going to ask where you think you're going.'

'Don't try and stop me,' I said, which sounded far more like a threat – given the fact I was facing a woman in the half-dark – than I'd have ever wanted. I just meant I'm going, and no amount of well-reasoned argument's going to deter me.

She looked at me. I could see the sympathy in her eyes. But there was steel there, too. They were the eyes of someone used to facing down people far more intimidating than me every day of the week. Sometimes you forgot the kind of lives other people must have lived.

I heard Nora coming down the stairs, behind me.

'You can't do any good out there, Alex,' she said, before she reached the bottom. 'The best thing you can do is get some sleep. Tomorrow is going to be a hard enough day without you being exhausted before you start.'

'I can't sleep,' I told them both. 'I'm going out of my mind up there imagining things . . . and now they've found her car . . . I've got to be there. I have to be.'

'So, you can save her?' That was Olivia.

I blew out my cheeks, that question like a needle popping the balloon of my superhero complex with one neat jab. 'Even if I'm just an extra pair of eyes . . .'

'Because you think you might see something the police miss?' Nora this time.

I nodded.

'I know it's irrational . . . but it's not like I'm doing *anything* here. You told me to sleep. I've called through the list; I've talked to every single one of our friends. I've run out of use here. But there at least I can do *something*.'

'You're right,' Nora said, and for a heartbeat I thought she was agreeing with me. 'It's irrational. What if Morven tries to call you here?'

'I've got my mobile. She wouldn't use the landline. The only time that thing rings it's cold callers trying to sell us shit.'

'What about that little girl upstairs? She needs you.'

'Olivia can do the family part of her job,' I said, sounding far more dismissive than I meant to. 'Besides, it's not far. I can be there in half an hour at this time of night, if I ignore the speed limits, and back before Poppy ever realises I'm gone.'

'You've got all the answers, haven't you?' Olivia said, still standing in my way.

'Apart from the important one, where is my wife?'

'I can't let you go by yourself. Not in the state you're in, Alex. You understand that, don't you?' Nora said. Up close, her eyes weren't washed-out, they were steely grey, reminding me that today's kindly grandma was yesterday's warrior queen. 'It's irresponsible. I'd be letting you put yourself at risk if I stepped aside. I'm not trying to stop you because I'm some old bitch. I'm not going to lie to you, I'm frightened for our girl, but when we find her, she's going to need you. I honestly think you can do more good here, but I know you don't believe me.'

When. It was a deliberate choice of words. No ifs. No room for doubt.

'I've got to do something,' I said again, sounding like a needle stuck in the groove, and so much less convincing this time around.

'I'll take you. But on condition,' Nora said, reaching for her own coat. I heard the rattle of car keys as she dipped a hand in her pocket. 'When I say it's time to come back, we come back, no arguments. No rushing off on your own. And no getting in the way. Whatever you may think, Olivia isn't an unpaid babysitter.' I nodded. 'Okay, let's take a ride.' She dangled a set of keys in front of me. There was a KIA logo on the keyring.

Olivia opened the door for us.

I saw the silhouette of an old model Sportage under the sodium-yellow of the streetlight across the road. There was barely room to wriggle out, with Olivia's car in what would normally have been Morven's space, Nora's was an extra car in an already crowded street, squeezing everything closer together, no doubt to the curses of the neighbours. But that was London encapsulated in one frustrating snake of cars. There just wasn't the room.

Nora came out of the house behind me and pressed the button on the key, I heard the *thunk* of the central locking disarming, confirming that her car was the rust-orange Sportage.

I made my way to the passenger side and clambered in as the overhead light came on. Nora got in beside me, telling me to 'Clunk click every trip, young man.' That was something I hadn't heard in forever.

'I'm not sure we're allowed to say that anymore,' I said, belting up.

She looked at me, confused.

'Don't worry about it,' I said, not sure I had the energy to get into the whole Jimmy Savile thing.

Nora was a careful driver. She went through the motions in the same strict order she'd been taught for her test: mirror, signal, manoeuvre, and negotiated the narrow streets around our home keeping a strict five miles an hour below the limit. The night city was a strange beast. It was too late for drinkers finding their way home, and had turned itself over to the night people, the bakers and delivery drivers, the butchers and market men off to Billingsgate and Smithfield, the cleaners on their way home from the night shift, and the Uber drivers too stubborn to give up the ghost. All of this went by to a soundtrack of Tori Amos that surprised me. It shouldn't have, Nora would have been maybe forty when *Little Earthquakes* came out. How could an album with a track like 'Me and a Gun' not resonate with a woman like her, given everything she must have seen? It was just that unconscious prejudice that something I liked couldn't be something a pensioner would love, but that was just me getting older and refusing to admit it, like the fact I was part of this peculiar generation that spanned inches and millimetres like they were the most natural measurements in the world and miles and metres like there was no contradiction in how we were seeing the world. Seventy miles an hour, sounds like a decent speed limit, one hundred kilometres an hour sounds reckless, and being just shy of six feet rather than one hundred and seventy-seven centimetres sounded so much more imposing, because six feet has always been the magic number.

We paralleled the river. Nora didn't accelerate until we made it out beyond Brampton Road and onto the Hammersmith Flyover, and that only lasted as far as the Hogarth Roundabout, where we left the river behind.

The first few fat drops of rain splattered against the windscreen before we reached the motorway.

By the time we were on the M25 the heavens had lost all the romance of the starry night and the bullets of rain were drumming off the roof, bonnet and windscreen so hard I could barely hear the music. We drove the rest of the way to the soundtrack of the windscreen wipers imitating R2D2 as they scraped across the glass.

It was miserable out there.

TEN

The only other vehicles on the road were the lorries heading down to France and Spain as Europe opened up to them by way of Portsmouth's docks. Up ahead, I saw the blue lights.

We were still a mile or so short of Fleet, along a long stretch of the hard shoulder. The shadows of tall trees lined the side of the road. A recovery vehicle was parked up in front of our Golf, its warning lights spinning and hazards blinking. There were two police cars behind it, lights going.

The dashboard clock said it was still only quarter to four. The lorries thundered passed with a regular *dub-dub* as their tyres rolled over a drainage grille.

Nora killed the engine.

She looked at me, waiting for me to get out, but confronted with the reality waiting a few cars away, I couldn't bring myself to open the door, like it somehow became more real the moment I broke the seal and let it into my life.

'You don't have to do this,' Nora said, voice filled with kindness. 'I can start the engine, turn the car around and we can go back home and be back before Poppy's awake. Nothing says you need to be here, Alex. Nothing. You don't get points for being a hero.'

'How about a drenched one?' I said, opening the door.

I clambered out into the rain, and by the time I had covered the thirty feet to the Golf the front of my leather jacket was streaked with tears of rain and my hair was plastered flat to my scalp. One of the officers, seeing my approach, looked up, and must have assumed I was a detective because he broke off what he was doing and came over, face grim.

'What have we got?' I asked, not giving him a chance to get beyond his first impression. It felt like the kind of thing a senior officer would say rolling up to the scene.

'Car's been abandoned for most of the day, no sign of a struggle, key still in the engine though, which is odd, unless she was hoping someone would steal it.'

I nodded. 'Not impossible if she was running rather than taken. No way of knowing if she walked out of here or hitched a ride?' I turned to look back the way we'd come, but there wasn't much to see through the curtain of rain. The lights of Farnborough were long gone.

'There's houses and offices on the other side of the embankment,' the officer indicated the trees. 'She could have scrambled up there and disappeared into the wildlife reserve.' He could see my confusion. 'Fleet Pond's a stone's throw that way. Bit of a dogging hot spot this time of night, not much else to recommend it,' he shrugged. 'Train station is less than ten minutes' walk that way,' he indicated two slightly different paths, both involving scaling the embankment. 'Or she could have hiked on down the hard shoulder looking to pick up a ride at the services, and from there hitching a ride north or south just as easily,' he hooked a thumb over his shoulder. 'Not that I'd fancy walking along the side of the motorway for a couple of miles the way people drive.'

'Or she could have been picked up by someone expecting to meet her here,' I said, trying to think things through. She'd planned this, I just didn't know how well, and that thing about an affair had put a niggle in the back of my mind and set it gnawing away, even if I knew it was absurd.

'Sir.'

'Who found the car?'

'Numerous calls in to the local police flagged it as a hazard, but it wasn't until we got word from London to be on the lookout that anyone put two and two together. Cars get left every day. Drivers misjudging what's left in the tank, thinking they can crawl to Fleet on fumes, a blowout and no spare, that sort of thing. Local garage has a nice little tow truck side-line going on.'

I nodded.

'I can imagine. Nothing in the car to suggest where she's heading?'

'We're waiting for SOCO to go over it, but I wouldn't hold your breath.'

I heard the car door slam behind me and knew Nora was about to put an end to our little case of mistaken identity. I had maybe one question and half an answer before he knew I wasn't his superior and stopped talking, so needed to make it count. I blew out my lips. 'Anything at all strike you as off or out of place?'

'Other than the whole abducted by aliens vibe it's got going on?' He scratched at his temple, then ran a hand through his hair, lifting it out of his eyes. 'Not really. I guess it's the coincidence that raises an eyebrow. Of all the miles of motorway she just happened to abandon the car comfortable walking distance from a train station? That seems . . .'

'Improbable,' I agreed. I'd been thinking the same thing since he'd mentioned the alternative ways out of here, but I'd also caught myself thinking the proximity made it feel obvious, and obvious made it less likely if she was trying to cover her tracks. It all hinged on whether Morven was actually running, or if it was more reasoned than that, and she was hiding. And that, in turn, hinged upon who she thought was after her – and just what they were capable of.

'Officer,' Nora said, joining us. The rain seemed to wash off her rather than soak her; maybe it was a respect thing? The elements recognising her as so much better than us. 'I'm Nora Flynn,

Protected Persons Unit. This is Alex Kerr, the missing woman's husband.'

The young officer's face as the realisation sank in that he'd been flippantly talking about alien abduction with me, and my relation to the abductee, would have been priceless if it wasn't so fucking tragic. Flustered, he said sorry half a dozen times, shaking his head.

'Nothing to be sorry about, mate,' I assured him. 'And you're right, there's a really creepy alien abduction vibe about a car left at the side of the road with the keys still in the ignition, and no one in sight.'

'Do you want to look inside, see if there's anything missing or that strikes you as out of place?' I nodded. 'Just don't touch anything. I'll get shot.'

'My prints will be all over the car,' I reasoned. 'We share it most days.'

'Still,' the young officer said, nodding, but not willing to concede that all things considered it was a stupid request.

The overhead light came on as I opened the door. It lit up the inside bright as day. I slipped into the driver's seat. The keys still hung from the ignition. A little piece of my soul was crushed in that moment, looking at the diamond shoe keyring hanging there.

Who needed to imagine monsters when something so banal had the power to break you?

I looked around, but he was right, nothing was out of place because there was nothing to be out of place. There were a couple of CDs jammed into the space above the player, but there was no secret message being spelled out by their selection. I checked the glove compartment. Aside from the manual there was nothing in there apart from a scrunched-up Mars wrapper I'd forgotten I'd hidden a few weeks ago. Gone were the days of well-thumbed *A to Z*s with their dog-eared pages and bits of envelope torn off to mark the destination across several pages of the map. It was all on GPS now, tracked by phones and satellites like everything else these days. I closed the glovebox and felt around under the seat, knowing there would be nothing under there but doing it just the same.

I thought for a second my finger brushed up against something, paper, and I twisted, trying to fish it out, thinking it might be a receipt or something else that could tell its own part of the story. But it was nothing so useful. I held a scrap from a fast-food wrapper pinched between fore- and middle finger and turned it left and right, so that I could view the ketchup stain on the back like it might suddenly provide enlightenment.

But maybe it did, because it wasn't mine, and Morven wasn't big on junk food at the best of times. At least I didn't think she was. It was weird to think that I couldn't even be sure if she was a secret burger binge-eater. I dropped the scrap of burger wrapper and gave up the search.

'Anything?' The young policeman asked as I clambered out of the car.

I shook my head. 'A scrap of burger wrapper, nothing to get excited about.'

'Sorry,' he said, a slight tilt of the head, a slighter rise and drop of the shoulders, and I realised he'd let me search for me, not for him. He hadn't been hoping I'd find something. It was a little act of humanity, that was all, and it drove home the futility of looking for one woman in a population of sixty-six million. I could stand on every street corner I knew, pushing her photograph under the nose of every passer-by, and be no closer to finding her before I died than I was now.

I looked at Nora, who had that same expression of *we can do anything you need* on her face as she looked at me, and that just rammed home the truth of this whole middle of the night trip – it was about appeasing me, not about letting me help. To be honest, I'd expected the site to be swarming with cops, with a full search to be mounted and them out there with their torches, scouring the countryside to see if she was in trouble, looking for footprints in the mud or scraps of torn fabric hanging from branches to flag the way.

'Let's go home,' I said, admitting defeat – partial defeat, at least.

She rested a hand on my arm, nodding gently, like I'd finally come to my senses, and guided me through the driving rain back to the warm dryness of the car.

'Actually, can we make a quick stop at the services? I could do with the loo.'

That earned a wan little smile and an 'Of course.'

She turned the ignition and Tori re-joined us in the musty car as our soaked clothes slowly steamed. She indicated, waiting for a huge eighteen-wheeler to thunder by, then pulled out into traffic, getting up to speed fast.

I couldn't help myself; I turned sideways to look out of the window and watched the Golf blur by, and then it was gone, just like that.

The off ramp was two and a half minutes' drive away. I saw the eighteen-wheeler leave the three-lane motorway and climb, slowing for the curve that opened up on the huge car park of the Welcome Break. The lights of a Days Inn promised rooms, but they were the very first place the police would look. More signs promised Pizza Express and Burger King, and for a moment I wondered if that might have been the source of the ketch-up-smeared burger wrapper, not sure what that would tell me?

We followed the eighteen-wheeler up the off-ramp, decelerating as Nora went down through the gears to navigate the mini-roundabout, and slowed to a stop outside a Starbucks that appeared to be open 24 hours. Across the forecourt I saw the lights of a KFC and a Subway. This little strip of concrete and steel was a fast-food heaven. More lights came from inside.

'Do you want anything? A coffee maybe?'

Nora shook her head. 'I'm good.'

'Okay, I'll just be a minute.'

'Take your time.'

I half-jogged across the parking lot towards the lights, head down until I reached the cash point on the corner, then slowed down as I came under the sheltering canopy of the building. I scanned the underside of the roof and the outsides of the windows as I walked around to the sliding doors, looking for cameras and trying to get an idea how much, if any, of the cars beyond were covered. I saw a line of what looked like charging posts for electric cars. Never had there been a more obvious indication of just how quickly the world was changing.

Inside, a young woman was on her knees, changing the news headlines behind the wire grille of the newspaper stand, despite the fact no one bought papers these days. It was one of those little rituals of life that would die out soon enough, lost to clickbait. She looked up, smiling at my approach. I was the only other person inside, despite the lights. Most of the restaurant shutters were down.

The piped music was still playing, not some canned Muzak. The Pixies. 'Debaser'. It was a surreal tune to hear in a place like this.

I raised my eyebrows. It was a little quirk that drove Morven mad. She kept telling me how stupid it made me look, but after a lifetime of doing it, no amount of trying not to was going to break that ingrained habit. I crossed the mosaic tiles of the floor and pointed beyond the empty food court towards what I assumed were the toilets.

The sign above the archway promised a lot more than a simple toilet stop, with showers, baby changing facilities and more. And inside was a lot cleaner than my toilet at home. I relieved myself, then washed my hands, and was halfway back to the car before it occurred to me to show the shop assistant Morven's photo on my phone. I doubled back, opening the photo app as I ducked into the newsagents. This time they were promising 'Here Comes Your Man'. The tracks were short. It meant I'd been in here less than five minutes. I grabbed a bottle of Pepsi Max from the fridge and went up to the counter.

She smiled the smile of shop assistants everywhere, and scanned my item: 'You can get a king size Mars, Snickers, or Twix for an extra 20p.'

'It's fine,' I assured her, smiling at the thought of the perfect accompaniment to a diet soda being a full sugar hit of chocolate. Or maybe it was. Feel good for buying the low sugar alternative, so you don't feel so bad about buying the chocolate, giving yourself a free pass. 'Can I ask you a favour?' Her smile didn't falter, but I could sense a slight tensing in her posture. I held out my phone. 'Have you seen her in here?'

She leaned forward, but didn't really look before she said, 'Sorry. We get thousands of people in here every day.'

I nodded, seeing the slight confusion in her face. She'd expected someone younger. I wondered how many fathers came through this place looking for runaway daughters and sons? Officially, something like seventy-seven thousand kids ran away every year. That was another one of those harrowing statistics I'd picked up from the bullying documentary. The numbers beggared belief.

'It's my wife,' I said, needing to fill the silence and keep the conversation going. 'The police found her car a mile from here. I'm trying to find her.'

'Shit. Was there an accident?'

'No. She just . . .' I didn't have the words for that part of the story. There was too much to unpack to try and explain how the woman I'd married wasn't the woman I thought she was, or that a ghost from her past had come hunting for her. 'I need to find her.'

'You should check with Gregg,' she said, offering a lifeline. 'He was in all day.'

'Gregg?'

'Gregg Harrison, the Services Manager. It's a fancy title for what he does,' she grinned. 'He should be around somewhere. His office has got all of the security cameras and stuff, if anyone round here can help it's probably him, but like I said, thousands of people come through here every day, so the chances of anyone standing out enough to be remembered are slim to none.'

'You know what, I'll take that Mars Bar, thanks,' I said, fishing out a few coins from my pocket.

'It's on me,' she said. 'Hope you find your wife.'

'Me too,' I said, unpeeling the wrapper and taking a big chocolate and caramel bite.

'The offices are through the service door beside the KFC. You can't miss it when you know it's there,' she assured me.

ELEVEN

And she was right. For all the shopping mall camouflage at play, once you knew the door was there it was pretty obvious.

There was something unnerving about the soundtrack now. It had moved on to 'Monkey's Gone to Heaven' as I pushed the door open. It swung wide onto a concrete corridor that took me behind the curtain into an ugly concrete and breeze block Oz. There was a narrow metal stair at the far end that led up to an industrial-style office door. Light crept beneath it. I climbed the eleven steps, my footsteps ringing out in the cramped confines of the service corridor, and knocked on the door.

Gregg was a mop-headed blonde kid who couldn't have been much older than my trainers. He still had a rash of angry zits pocking his cheeks and ingrown hairs along his jawline. But he had the brightest blue eyes.

'Can I help you?'

'Gregg?'

'That's my name or was the last time I looked. Same question.'

'Yeah, I hope so. The girl downstairs said you were working yesterday?'

'Some of it,' he agreed.

I took my phone out of my pocket and brought up Morven's photo.

'Did you see her?'

Looking at it, he shook his head. 'Sorry.'

'It would have been fairly early on, I think, maybe ten or eleven.'

More head shaking. 'Sorry, mate. Wish I could help.'

'Do you have security cameras?'

'We do, but you don't get to look at them. That's just the way it is.'

'That's fine,' I said. 'The police will be coming in a few hours. Just giving you a heads up. You might want to dig the tapes out.'

His lips quirked into a wry smile at the mention of tapes. 'They're more than welcome to. You know how it is, as much as I'd love to help, I just can't unless it's official, there's all sorts of privacy laws and stuff. I'm not sure they'd be much help, anyway. It's a small island we live on. We're talking nearly twenty-four hours ago. She could be tucked up in a B&B in the Outer Hebrides by now counting Scottish sheep.' Which was hard to argue with, but that wasn't a helpful way of thinking. 'And to be honest, you look nice and normal and all that, but I don't know you, you could be some complete nutter who's obsessed with this poor woman.'

Thinking of the music being piped into the food court I nodded and said, 'That's true. I could have a switchblade in my back pocket, slice up your eyeballs and just go look myself.' There was a moment then, a heartbeat, when he absolutely didn't realise I was quoting the soundtrack I'd just walked through, and I felt guilty for scaring the crap out of the poor kid. I mean, it was four in the morning, and he was alone up here with a stranger. If I had been a psycho he was screwed. 'But I'm not, and I don't, and the eyeball thing is just a lyric from the song that was playing when I came in here. The Pixies. Sorry about that, I've got a really shitty sense of humour sometimes.'

He burst out laughing. It was as nervous a laugh as I'd ever heard.

'Haven't we all?'

Poor kid. He wasn't going to forget seeing me, that was for sure. I felt like I owed him something. Some kind of explanation.

'I woke up yesterday and my life was normal. Went down to have breakfast with my kid and my wife, more normal, kissed my wife goodbye and took the little one to school, and everything else, from that moment on, has been the absolute opposite of normal. I don't even know how to begin to explain it. I'm fucking terrified something is going to happen to the woman I love, and I'm helpless to do anything to stop it . . . and now I'm here, holding her photo out to complete strangers and like an idiot hoping one of them is going to say, "oh, I saw her. . ." when the truth is I don't even know if she came through this way. And even if she did, I know it was nearly a day ago and she could be half a world away by now.' I shook my head. 'I don't know anything and it's killing me.' Never a truer word has been spoken.

I felt like I was made out of Meccano and someone had just loosened all of my little bolts a turn. I sagged just a little bit.

I didn't have any more begging left in me.

'They'll kill me . . .' Gregg sniffed, like a kid with a bad habit, but said, 'Come on, this way.' He pushed a second door open, beside his office, just off the stairwell. 'And if anyone asks, I dunno, tell them you hit me over the head or something . . . pity you don't have that switchblade after all,' he gave me a cockeyed smile and I found myself quite liking the kid.

The door opened into a security room with half a dozen screens showing black-and-white images of all around the service station, covering inside and out. There were a couple of chairs, and the mic from a PA system that no doubt told kids separated from their parents to meet at the assembly point half a dozen times a day, in between encouraging people to spend spend spend. The screens cycled through a number of different angles, offering maybe fifty different views of the parked cars, shops and the dining areas. It was easy to imagine that every single angle was covered. After less than a minute of watching the screens I saw Nora leaning against the side of her car having a smoke. No. Not

67

smoking. It was a vape pen. There was something quite wonderful about watching someone in her late sixties vaping.

'What time did you say?' Gregg said, settling into one of the two leather seats in front of the console.

'Yesterday morning,' I said, 'Not before ten, I doubt after twelve. But I can't be sure about that.'

'Two hours. That's a big window. Do you feel lucky, punk?'

'Not right now,' I said, sinking down into the seat beside him. 'Let Operation Needle in a Haystack commence.'

He punched some commands into the console, one of the screens going dark for a moment as it reset, before coming to life again as if the power had cut for a second. The image on the screen was time-stamped 10:00:00 and there must have been fifty people in the frame, parents, kids, a couple of heavy-set truckers, and as he scrubbed forward through the footage it quickly became apparent that all human life was here, just passing through to somewhere more important. That is one of the stranger things about a place like this; no one comes here because they want to, and no one stays. It's a passing place. The scale of what we were trying to do was all too obvious after a couple of minutes at the console, when I must have looked at three thousand faces and been no closer to finding Morven. I saw couples holding hands, I saw parents wrestling with push chairs and trying to wrangle kids who scattered like Brownian random motion in the flesh. I saw pregnant women and sweaty truckers in band tee-shirts. I saw salesmen in their slick suits with slicker hair, carrying their sample cases. I saw goths and punks and a lot of denim. Ninety per cent of people rolling through seemed to be wearing jeans.

What I didn't see was my wife.

I was doing this all wrong. I could stare at these faces all day and not see her, even if she was there.

The problem was, I didn't know what was the right way to do it.

I was about to give up when a flurry of movement caught my

eye near the top of the screen. I recognised the dress before I recognised Morven. She hurried through the shot, looking over her shoulder twice. She held something in her hand. It was hard to tell what, given the relatively poor resolution, but it could have been an envelope. One of those larger manila ones. She was only in the shot for a few seconds before she was out of frame again.

'Do you have another angle of this?' I said, reaching up to point at the screen she'd just walked out of.

'Sure, gimme a sec,' and good to his word a second later another shot filled the screen, picking up from the same time stamp, offering a view of Morven breezing through the food court towards the trays where all of the rubbish was being dumped out by still-hungry diners.

It took me a moment to realise what I was seeing, and then to be sure I had seen what I thought I'd seen: Morven dropped the envelope in the bin with the fast-food wrappers without looking back, then walked across to one of the concessions to buy herself a hot drink, some sort of fruity tea no doubt, before heading back out.

'Is that her?'

'It is.'

'What's she doing?'

'I'm not sure . . .'

He paused the image on the screen as Morven turned to face the camera, scalding hot tea to her lips. She didn't look like someone running.

But what does someone running look like?

She didn't seem to be under any sort of duress.

And I almost managed to convince myself the envelope she'd dumped in the bin was trash when she started moving again. The camera didn't follow her. I could have asked Gregg to change the focus again to another of the angles, but because I didn't, I got to see an older woman, in heavy knitwear, like a country farmer's wife, push herself up from one of the cheap faux-leather banquettes, and go over to the same bin and dip her hand inside. It was a blink-and-you-miss-it thing. She took the envelope out of the trash and stuffed it into her shopping bag, then turned her back to the camera and walked away.

'What the actual fuck . . . that was a dead letter drop, wasn't it? Is your missus some sort of spy?'

I nearly laughed, honestly, it was right there on my lips, only it wouldn't spill out of my mouth. The head shake was negligible. I was trying to see the other woman's face. 'Can you get an angle on her? Somewhere we can see her face?'

'I can try,' he said, 'but I'll be honest, this is a bit what-you-see-is-what-you-get, no guarantee. We're not exactly hi-tech in here. No real need, given the biggest threat is someone burning a copy of the *Sun*.' Another twitch of a smile. I caught the tinge of suppressed accent and realised he was a northern lad. Liverpool, most likely, not the city itself but the fringes where middle class took the rough edges off.

He input a few more commands to shift through different cameras following along with the same time stamp, but it quickly became clear that the woman was aware of the cameras and made sure she kept her face away from them as best she could. There were a couple of glimpses of her in profile, but not a single good full-face image. But he kept looking.

I hadn't realised how long we'd been at it, until I noticed Nora was no longer standing beside the car, vape long since vaped, and was walking through the food court looking for me.

I leaned into the mic and pressed the green broadcast button, earning a crackle in the speakers all around the place, and said, 'Nora, we're up here,' which made the old woman turn and look to the heavens like she expected to see the face of God in the acoustic tiles. 'Security office, the door is over by the KFC.' She nodded and changed direction. There was a moment where she appeared confused by the seemingly solid wall, then she reached out and pushed tentatively, and the hidden door swung open on the concrete back passageway.

'I've got an idea,' Gregg said, behind me, and instead of trying to scrub all of the footage for a single usable shot of her face, he changed tack and the on-screen image shifted to the car park.

I opened the door and called, 'Up here,' and heard the echo of Nora's heavy feet through the concrete corridor.

Gregg punched the air triumphantly. 'Got her!'

I turned to see an image of the woman getting out of her car. I couldn't make out her face, as with every other angle it was partially obscured. I was about to say so, when he handed me a piece of paper with a registration written on it.

'You beauty.'

'I have my moments,' he agreed.

We had maybe fifteen seconds before Nora joined us in the console room. 'Kill the screen,' I said, making a decision I hoped I wouldn't live to regret. I couldn't tell you why I didn't want her to see what we'd found. It made zero sense. She was connected to the police, and through them had access to the PNC, a national computer database with every single make, model and registration of car, plus owner history. And I had, what? Google? Even so, rational or irrational, I didn't want her knowing about the woman and the envelope until I had no choice but to tell her. It was a split-second thing. Lives have been saved and lost on less.

I stuffed the paper into my pocket.

Credit to him, the kid didn't hesitate. By the time Nora stood in the doorway we were looking at a live feed of the food court and the picnic area outside.

She looked at the screen and realised what we'd been doing, but before she could ask how it was going, I cut her off with, 'It's pointless,' and shrugged. It wasn't too difficult to sound like a broken man, given how precariously I was teetering on that abyss line.

Nora looked at me, her face full of sadness. She understood my pain. Of course she did. That's why we were here in the first place, why she'd agreed to drive me out to the car, and why we were going home now. Morven had been part of her life for twenty-something years before she'd retired. She'd been a surrogate mother and protector. And now she was out there, lost and alone and vulnerable. And that was the key word, vulnerable. And that's why, I admit, my decision not to tell her what we'd just seen surprised me, but on some gut level I thought it was the right thing to do.

I'd like to say my motivations were noble, like I'd taken on the mantle of her protector when I'd said 'I do', but the truth is far more paranoid: I just couldn't trust anyone at that moment. There was nothing personal about it. Trust isn't given freely, it's hard earned. This little niggle at the back of my mind kept prickling away, and it wasn't until I'd seen the image of Morven up on the screen that it occurred to me: she'd lived this new life just fine for over thirty years, no breaks in her identity, no threats from the past. Until now. Of course, it could just be bad luck and coincidence, but what if that was because someone had betrayed her? Which then begged the question who would have even known her truth to betray it? This stuff was rooted in the darkness of my fears and had been ever since the moment I'd seen those five happiness-shattering words *I know who you were* on her phone. Maybe it's down to the coded messages embedded in every cop show since *The Sweeney* all the way through to *Line of Duty*. As Ted Hastings would say, it's all about bent coppers.

Right now, there was too much going on here that I didn't understand. Not least of which was, who was Morven Kerr, really? What had she witnessed that they'd decided the only chance she had at a normal life was to shed the skin of her old one and start all over again? What kind of enemies did she have out there, that simply knowing who she had been when she was eighteen put her life at risk now?

I wanted to pretend that it was hard imagining that any kind of grudge could fester for that long, but it wasn't. It was far too easy to imagine the kind of thing that could have someone hating you for the rest of their lives.

'Come on, Alex, let's go home. Let the police do this later. Poppy's going to be waking up any minute, and she's going to wonder where you are. We don't want to frighten her. She's got some strange enough days ahead as it is.'

I nodded. I didn't mention my little girl's superpower, that she could sleep like the dead. I thanked Gregg, who gave me a conspiratorial wink as Nora turned her back and walked out of there knowing I was risking Morven's safety by lying to her retired protector.

As I followed Nora out across the food court towards the car, I realised that the music being piped into the place had changed from the discordant jangle of The Pixies to much smoother stuff. It took me a moment to recognise 'Forever Autumn'. It's one of those songs I've always loved, despite it being nothing like the stuff I listened to either before or after. There's just something about it; the ache in Justin Hayward's voice, the haunting flute, the reverb, the plucked strings and the spiralling sound. I could listen to it again and again and again without ever growing bored by the chord progressions or the repetitions behind the building sound.

It always struck me as curious, or maybe more real, that he sang about a life remaining forever autumn because the woman he loved wasn't there. Not winter, not filled with despair, but with that slowly dying hope like the leaves turning golden brown before they fell.

Stepping out into the early morning, I realised I was crying.

TWELVE

If Nora noticed, she didn't say anything.

She turned over the ignition and rolled slowly out of the car park to join with the traffic back to London. Not that there were more than a handful of cars on either side of the road.

I saw the flashing blue lights on the roadside but didn't twist to look at our car as we swept past. There was nothing to be gained by torturing myself.

Nora didn't talk much on the return journey. Maybe she wanted to leave me alone with my thoughts, or maybe there was just nothing left to say? Either was fine by me as it meant I didn't have to lie to her.

'Do you mind?' I asked, leaning forward after maybe ten miles, to turn the radio on.

'Help yourself.'

After surfing through the channels for a few seconds I settled on one of the variants of Absolute Radio, which, I confess, even after all these years I still called Virgin. I'd recognised a few bars of something and that had been enough to win my loyalty for a couple of miles, at least, while the road beneath us changed from tarmac to a louder concrete for a stretch, then back again. The music was just a distraction. I was trying to think. How could I convert the registration plate in my pocket into a genuine solid lead that was worth following?

Call in favours.

That was the only answer that made any sort of sense. But it was a big ask. The kind of ask that could cost my contact his job. Thing is, it wasn't even a dilemma. Of course, I was going to put him on the spot. What choice did I have?

Of course, it wasn't something I could do with Nora or Olivia babysitting me, which meant I needed to get some alone time without looking like I was desperate to do it.

Absolute Radio didn't let me down. We were treated to a succession of what the kids would call bangers. The best thing about it was it meant we made it all the way back to the house without having to say a word, but with no uncomfortable silence.

It was nearly six when we pulled up outside the house. Unsurprisingly, someone else was in the spot we'd vacated, so Nora was forced to trawl around looking for a space. We eventually parked a good five minutes' walk away. After an hour in the passenger seat, it was good to stretch my legs. There's something quite nice about London at this time of the morning, the calm before the busy weekend storm.

The front door opened before we were halfway up the short garden path. 'Everything okay here, Officer Mendes?' Nora called.

'You better come in,' she said in a tone that promised there'd been developments. And not of a good kind. I felt my heart calcify, and in the moment that should have been between one heartbeat and the next, wanted nothing more than to turn and run away. Nothing in the world was going to make me want to hear what she had to say. But I followed Nora inside.

Mason, looking like he hadn't slept a minute, sat on my couch waiting for our return. He half-rose as we came inside, then in this weird role-reversal of guest and host gestured for me to take a seat in my own armchair.

'What's going on?' I asked, no preamble.

Mason was equally forthright. 'Is there any reason you can think of why Morven might have withdrawn a large amount of money from your joint account yesterday?'

The envelope.

'One,' I said, thinking on my feet. The next few seconds scared me, because they proved just how good a liar I actually am. I blew out my cheeks and shook my head. 'She's out there alone, right? She's running and unlike us, she knows who she's running from . . . she knows that you can track stuff like credit card transactions, right? We've all seen enough crime shows to know your digital footprint is there for all to see . . . that's why she left her phone . . . so, she takes out enough cash to keep her going for a decent chunk of time. Instead of leaving a trail of credit card receipts, she pays for everything in cash. The roof over her head, the food in her belly . . .' I couldn't read his face. It was plausible. Hell, if it wasn't for what I'd seen in the Service Station I would have given exactly the same answer. But I had seen what I'd seen, and now I knew that a chunk of change had been in that envelope she'd dumped in the bin to be collected by the other woman. She was being black-mailed. I don't know if that was better or worse than being hunted by whoever she was being protected from, but it felt like it was beginning to make sense.

Someone had worked out who she was and was blackmailing her to ensure their silence.

She'd run to protect us in case they weren't good for their word. That made sense, I mean, who's to say they wouldn't take her money then turn her over, making a killing? 'Train tickets.' I added, not sure if he'd follow my breadcrumbs. 'We were just there,' I looked over at Nora. 'Where she dumped the car. The officer said there's a train station a few minutes' walk from where she left it, straight road. Can't be a coincidence, right? Buy a ticket for cash, you can pretty much go anywhere in the country, leaving no trace.'

'Not exactly no trace,' Mason corrected, 'but you are right, following cash is a lot more difficult than following credit card transactions and GPS transponders.'

'How much money did she take?'

'Over five thousand pounds.' Which would have pretty much cleaned us out. We weren't exactly pay cheque to pay cheque people, but there wasn't a huge buffer between that and starvation. She'd left enough in the joint account to get us through a month's bills without panicking. But only just.

I closed my eyes.

I didn't want Mason reading my mind.

The breath that leaked out between my lips was heavy, a real sigh as I struggled with the implications of everything I'd learned in the last few hours. My head was spinning. Mason would have expected it. Anything else would have been weird.

So, did this mean I could trust everyone in this room?

Probably, but the problem was it still didn't mean I could trust everyone they were connected to. Like it or not, I had to act as if there was a leak somewhere, rather than just accepting that this ghost from her past was some sort of random haunting. There was nothing to say the woman blackmailing Morven wasn't connected to the police somehow.

What was that old saying? Just because you're paranoid doesn't mean they aren't out to get you.

I rubbed at my chin.

'What am I supposed to do?'

'Ideally, not go running around the country trying to play the hero,' Mason said, and while his tone was even, there was an unmistakeable edge to it. He wasn't trying to be funny. He was putting me in my place, and as far as he was concerned my place was here. These four walls.

I heard the clump of not-so tiny feet upstairs.

Madam was awake.

Which meant I was a couple of minutes away from an uncomfortable conversation.

I wasn't looking forward to this.

Honestly, I could have happily put it off until Monday when Morven was due home, but that would have meant some creative thinking to explain the police presence in our home, and that we couldn't talk openly about what was happening. There was only so much 'Go and play in your room' I could get away with.

Give Olivia her due, she read my mind and shook her head. 'Not a good idea. Is there somewhere she can stay for the weekend? Your folks, maybe? Uncle or aunt?'

Mason nodded, reinforcing the suggestion. 'That's a good idea. No need to worry the poor kid unduly. Not when her mum could come walking back through the door on Monday like nothing's happened.'

Which sounded fine in theory, but right at that moment felt like putting your faith in the Tooth Fairy. But Olivia was right. Not for the reason she thought, though. I was going to need to move about freely if I was going to try and follow Morven's foot-steps. I couldn't do that if I was worried about Poppy. 'I'll give mum a call,' I agreed, already working on my excuses. 'Either of you want a coffee? I'm going to make myself one.'

'Please, two sugars, no milk,' Mason said.

I nodded. 'How about you? We've got a veritable coffee shop in the kitchen, you name it, I can whip it up in a couple of minutes.'

'Hmm, hazelnut latte?'

'Challenge accepted. Nora?'

'Surprise me.'

I reckon I'll do that in the not-too-distant future, I thought, and grinned as I headed through to the kitchen area, sorting out Poppy's granola and yoghurt before I put fresh water into the espresso machine and powered it up. I spent a second staring at the open cupboard trying to decide what mugs to use, while the machine chugged away, cleaning the pipes out. I did Mason's Americano, then Olivia's hazelnut latte, which was as complicated as putting some milk in the frother and pressing a button, then had a look along the line of syrups and other stuff we've accumulated due to my coffee obsession and decided on a nice chocolate-infused coffee.

The grinder was whirring on those beans as Poppy came trudging into the kitchen, bleary eyed, in her pyjamas. No unicorns or little ponies for my little girl. She was baby Yoda all the way. She stretched theatrically and hopped up onto the breakfast bar stool, spoon already in hand regardless of the fact her eyes weren't actually open.

'Morning star shine,' I said, transferring the coffee grounds into the portafilter and tamping them down. A button push later the thick chocolaty liquid was trickling out of the espresso spout. I'd frothed enough milk for both drinks. 'How'd you feel about spending the weekend with nan?'

'You trying to get rid of me?' She said, around a mouthful of granola, and making sure she let me see more yoghurt than I really wanted to in the process.

'Never. Some work stuff has come up, and with mum away I need to make sure you don't get up to mischief.'

More munching.

A nod.

I took the coffees through, then grabbed my mobile and went up to the office to call mum and ask her to look after our little Popsicle.

Mum answered on the first ring, like she'd been sitting on the phone. Which, given it was a Saturday morning, she probably had. She was a creature of habit. Saturday morning, fresh bread from the local bakery, Nescafé, and the crossword. She didn't move from the kitchen table until the last square was filled in, even if these days that meant resorting to the internet to cheat when she'd given up wracking her brain.

'Hey ma, some stuff's come up. Is it okay if I drop Poppy off at your place for the weekend?'

'Of course it is, love. Everything okay?'

'Not really, but I can't get into it. I'll drop her off in half an hour.'

'Okay sweetheart. You do what you've got to do, we'll keep trouble occupied.'

'Cheers, mum. Love you.'

I hung up before she could send her love back and went back downstairs to tell Poppy to get a shift on. 'Leaving in fifteen minutes.'

'Are you?' She said and giggled.

'You too.'

'Hmm. It's good to have ambitions, I suppose.'

'Fifteen minutes.'

I chuckled and left her to it. At some point I was going to have to come up with a better excuse to square away the presence of Nora and Olivia in our home. Poppy was nine, she wasn't stupid.

'Okay,' I said, returning to the lounge. 'I'm going to run Poppy round to mums. It's fifteen minutes from here.'

'That's fine,' Mason said, already on his feet. The entire purpose of his visit had been to see my face as he delivered the news about the missing money. I guess I'd passed the test.

'There's a spare room upstairs,' I told Nora. 'You're more than welcome to crash if you feel like you need to be here. Christ, that sounds like I'm trying to get rid of you,' I back-peddled. 'That's not what I mean, it's just you've been up all night, you've got to be exhausted.'

She smiled softly. She had that grandmotherly thing down perfectly. 'It's fine, I'm going to head home, too. You know what it's like, there's something special about your own bed.' I nodded. 'Olivia will stay here. If anything comes up, she'll call and wake me up. Now, in all seriousness, Alex, you need to get some sleep. You're no good to anyone if you're running on empty. Tired people don't think straight. They make mistakes. And do stupid things.'

80

There were more mind readers in my front room than at Centre Parcs.

I nodded. 'I will. I promise. But first things first, need to get madam to mums.' I wasn't about to say what second things I had in mind though. That was between me, my mobile phone and the piece of paper I had scrunched up in my pocket.

THIRTEEN

I'd bent the truth. At this time of the morning it was more like ten minutes to mum and dad's, not fifteen. I wanted those extra five minutes either way to myself.

Parked up at the side of the road, beneath the hanging branches of the urban jungle that was their fancy part of town, I took my mobile out and thumbed through my contacts, looking for a name.

Mac.

Dylan Mackenzie.

He'd done some consulting on the teen suicide documentary. Three years ago, he'd been an Outreach Officer in Kentish Town, but before that he'd been part of Youth and Family Services, and regularly worked with Missing Persons helping to track down runaways. That meant he knew the procedures, all the stuff they'd be doing to look for Morven, and could help steer me through it, anticipating next moves and pitfalls. I didn't envy him. Best I could tell, most of his day was taken up patching up kids who found themselves on the business end of a knife. The city had changed a lot since I'd grown up. I think the first time I really noticed it was when that kid was stabbed outside the big McDonald's on Oxford Street. The idea that we were paralleling the gang culture of New York felt so far-fetched back then, yet within a few months you'd be seeing teens wearing do-rags and gang tags spray-painted on shutters and red brick. Mac had explained how it was all about intimidation and glorifying the gang. That whole need for territorial dominance translated into stabbings and beatings to send messages between rivals. He was a good guy, but he was on a hiding to nothing. It was a war we were never going to win when we didn't even understand the terms of engagement, we were that far out of touch. That was just the depressing truth.

I hit the call icon.

It rang three times before Mac picked up. 'Al, long time, mate. What's up?'

It was good to hear his voice again. Big, booming, Brian Blessed-like. There are just some people who are full of life. They've got this natural gravitas. You can't help but be drawn to them. It helped that he was basically the genetic template they perfected a few clones down the line from Idris Elba. He was a little less imposing, a little less muscular, eyes a little less piercing, but let's be honest, that's a little less we'd all have no problem being.

'Blunt version, or the sugar-coated one?' I said, smiling even though he couldn't see me.

'You need something?'

'I need something and you're not going to like it.'

'Ah my favourite kind of phone call from someone I haven't heard from in two years. Hit me.'

I took the crumpled paper out of my pocket and smoothed it out against the dashboard.

'I need you to run a license plate for me.'

'Not a fucking chance, pal. I mean, I love you like a brother that I never talk to, but I'm not going to risk my job for you. Sorry.'

That was the answer I'd expected, the question was, did I give up now, or did I beg – and in begging, tell him what was going on?

He was a cop, after all, even if his uniform was jeans and band tee-shirts. He had loyalties that he couldn't compromise, even as a favour to an estranged brother.

'I'm desperate, Mac. I can't say why.'

'What part of "can't do it" don't you understand, Alex? I get a reg run through the PNC I need to give my badge number. There's privacy laws and so much other shite. Even if I trust you, if it turned out something happened to them and the investigating officers see that I ran a PNC check against their car there'd be so many questions I've got no answer to. I'd be crucified.'

'I get it, I really do. But—'

'Don't *but* me, Alex. No exceptions. Not even if your life depended on it.'

'What about Morven's life?'

Silence.

Breathing at the other end of the line.

Then: 'I fucking hate you, Alex. Tell me it's bullshit.'

'I wish it was,' I said, looking out the window at a couple of kids playing in the street. Their tennis ball bounced away down the gutter.

'I'm going to regret saying this, aren't I? What kind of trouble is she in?'

This time it was my turn to be silent.

The kids moved off, chasing each other. Plenty of laughing and joking. I remembered when life was about as complicated as that. 'She's missing.'

'Shit, have you—'

'Yeah. There's a family liaison officer in my lounge right now and I've just dropped Poppy off with my parents.'

'Okay, that's good. Talk me through it.'

I did, the basics, bare bones, skirting around the fact that as much as I wanted to, I couldn't trust the people supposedly helping me because of who my wife might have been. But I was going to have to if I was going to convince him to stick his neck out. 'I've got a registration plate. I think whoever owns the car is blackmailing her. I need to find them.'

'Then give the number to your FLO. That's what they're there for. They can run the plate. If I do it, it's a crime.'

'I can't,' I said.

'Of course you can, mate.'

'I can't,' I repeated.

'Okay, give me one good reason why you can't?'

I looked at myself in the rear-view mirror. I looked battered. Not just tired. Battered. All or nothing. I closed my eyes, not wanting to see myself as I betrayed her secret. 'She's been living under a new identity since she was a teenager. I don't know what happened back then, but someone has breached her new name and linked her to who she was. I can't be sure it isn't someone with access to her files, meaning it could be one of the people sat in my front room right now . . . I want to trust them. You have no idea how much I want to trust them, but . . .' I let my voice trail away.

Mac finished my train of thought for me, 'Even if they're not the source, any one of them could be working with them, feeding stuff about her to whoever we're hiding her from because they're the only ones with access to her files. I get it. I know the way your mind works, my friend, but fuck me, you keep thinking that way, you'll go out of your mind, mate. Shit happens. Random shit. Someone might have seen her in the grocery store or outside the school gates or pretty much anywhere else, and just had a double-take moment and realised they recognised her. It doesn't have to be some grand conspiracy.'

He was right, of course, but that didn't help me in the slightest because the doubt was already living in my head.

'She's kept her secret for over thirty years, suddenly some bastard's blackmailing her and she's disappeared? It doesn't matter how it happened. Not really. She's out there alone, Mac. She walked out of the house and decided for whatever reason it was better she disappeared than tell me what she was running from . . .'

'Then you have to trust someone,' Mac reasoned.

'I do. You.' I looked at the clock on the dashboard. I have

to head home soon, or they'll start to wonder what's happened to me.'

'I'm saying this with love, brother. I really do fucking hate you.'

And I knew he was going to help me.

I gave him the registration.

FOURTEEN

I walked back into the house as if I hadn't just been plotting away behind their backs, not exactly all smiles, but like someone who was glad to see them.

Olivia was making a fresh pot of tea in the kitchen and Siri was busy playing her some background music that was going to completely screw up my recommendations. I'd told her to make herself at home. Truth was, I was glad of the noise, normal life puttering around to come home to; the house felt empty without Poppy and Morven. It was a Saturday morning, normally the front room would have been filled with the cackle and buzz of her programmes. Civilisation had come a long way from the world of *Tiswas* and *Swapshop* I'd grown up with, but the Saturday morning TV ritual was sacrosanct. The more things changed the more they stayed the same.

'Everything okay?'

'All good,' I assured her. 'Well, within limits.'

A slight twitch of the lips that wasn't a full-blown sympathetic smile. A nod. And the glass kettle chimed three notes as the water didn't reach boiling point. It was one of those fancy kettles with a temperature gauge and slider set to 85 degrees, which was supposedly optimal for a lot of teas according to the manual. Like I said, the world has moved on a lot.

Sometimes I look at my little girl and think how weird it is that she will never know a world without social media, the demand of likes and influencers.

'You don't need to stick around,' I said, rooting about in the cupboard for a mug to make my own brew. 'I've got work to be getting on with, and honestly, there's got to be a better use of your time.'

'It's fine, for today my job's no more complicated than making sure you're doing okay—'

'Which is a big ask, all things considered,' I said.

Another twitch of the lips. This time a slight incline of the head. 'That you feel like your questions are being answered and to ensure that you have a point of contact with the main investigation.'

Which all sounded great, but for the fact that it wasn't the truth, the whole truth and nothing but the truth, so help her God. She was here to investigate our lives from the inside, me and Morven. To get to know the dynamic of the house, to dig around and see what she could learn that might lead to a breakthrough out there in the real world.

'Why don't we have a chat over these,' she said, raising her cup. 'You can tell me about how you guys met.'

And just like that she was back at work. Instead of going back through to the lounge, we sat in the snug, which was a posh way of saying we sat before the open fire in the other half of the kitchen.

'You're going to be disappointed,' I warned her. 'It's not some meet-cute. I tagged along with a friend who wanted company on the long drive up to Edinburgh for a reunion with some of her Uni mates. We were at that age, you know, when your friends are your family, and you do stupid stuff like sit in a car for sixteen hours there and back to keep them company, and think nothing of going to a reunion for a class you weren't part of.' That earned another of Olivia's smiles. No doubt she'd discerned some deep quirk of my personality from my confession that I crashed other people's reunions.

'It was a decent night, though there were lots of in-jokes and shared memories. Morven was there. But like me, she hadn't gone to the university either, and was just hanging out with her friend, which meant the two of us gravitated towards each other as the cuckoos in the nest. And we had a great time. I mean tears rolling down the face fun. We talked from six, when we walked through the door, until two in the morning, without taking a breath. And then we went our separate ways, me back down south, her, somewhere in Northumberland, I think.' It was good to remember this stuff.

'What I remember most about the night, and it's a weird little memory, isn't the place – I couldn't tell you where it was, a pub, that's about it – I couldn't tell you who else was there or what anyone looked like, what I remember is that first impression, that she smelled like Fruit Pastilles.' I chuckled at that. 'It's a really stupid memory, but it's seared into my senses. Fruit Pastilles. I have no idea what perfume it was. It was one of those moments of chance that utterly reshapes the trajectory of your life.

'After a week I couldn't get her out of my head and I was kicking myself for not asking for her number, but there was that whole different ends of the country thing. It felt like a much bigger place back then. I didn't drive. I wasn't earning much. Hell, I'd had to borrow two hundred quid from a friend to pay the bills that month. So, the idea of falling for someone who lived so far away was stupid. But – there's always a but, right? But I couldn't stop thinking about her. So, I wrote to my friend and asked her if she'd ask her friend if they had a way to contact her.

'What I got in return was a scathing letter from Tamsin, my friend, asking what was it with the arrogance of men that they always thought someone had to be interested in them, and making me feel about six inches high. I apologised. I remember that. I don't remember exactly what went into that apology, but it was sincere. I tried to explain how it was just that I'd had a great night and it had felt like there was something . . . you know?' Olivia nodded along as I trawled twenty-four-year-old memories for the truth, or a version of it, filtered through the looking-glass of time.

'A week went by, maybe more, remember this was before everyone had email in their pockets, and lots of us still relied on good old-fashioned lick-a-postage-stamp stick-an-envelope-in-the-post mail,' my turn to quirk a smile that said yeah, we're old. 'Then I got another letter back from Tamsin. I remember the first line. *God, I'm sorry.* Turned out Morven had asked her friend about me, and if she'd reach out to Tamsin to put us in touch. She'd put her phone number in the letter and put the ball very much in my court. If I wanted to complicate my life all I had to do was dial that number and say hi.'

'You called?' And a heartbeat later. 'Of course you did.'

'Of course I did. But it wasn't easy. I don't remember how long it took me to summon up the courage. A few days at least. Then I finally rang, and she wasn't in. Her flatmate answered.'

'Oh God, what an anti-climax!'

'Yep. But at least she was glad to hear from me. So, we kept on talking until Morven got back from work, about an hour later.'

'Hah. Well and truly vetted then.'

'Yep. We arranged to meet up that weekend, halfway, so a dirty weekend in Sheffield of all places. We walked around the city getting to know each other. We invented strip bingo, which is every bit as weird and wonderful as it sounds, and scavenged the racks of used record stores and second-hand bookstores, and just talked. And it was good. But I mean, we hadn't even had a first kiss and we had the weirdness of needing to find a hotel or to get the trains home that evening. It's kinda funny to remember it all, we weren't exactly sophisticated. It was dinner at Pizza Hut, a couple of beers at a real ale pub, and then aimlessly walking around looking for a room because we'd missed the last train.'

A memory hit me then of Morven emerging from the toilet in the pub in tears. I hadn't thought about that in half a lifetime. I remember thinking I'd done something wrong, but her period had started while we were in the pub and she was gutted because she thought it would ruin our night. I don't claim to know what she thought about me back then, but the idea that sex was expected or everything would be ruined was kind of sad. We'd ended up in twin beds that we pushed together, and after about six hours of foreplay fell asleep together. It was a pretty good way to start a life together. If I'd never seen her again it would still have been the most memorable night of my life.

'And you said it wasn't a meet-cute,' Olivia said, shaking her head. 'Sounds pretty cute to me.'

Another random synapse fired, and I remembered one of the songs that had been playing in one of the second-hand record stores, 'Cornflake Girl' by Tori Amos. I'd spent my last tenner on it the next day before we went home and joked we'd always have Tori. I wondered if it was Morven that had got Nora listening to her?

'It would never work in Hollywood,' I said. 'And I'd be lying if I said it was plain sailing after that. It took me nearly two years to convince her to up sticks and move south. But those two years of long-distance phone calls and hours of the intercity up to Newcastle were pretty good years. And given where we ended up, I wouldn't change them for a thing.'

'And that's what counts,' Olivia said. 'So, Northumberland, eh?'

'God's own country,' I said.

'I thought that was Yorkshire?'

'Only if you've never been to Northumberland,' I countered, 'He might have made Yorkshire, but it was only as a test run for Northumberland.' That earned a laugh.

'Did you spend a lot of time up there?'

I nodded. 'We did. And we still go back for holidays.'

I could almost see the cogs and gears whirring away behind her eyes. 'Anywhere of special significance?' Meaning somewhere

Morven might retreat to. I'd been having the same thoughts. Was there somewhere up there where she still felt at home, because that's what we do, isn't it? We run to somewhere or from somewhere.

I felt my phone vibrate in my pocket. It was on silent. 'Sorry, I've got to get this,' I said, pushing myself up out of my seat. It was Mac. I headed towards the door before I answered, and even then it was only to say, 'Hey man, how you doing?' I took pains not to say anything that might raise an eyebrow. I sat on the stairs, knowing that retreating to the privacy of the study would only make Olivia think the call was something I didn't want her over-hearing, which would send her cop brain jumping to all sorts of conclusions.

'I can't believe I'm about to do this . . . I've got an address.'

'Okay.'

'I'm not going to give it to you.'

'Okay. Why not?'

'I'm not going to let you do something stupid, Alex.'

'Would I?'

'We both know you would.'

'That is true,' I admitted.

'I'm going meet you and we'll go together.'

'Okay. You need me to come in?'

If he wondered why I'd phrased it like that he didn't let on, beyond a wry, 'Be hard to get there otherwise.'

'There's a couple of things I've got to do here first. Give me an hour to get over to you.'

'It's okay, I'll swing by and pick you up. I'm over by Liverpool Street anyway.'

'Okay, I'll head out in a few. See you at the office,' which was relying on Mac remembering I did most of my work in the Jamaican café around the corner from Poppy's school.

'If you're there before me, I'll have one of those coconut cake things.'

He remembered.

'My treat,' I promised.

'Damned right it is, mate.'

I killed the call and looked up to see Olivia standing in the doorway, cup in hand. 'Problems?'

'Always,' I said. 'Work. You know how it is.'

'You need to go in?'

'Yeah, won't be long, I'm sure. We've got some material on the new documentary we're cutting,' I said, and shrugged, like it was obvious what the problems would be, and how they couldn't cope without me.

'Don't worry about it. I'll head back to the station. You've got my number if you need me. If Morven reaches out . . .' I nodded. The rest didn't need saying. Non-verbal communication. We understood each other.

'Right back atcha.'

'We'll find her,' she promised. What she didn't say was that it was going to be okay. That was the kind of promise she couldn't make without tempting fate.

'I'll think about those special places,' I told her, picking up the conversation that Mac's call had cut short.

'That would be really helpful. Anywhere that means something to her, or to the both of you. That's our best chance of finding her right now. People don't tend to hide to somewhere they have no connection with, they look for the comfort of the familiar and the meaningful.'

I nodded. 'That makes sense. I'll wrack my brain.'

'Okay, now get yourself off to work and save the day.'

'Some of us superheroes don't wear our undies on the outside of our jeans,' I joked, handing Olivia her coat from where it had been draped across the banister. It was something my dad used to say – but he dreamed of flying naked above the city most nights, so. . .

'Good job. That would get you sectioned these days,' she came back, another twitch of the lips. There was definitely a sense of humour in there fighting to get out. It must have been a difficult thin blue line to tread, that whole building a rapport without looking like an insensitive arsehole laughing and joking at someone else's misfortune, especially when the other person seemed to be holding it together. 'I know it's hard,' she said, 'and I know it's a dumb thing to say, but try not to worry. Go to work, do your job, let us do ours. We're good at what we do.'

I grabbed my own jacket and followed her out, locking up behind us.

We parted at the garden gate, another little nod of the head between us, Olivia heading across the road to her car, me walking down the street in the direction of Poppy's school and Maggs' café.

FIFTEEN

I'd been nursing my coffee for ten minutes before Mac's imposing figure loomed over the yummy mummies. He inclined his head an inch, it was as close as I was going to get to a greeting. However, he was all smiles for Maggie, who knew what he wanted on sight. But that was Mac, once you saw him, you didn't forget him. Some people are just like that. They make an impression.

He sat down beside me, beating his thick black coffee by about half a minute. Maggie set the coconut toto down beside the mug, and as Mac went to pay, put him off with a 'Don't worry yourself, my treat. Nice to see you back.'

'Nice to be seen, Maggs. Looking mighty fine if I might say so.'

'You might,' she grinned, and retreated back behind her counter feeling very much like she'd been seen.

Straight down to business, Mac cut through all the noise and asked me, 'Like I said on the phone, I've got an address. The question is: are you *really* sure you want to do this?' I nodded, but that didn't stop him from going on. 'If this really is the person making Morven's life hell, we aren't equipped to deal with it, you know that, right? This isn't some vigilante movie; we can't wade in there swinging baseball bats. We're literally helpless, with no idea what we'll be walking into.'

'I've got no choice,' I said which was patently untrue, but Mac nodded anyway.

He took a bite of his toto and licked his lips, giving the thumbs up to Maggie behind the counter. It was a nice normal little inter-action in the middle of a bigger one that was anything but.

'I thought you'd say as much. You're wrong, but fine. I'll humour you. But we're doing this on my terms, Alex. I'm serious. If I say it's off, it's off, we walk, no questions, no arguments. You said you trusted me, this is what I do, I need you to prove it. Words are easy. We go, we scope out the place, and if there's even a hint she's there, or anything smells off, we call for back up. No argu-ments. We do this properly or we don't do it at all.'

I didn't have much choice as long as he had the address and I didn't, so I agreed.

'Good. It's going to take us a few hours to drive up there, more with Saturday traffic, day trippers getting out of the city for the long weekend. Ideally we should have been on the road hours ago.'

'I was,' I told him. 'That's the only reason we've got this address to chase down.'

Mac shook his head. 'What sort of mess is your missus wrapped up in?'

'I wish I knew.'

He took another huge bite of his toto and washed it down with the last of the coffee. 'Get your shit together then, my friend. Road trip.'

'I'm not sure my shit will ever be together, mate,' I said, know-ing I sounded sorry for myself. 'But I'm as ready as I'll ever be.'

'Good enough. Come on then.' He blew a kiss towards the counter and was out of the door, leaving a pheromone trail in his wake.

I followed him to his car, which, like him, was larger than life. A racing green e-type Jag with wire rims that was lovingly pol-ished and buffed to within an inch of its rusty chassis. Its curves looked so unlike anything else on the road, its headlights like sad eyes, and even though the matching green leather interior was as cracked and pitted as my teenage acne, it was one hell of a car.

Turning over the ignition my ears were treated to a bass boom of desert eagles, so much rage and despair and the glory of dying young for some stupid honour debt as some nameless hip hop voice ripped out of Queensboro rapped through a tale as old as the car itself.

Back in the sixties it had been a fast car. The way Mac handled it, negotiating the narrow streets of Shoreditch out towards the M40 with increasing bursts of acceleration, getting from nought up to sixty before more lights or crossroads forced him to decelerate hard, proved age hadn't slowed it down any.

With the roof down, we were living proof of evolution, sitting a good five inches taller than the car had been designed for. The wind in our faces whipped away our words. The one mercy was that it whipped away the rapper, too.

We were two hours on the road, a good part of them the most frightening minutes I'd spent in a car, with our low profile putting us level with the wheel nuts on the lorries we wove around, Mac seemingly oblivious to the fact they'd crush us like a bug if he put one foot or gear change wrong. It felt more like a computer game than the last computer game I'd played.

The nature of the roadside changed almost as fast as we travelled, going from city to wildwood in little over ninety minutes, with Mac following signs I barely had time to read. The roads narrowed and narrowed again, eventually down to a single-track farm lane that cut through a tree tunnel grown out of the leafy canopy of the ancient Wychwood forest. We were less than two hours from London. We might as well have been a lifetime away. There was no way of reconciling the beauty of this place, seemingly untouched by the presence of man, and the choking pollution of the city. Another turn took us to a farmhouse gate with a cattle grid behind it.

'Last chance to turn back,' Mac said, slowing to a stop in front of the five-bar gate.

I looked out over the top of the windscreen. I could taste the pollen in the air and the green odour of the leaves. The entire world outside the car felt more vividly real than I was ready to deal with. The approach to the farmhouse wasn't exactly secluded. There was no way whoever was in there would miss us coming, put it that way. No element of surprise.

'I'd never be able to live with myself,' I said, and opened the door. The e-type rode so low it was a struggle to lever myself up out of the passenger seat. I felt Mac's hand on my arse giving me a push.

The handle on the gate was rusted, and I needed to lean in to push it back against the hinges to get it to lift, but a moment later its weight was swinging it wide open. I stepped back to let Mac drive over the cattle grid, then went to close it behind us, but Mac shook his head. It made sense. There was no way of knowing if we were going to have to make a sharp exit.

I clambered back into the car, and we drove the half-mile approach to the farmhouse.

There were two barns to the left of the main house, as well as a garage for tractors and other farm machinery beside them. I saw three cars, including a '70s Land Rover that was bricked up, one of its wheels on the ground beside the front axle. None of the cars looked like they were in any fit state to go anywhere. A huge red plough with two dozen claws looked like it was about to take a huge bite out of the ground.

Mac killed the engine.

There were no lights on in the main house.

No dogs barking.

We didn't get out of the car.

'So, what's the plan, walk up to the front door, knock, and tell them to leave your wife alone?' Mac asked.

I have to admit, even with the two-hour drive to the farm, I hadn't thought this part through. 'The first part sounds about right.'

'And when they open the door?'

'One step at a time,' I said.

'Let me call it through. We don't have to be the first through the door. This isn't a game any more, Alex.'

'It never was,' I said, but I knew what he meant. I got out of the car and walked up to the door. It was as green as the car, with a leafy head with a brass knocker in its mouth in the middle of it.

I heard the crunch of gravel behind me. Mac hadn't slammed the car door. I didn't turn around. I only had eyes for the farm-house – not that I could see through the thick oak door.

I knocked. Three times. Hard.

Mac didn't wait for an answer; he went over to one of the windows, cupped his hands above his eyes as he leaned in, trying to peer inside through the yellow nicotine-stained net curtains. There was nothing to see through the dirt and grime.

'I can't see anyone,' he reported back, moving on to the next window and slowly working his way around the house while I knocked again.

No matter how hard I hammered against the door, no one came to open it.

The anti-climax was a gut-punch. I'd wound myself up in anticipation of the face-to-face and, denied all of that, pent up tension rushed out of me in a disappointed sigh. I don't know what I'd expected to happen, but it wasn't this.

Mac emerged from around the back of the house. 'No one's home. So, what do we do?'

I scratched at the roots of my hair, as though I might be able to excavate an idea.

'You check the barns,' I suggested, 'I'll go see if there's anyone around the garage.'

Mac nodded, content to do my bidding. If he'd realised I'd sent him as far from the farmhouse as I reasonably could, he didn't say.

I turned my back on him, as though heading off to the open

garage. I walked around the corner of the house, out of sight. I had different ideas. I looked about the yard for something that might work. I wasn't picky, a decent-sized stone, a piece of pipe, some sort of tool, it didn't matter, it only needed to break the glass. I fixed on a six-inch copper pipe, ragged at the end with weld, and hefted it, banging it against my thigh as I walked towards the back door.

The normal thing to do with no one home would have been retreat, wait, see who arrived. But I was done with normal. I had been from the moment I decided to withhold a vital piece of evidence from the investigation into my wife's disappearance. Now, I was embracing the abnormal. Five strides straight to the door, moving with purpose, and a single sharp rap against the pane that sent glass showering inside. I reached in, and reached down, fumbling the lock with my fingers and cut myself, a deep stinging gash as I pulled my arm back out. The blood ran in a thick rivulet down the pale skin of my inner arm to my wrist. The cut was deep, but the adrenalin high meant I barely felt a thing. The pain would come, along with stitches.

I pushed the door open and went inside.

I'm not sure what I was expecting to find. A cell with a huge wooden X on the wall and leather cuffs dangling from it on chains? Darkened windows and tortured cats hanging from string ropes with the owner using them to practice the dark arts of vivisection? Or a nice oak refectory table big enough to comfortably sit ten, with high-backed oak chairs around it that bore the wear and tear of everyday life hard on their legs?

Dishes lay drying in the rack beside the sink. There were plants in the window. It wasn't a modern kitchen, there was no fancy tiled splash back or high-pressure mixer tap on a cord.

There was a pair of green Hunter wellies beside the door, the soles caked in thick dried mud like victims of Vesuvius.

I saw a tea towel on the side and wrapped it around my wrist to soak up the worst of the blood. The last thing I wanted was to leave a trail of DNA-rich breadcrumbs across the floor.

I glanced around the interior, not sure what I was looking for, and trying to think like someone who'd just returned home with an envelope stuffed full of cash. I wouldn't necessarily move to put it somewhere safe, this was my home, the whole place was safe, so I'd be just as likely to leave it lying around on a table, same with anything else that might give me a clue as to what the fuck was going on.

So, I went deeper into the farmhouse.

The kitchen opened into a hallway with a wooden stair leading up, and two more reception rooms downstairs. With a choice of left or right, I went right knowing I only had a few seconds before Mac realised what I was doing.

This room was not much better than the last, there was a stuffed armchair, worn through on the arms so that tufts of foam poked up through the fabric, and a settee that was covered with a crocheted blanket that did little to protect it from the dirt and grime of the farm. I saw an assortment of figurines, the kind of tacky ceramics my grandmother used to collect, and a number of ballerinas and dancers in clear plastic display boxes. There was one in a toreador's outfit, another in the flowing pink skirts of a flamenco dancer, fans raised, and all sorts of others around the room. There was an air of sadness to the collection. They were out of time. An inheritance that the receiver was too guilty to throw away but didn't really want.

And on the coffee table beside a chipped bone china cup on a mismatched saucer, the envelope.

I didn't think about it. I crossed the room quickly, snatched it up, expecting to hear Mac's, '*What the fuck do you think you're playing at?*' at any second, and fumbled it open. It was thick. Stuffed full. Five grand would do that, I supposed. It felt weird, stealing my own money back.

But nowhere near as weird as tearing the envelope open and realising there was no money – it was stuffed full of clippings and photocopies.

I found the note on top, Morven's handwriting unmistakable.

You know nothing about me.

I flicked through the cuttings and all the rest of it.

They were all parts of our life.

There was stuff about my documentaries, including a photo of us as a family on the red carpet for the BAFTAs a couple of years back; there was more about our wedding, including photos from the cloister in Sorrento where we'd said 'I do', a copy of our marriage certificates, in both Italian and in English after we'd come back to get it ratified here. There was a copy of Poppy's birth certificate, listing her mother and father as Morven and Alexander Kerr. There was a black-and-white photo of a school sports day that must have been some time back in the '70s, and a girl I assumed was Morven tearing down the hundred metre dash with her thumb over the egg to make sure it didn't spill from her spoon during the race. She looked absolutely fixated on the egg, oblivious to the camera, and so incredibly like Poppy in that moment it broke my heart.

I kept shuffling through the stuff.

There was an entire life in here.

Two.

The life before me, and the life after.

But everything in here proved beyond any doubt that she was Morven Kerr, née Muir, the woman who'd smelled of Fruit Pastilles when we met and served as co-inventor of strip bingo.

She was my Morven, had always been my Morven and always would be my Morven.

It was a full family archive, everything imaginable, photographs of birthday cakes with their candles being blown out, more photos of ice cream sundaes on the beach and soaking wet swimming costumes, all of it just so utterly normal and unremarkable.

There were even pictures that I assumed were of her parents, back when she was barely waist high and swung between them as they laughed their way along a road somewhere.

The problem was I knew that wasn't true.

At least none of it before that night in Edinburgh when our worlds had collided so wonderfully.

I was looking at a well-constructed lie.

I had to be, because Nora had told me as much. Morven Muir was a name she'd made up.

'What did I tell you about doing something stupid?'

I hadn't heard Mac come in behind me.

'Not to,' I said, holding up the envelope.

'What's that?'

'I thought it was my money. It's not. It's her denial. It's all of our lives, mine, hers, Poppy's, crammed into an envelope and begging whoever it is blackmailing her to just let her get on with living it.' Mac looked confused. I couldn't blame him. 'It's proof that she isn't who they think she is,' I said.

'But we both know she is,' another voice said.

SIXTEEN

'Who are you?'

I looked up to see the double barrels of a shotgun levelled at my chest, twin black holes promising to swallow the life in the room whole. The woman behind them glared. I could sense how desperately she was itching to pull the trigger.

She looked older than she had in the security footage. Broken by the wheel of life, I guess.

The pain in her eyes was as old as time.

'Give me one good reason why I shouldn't just pull the trigger?'

I didn't have one.

Mac did.

'Because if you do, you'll be shooting a policeman, and that would end very badly for you,' he said, careful not to make any sudden moves that might cause her trigger finger to get itchier. He took a step towards her, hands out placatingly.

She looked at the bloody tea towel wrapped around my wrist.

'Not good enough. Don't take another step unless you want me to give you a gut full of lead shot. Now, who are you and what are you doing here? Don't bother trying to feed me some bullshit line, either. You break into my home, I find you rooting around in my things, I'm well within my rights to defend myself. So, explain yourselves. You say you're with the police, then show me your warrant, policeman.'

'I'm not lying,' Mac assured her. 'But you're going to have to take my word for that. You know we don't have a warrant to be in here.' He held his hands up, palms out to her, not that they would have been much good against shot. 'I'm truly sorry. It's no excuse, but my friend got carried away and did something stupid – but he did it for a good reason. Not that it makes a difference. I came in here to haul him out on his arse, but that doesn't make things any better. If you'll let us explain, I'm sure you'll understand why he did it.'

'And you think why is important?'

'I do.'

'I'm listening, but I am not sure I want to listen to a pack of lies.'

'If you'll let me reach into my back pocket for my wallet, I'll show you my ID, okay?' Mac reached back slowly.

She didn't shoot, which was something.

But she didn't lower the shotgun.

She gestured towards the busted couch. 'Over there, the pair of you, sit. Keep your hands where I can see them.'

Mac nodded.

I was a couple of steps slower but sank down beside him into cushions that threatened to drag me down into the belly of the couch and swallow me whole. I cradled my injured wrist, holding the tea towel tight. It stung, but it wasn't any kind of agony, which I hoped was a good omen, despite how much blood the tea towel appeared to have soaked up.

I didn't wait for Mac to explain our presence. I felt like everything was slipping away from me. I only had the one question. I looked at the woman. 'Why are you doing this?' I couldn't help myself. I knew it was only going to escalate the situation, but she was the one pointing the gun, not us. 'What has she ever done to you?'

'What?' The woman said.

That threw me.

I ignored the black-eyed stare of the shotgun. 'You heard me,'

I said with considerably more courage than I felt. 'What gives you the right to turn my life upside down? Last week my whole world consisted of school runs and arguing about who had control of the remote, then you started sending my wife threatening messages, blackmailing her. What gives you the right to think you can destroy my life?'

She shook her head. Not much, but it was unmissable.

'Look at me,' she dipped the shotgun, then raised it again, like she was trying to make me lift my eyes from the barrels to her face. 'I said *look at me!*' I don't know what I was supposed to be seeing, but whatever it was, I wasn't seeing it. 'Do I look like someone who sets out to destroy anyone's life?'

My first and absolutely worst instinct was to say something clever, but I was just too wound up, the words all cramming to the front of my head. I kept my mouth shut.

I looked at her.

She was right.

I stopped seeing the enemy in front of me and instead looked at her for what she was, a pensioner dressed in a heavy knitted cardigan with patches across the elbows and a flower over her heart where it had been mended. It was far too heavy for the weather. And like everything else in her house, it was old.

She turned her cheek away from me, just slightly, changing the way the light and the thick shadows settled across her features and for a moment they conjured up another face altogether. My imagination was playing tricks on me. But there was a resemblance, wasn't there?

My confusion lasted less than two seconds. 'You want the truth? That girl ruined my life . . .' She said, bluntly, but there was such incredible sadness behind those words.

'I don't—' but I did. I understood. I didn't *want* to, but that was different.

The shadows weren't lying to me, they were where the truth

106

hid. I saw Morven in there, reflected in the wrinkles and worry lines and weather-beaten skin, an older version of her, sure, with the sharpness of her features worn down by time.

Which meant I could only be looking at her real mother.

'You really don't know, do you?' The sorrow that had been there was joined by confusion. Another question. 'It wasn't you?' I had no idea what she meant with that. 'You poor bastard.' That was something we could both agree on. 'Do you even know who she was? I mean back then, before she got to reinvent herself?'

I shook my head. I realised my hands were clasped, like I was praying.

'Oh God, I pity you. I really do.' Gone was the hostility towards us, not because of Mac's calming reassurance but rather because of some secret past she knew and I didn't. It felt like half a lifetime since I'd last thought ignorance was blissful.

'I know she had to change her name, that's all. And I only found that out yesterday.'

'So, you really didn't send the message?'

I shook my head again. 'What message?' But it had to be similar to Morven's, didn't it? *I know who you were.*

'The first one came a few days ago. I don't know who it was from. They protected their identity. It said they'd found my girl. I didn't believe them. People can be cruel. The number of times I've had threatening letters, phone calls where there's no one on the other end, or there's just this heavy breathing, then there's the ones where they'd promise to hurt me for what she did . . . Believe me, after a while you start to dread the phone ringing.'

'I can't even begin to imagine,' Mac sympathised, a few kind words to draw the rest of her story out. 'What did you do?'

'I wasn't going to respond . . .'

'But you did.' Not a question.

She nodded. 'I couldn't not . . . she's still my little girl, whatever else she is . . .'

107

'What happened?'

'Nothing for three days. Then I got another message. It said they'd bring her to me, let me see her for myself. It's been over thirty years. She's been gone a lot longer than she was with me . . . I wasn't going to go. But . . .'

'But how could you not?' Mac was on her wavelength. He was telling her he got it, he understood her pain, he'd have done the same thing. He leaned in a little more. He wasn't bothering with his badge or proving his credentials, he was being human and that was buying him more credibility than a warrant card would. I tried to put myself in her shoes, but they were more uncomfortable than my own.

Listening to Mac, he had a way with her. It was similar to how Ellie Underwood had been with me last night.

Was it only last night?

Christ, it felt like a lifetime ago already.

I picked at the tea towel, the cloth scratchy against my skin.

'They told me not to approach her, just to sit and watch. I didn't know if they would be watching me, but if they were, I didn't want to risk them scaring her off . . . so I just sat with my coffee while it got cold, and then colder, waiting. I got there more than an hour early. I didn't want to miss her. But,' another shrug, like how was she supposed to just accept a passing resemblance in a stranger's face after more than thirty years? 'I didn't recognise her at first, not when she walked through the door, but there was something about the *way* she walked, if that makes sense? It was like looking into the past and seeing myself walking towards me . . . She had changed so much, but it was like she hadn't changed at all.'

'It makes perfect sense,' Mac assured her. 'You didn't talk to her? Not even when you were sure?'

The woman shook her head. 'I didn't know what I'd say . . . too much time has passed. I could have said I missed her, but that would have turned into how she'd broken my heart and ruined my life if I couldn't keep my emotions under control . . . sometimes it's better to say nothing at all.' Both Mac and I nodded. 'I saw that she was clutching this envelope.' I knew exactly which envelope she meant. 'She didn't look around. She walked straight up to a bin and dumped it, then turned around and walked out. She didn't see me, but she wasn't looking for anyone. She was only interested in getting out of there as quickly as possible. I don't know what possessed me, but when she was gone I went and fished it out of the rubbish.' She nodded towards Morven's life stuffed inside the envelope. 'I thought about following her, but what would that have achieved?'

'So, you had no idea what was in the envelope?'

'None whatsoever.'

'You weren't expecting her to bring money?' I asked.

'Money?' She laughed then. It was a broken bark. 'No. He just told me to be there and I'd get to see her again. And I'll tell you this for nothing, I wish I had never laid eyes on her. I wish I'd stayed here yesterday and just let the world go about its business without me for once.'

'Why?'

'Because it hurts too much. It was easier when she was dead to me. I could get on with what was left of my life. It was an end, there was closure. It doesn't matter if she's someone else now, *my* girl is gone. She doesn't even have to pretend she's sorry, I don't have to pretend I forgive her . . .' she shrugged. 'She just puts on this new life of hers on like it's a frock . . . while the rest of us are left to pick up the pieces.' She looked at me when she said that, and I realised that I'd misinterpreted the pity in her eyes for sorrow.

She lowered the shotgun, finally.

'You think she's normal, don't you?' She asked me. 'A proper wife and mother. That she *cares*. That she's capable of love. But my girl isn't any of that. She's broken. There's a monster inside her.

It's always been there. I didn't recognise it at first, or didn't *want* to, because I'm her mother and I loved her. She's always been so good at hiding it, wearing her pretty mask over her monster face, but you need to understand, whatever else happens, she's always going to be the monster underneath. Believe me, I know my Lucy.'

'Lucy?'

'That's the name she was born with. She gets to pick herself a nice, interesting name, too. Lucy isn't good enough for her anymore.'

I fixated on Morven's real name, like it was the key to unlocking her secret self, the part of her I'd never known and never could know. Lucy. 'If you prefer the idea of her being dead and gone, why did you go?'

'I couldn't help myself . . . I just had to see her, one last time.'

'Which sounds like you are punishing yourself,' I said.

'You will too, one day when all this is over, and the monster is finally slain.'

'She isn't a monster,' I said.

'If you only knew . . .'

SEVENTEEN

'So, tell me. Make me understand. If she's such a monster I deserve to know, don't I? I get into bed beside her every night.'

The woman looked at me then, full focus on my eyes, as if there were only the two of us in the room. Mac ceased to exist. 'You do,' she said with such harsh earnest I felt the shiver chase down the ladder of my spine one bone-rung at a time. 'But it isn't easy to tell. Not without tying myself in knots, trying to explain things out of sequence, to explain the pain . . . it was a school trip, a few days in the Forest of Dean, staying in this old castle with her class, and a few siblings whose parents had the money to pay for the extra place. It took us months to save for Lucy, even though it was only a hundred and fifty quid, it felt impossible. That was a lot of money back then. We were living on maybe seventy quid a week, benefit money, for me, Garry, my husband, and Lucy's child benefit. But Lucy really wanted to go, so I got myself a little extra job, cash in hand, to scrape the extra cash together. She was so excited. It was her first time away. She was thirteen.' The woman seemed to lose her thread for a moment, swept up in some sort of nostalgia for days of benefit fraud and simpler times of happy families. 'Now I think if I hadn't . . . if I hadn't somehow scraped that cash together, if I hadn't broken my back to try and put a smile on her face, I might still have my Lucy, even if she hated me for not letting her go on that trip with the rest of her friends. She'd have got over it, eventually. Kids do, don't they?'

A little smile pulled at the side of my mouth. 'That's the thing, isn't it? The stuff we do for them, the unseen burdens they put us under, the costs. And barely get a thanks as they skip back through the door.'

'That week destroyed her life, and mine in the process, in so many ways.' She swept a hand out around the room, as though to say *see my kingdom*, or maybe *see what is missing from my kingdom* – no daughter, no husband.

'What happened?'

'She killed her best friend and her younger brother. Drowned them. He was only nine.'

'Jesus.'

'Had very little to do with my little girl,' she said, though she made the sign of the cross as her words slipped away into heavy breathing.

I struggled to wrap my head around the idea that Morven – *my* Morven, the woman I loved unconditionally, who made me laugh and lit up my world with every single smile and just as easily infuriated the hell out of me with any of a billion little quirks that were just part of what made our marriage what it was – was capable of killing anyone . . . let alone two kids, one thirteen, the other nine.

It went so far beyond horrific I simply couldn't give it space inside my head to root down.

'You don't believe me; I can see it in your face. You're trying to deny it. To find a way to tell me: *no, you're wrong. That can't be what happened. It just can't.* I know that look painfully well, believe me. I've seen it in a hundred faces. I saw it in the eyes of the jury, but then I saw it change into another look all together. And I'll see it change in yours, too. Up, on your feet. Come on.' She gestured with the barrel of the shotgun.

I rose from the couch, unsure what she wanted from me.

'Come with me.'

I followed her out of the room. She led me up the narrow

staircase to a musty old box room upstairs that was stuffed to overflowing with a hoarder's paradise of old papers, magazines, cuttings, picture albums and more, every shelf and cabinet straining to contain the stuff. The room had that old paper smell.

'See for yourself,' she said, not willing to cross the threshold. 'Pick a paper, any paper, there's something in it about Lucy's story. I'll wait.'

I looked at the devastation of the room, trying to grasp the sheer enormity of it, that her story could take up so much ink and paper, that there could be so much to say . . . but then, outrage sells newspapers and nothing fuels outrage like a child killing other children.

I took a yellowed tabloid off the top of one of the many piles. It was old; 29 April 1986. A family portrait dominated the front page. They were the picture-perfect butter-wouldn't-melt kids digging in the sand with their proud parents crouching down over them. They could have been any family on any beach in any era. The castles in the sand were crumbling on one side, the sand not wet enough to hold their shape. There was something melancholic in that juxtaposition, like the sand was offering a glimpse of the decay to come to one side of their perfect little family unit. The headline was garish set against the image, the two words TALGARTH TRAGEDY, set thickly enough to be visible fifty feet away. There was a single paragraph beneath it, crammed with the worst of the news to feed the reader's morbid curiosity.

A school trip to Brecon ended in tragedy as thirteen-year-old Chrissy Lang and her nine-year-old brother Scott drowned in the waters of Llangorse Lake. Police have remanded into custody an unnamed individual, thought to be a classmate of the tragic siblings. (Cont. Page Two)

I turned the page to see what followed, and beside a section about the continuing evacuation of Pripyat and the still unfolding horrors of Chernobyl, there was a box that included a short quote from a teacher, explaining that the kids had been on an outing to see the crannog and visit the site of the Dark Age royal fort. Obviously, everyone was devastated. And no, she wouldn't confirm what had happened out on the water. That didn't stop the reporter from speculating, though they stopped short of naming Morven. There was a class photograph reprinted in there, that was enough.

It was surreal, seeing the two stories juxtaposed like this. One of the greatest horrors of the modern world side by side with a much more intimate one that really only mattered to the handful of people wrapped up in it, no matter how awful it was or how many column inches it commanded.

I put the paper back on the pile and took another from a different stack. This one was a *Welsh Post*. The headlines were about another crime and another set of heartbroken parents, but thumbing through the pages I saw a grainy black-and-white shot of Morven in a school uniform of blue gingham frock and a navy cardigan that looked so incredibly '80s. As desperately as I wanted to believe it wasn't her, the resemblance was impossible to deny. I could see every contour her face would grow into, but it was the eyes that sold it. I knew those eyes, even reduced to the weird block and cross hatch of poor-quality print. It was her.

The newspaper listed her name as Lucy Galvin.

I knew that name as soon as I saw it.

How could I not?

The press had spent a huge chunk of my youth vilifying her as another Mary Bell, the ten-year-old from Scotswood who had killed two boys in the late sixties. The coverage had been fairly relentless, but I will admit, with the years in between most of it had faded into background noise and all I could remember – and most of that might have been at the prodding of the articles in the room – was that the girl had drowned her friend, then chased her brother across the water as he screamed for help and held him under until he stopped kicking. The image had been burned into my brain by a harrowing recreation I'd seen on the news – one that should never have been aired.

I rubbed at my jaw.

I shook my head.

My Morven and her Lucy couldn't be the same person.

They just couldn't.

Deeper into the room I found a letter from almost two months later. Actually, there were hundreds of letters, most of them threats, but the one that stood out was on a letterhead I recognised. It was a development company I'd worked with twice, though this was dated before my time. I read it in sickness and in horror, not quite believing that some faceless executive somewhere could be so heartlessly opportunistic as to write to the mother of a child killer offering money to buy her story, not as a documentary, which, reading between the lines, they were threatening to do if the offer wasn't accepted, but as a two-part drama with some then beloved and now forgotten actress in the lead. It was ever the way, exploitation and profit from tragedy, but it was hard to take when it hit so close to home.

I didn't remember the documentary, but that didn't mean it hadn't happened.

Seeing the letter in my hand, the woman said, 'Parasites.' That was all she needed to say. It conveyed her feelings perfectly.

I dropped the letter with the care it deserved and took up a magazine. It was one of those garish true crime things that had been popular back then. There was a double page spread on the drownings with a glossy colour map of the lakes, the drowning sites marked as though they promised some sunken treasure. X marks the spot.

There was a photograph of the woman, looking nearly forty years younger, giving an indication of how hard the intervening years had been on her. Susan Galvin, though it listed her maiden name as Hall, and said she'd gone back to living under it after the suicide of her husband, Garry, eighteen months after the murders. This was an unsympathetic scandal piece, with the implication that this survivor had brought it all on herself. The tone was like those bullying '80s tabloids, gloating over her pain. It absolutely refused the notion that there were more than those two young victims here.

Every inch of her life was in this stuff, pieces stolen from her diaries, quotes from classmates and parents; they even printed some of the drawings she'd done in class when she was younger and had some child psychologist spout bullshit about what a troubled child she was, as evidenced by the way she drew the house, the disassociation of the tree and the family unit from the home, and so much other shit. Sometimes a tree is just a tree, a house is just a house, and a kid can't draw. It didn't matter to these people. No stone left unturned; no dark secret not dug up as the muck of this family's lives was raked through.

It wasn't hard to see why Garry Galvin couldn't cope with this level of hell, or its endless nature, and unlike his wife he couldn't hide behind his maiden name.

There were scandal rags suggesting he'd had multiple affairs, others that he'd beaten his daughter. One paper called him the Rat King and made out that he'd been part of some Football Factory and was responsible for smashing the skull of a train conductor on one match day back when the Intercity Firm and the Headhunters had ruled. It had been a different time back then, of course, not the corporate affair football was now. It had been properly tribal, with those tribes going to war every Saturday.

There was one exposé with a photo of a coiled belt dominating one entire page, a line of blood dripped out from the buckle against the white, and beside it the inference that it was his belt and his daughter's blood.

It was the kind of sick stuff the British gutter press was distressingly good at.

I didn't see how any of it was remotely in the public interest, or what it had to do with the making of a murderer, but that was why I was a mere grunt, not some shark in the editorial pool, following the blood money as it churned the waters.

And at the end of it, eighteen months in, after court dates, after having his life torn apart, Garry Galvin reached the point where the only way out was hanging himself in the upstairs bedroom, using the same kind of belt made infamous by the tabloids.

I don't know how long I was in that room.

I have no idea how many papers I thumbed through, how many magazine pages I turned, how many sides of hate mail I read. I couldn't even begin to absorb the sheer soul crushing weight of it all. How she could live with all of this in the house, a constant reminder of the worst days of her life and everything that had been ripped away from her, was beyond me. It wasn't like it could offer her any sort of comfort.

What I can tell you is that it was as much a mausoleum to Garry Galvin as it was a museum to the memory of his daughter Lucy and the day she left their lives. Looking at this stuff I realised she'd been frozen in time as far as Susan was concerned, and with that came the understanding of why she had to go to that food court and see her daughter all grown up, even if only from afar.

There were more photographs of Morven, that same school photo repeated in dozens of them, but there were candid ones, too, including shots of her being hurried into the police station beneath the thick raincoat of the officer escorting her in. She looked so young in them. Sad. I don't know what I'd expected to see, but with all of the woman's talk of monsters in her I'd convinced myself there would be something . . . defiance? Rage? Pride? But there was none of that, she was just a little girl, lost.

But in every single one of them I saw the echo of my wife's face and knew the absolute truth of her story. She wasn't some witness kept safe from harm; out of reach of some crime family she'd testified against. She wasn't some innocent standing up against some great evil. She *was* the great evil.

It was a gut-punch.

'Seen enough?'

EIGHTEEN

I had.

More than enough.

There was only so much battering the soul could take.

If you'd asked me yesterday, I would have told you my life had been ripped apart. That wasn't even close to how I felt leaving Susan Hall's farmhouse. Hand on heart, I have no idea how she could have lived with it all these years. It wasn't a burden, it was a concrete block crushing down on my chest, with the delicate bird bones caving in on themselves one at a time. I took screenshots of the texts she'd received, along with the number they came from. I didn't expect any better luck following them than I'd had with the constantly repeated *I know who you were* threats Morven had received. The sender knew what they were doing.

It was a strange goodbye, too. It didn't feel right to hug, but she was my mother-in-law, and I suddenly found myself on her doorstep fumbling with my phone to show her a photograph of Poppy, her granddaughter, and telling her how like her mother she was. But of course she was, I'd just spent an hour looking at photographs of her at the same age. There was so little of me in her, no matter how I might have thought otherwise before today. The truth was in all of those newspaper cuttings.

'I don't know what to say . . . am I supposed to feel something?'

There was a cutting edge to the question, because of course she was. She was meant to look at my little girl and lose a little piece of her heart in the fairy tale version of this moment.

I shook my head. 'I just thought you should know.'

'And now I know.'

'Now you know,' I agreed.

Mac nodded like one of those bobble heads.

'You can keep the tea towel.'

I apologised for the broken window again.

We didn't say anything else until we were back in the car and watching the farmhouse recede in the rear-view mirror.

'Did you get what you came for?'

I scratched at the stubble coming through my chin. I looked at the clock on the dash. We'd be back in London for kick-off. That was how I always thought of 3 p.m. on a Saturday, even if television rights had completely changed that, with games strung out across the entire weekend now for the Sky and BT money machine. 'I don't know. I got answers I didn't want, and questions I'm not sure I can handle the answers to. But mostly I just found grief and I'm not sure either of us needed that.'

'Want to fill me in on what you found up there?'

'Not really,' I said, but I did it anyway.

By the time I was finished there was a tension between us that hadn't been there before. Mac said simply, 'I remember her.' And didn't take his eyes from the road.

I unwrapped the towel from around my wrist, expecting to see deep lacerations and serious damage, but the reality was nowhere near as bad as I'd feared. It had already stopped bleeding and was crusting over. Maybe I'd get lucky and wouldn't need stitches after all?

Some masochistic part of me wanted to ask more questions, like what he remembered from the police side of things, but of course he wouldn't have worked it. He remembered it the same way I did, from snippets of news reports, and from hearing his parents talk about how sick that kid must be. That was the over-riding memory I had, not the tabloid headlines. It made me very conscious of what got said in front of Poppy.

We made decent time back to London, traffic considering. Mac didn't share much of what was on his mind until we were close to home. 'Don't take this the wrong way, mate, but I'm not sure this is something you should be doing.'

'Look me in the eye and tell me you wouldn't be doing exactly the same thing in my place.'

Mac turned slightly, not really looking at me, not really looking at the road. 'I've got a different skill set, mate. This is what I do. It isn't what you do.'

'It is now.'

'That's so easy to say, but you know damned well the doing is different. You got lucky today, getting this far. And look where it got you.'

'Closer to the truth.'

'But ask yourself this, do you feel better for knowing the truth? Does it help that lovely wife of yours that you know it? Because I'll tell you this for nothing, I can't see any good coming from you knowing what she did back then. She served her sentence; she earned the right to a new start. Until today you knew none of this stuff, and she was your world. You loved her for who she was, simple as that. Hers was the face you saw every day; hers was the voice that lifted your heart and made the shit world go away; hers was the hand you took when you needed to feel comfort, and it was the hand you took when you wanted to steel yourself against the pain; hers was the only opinion that mattered; and more than anything, hers was the heart that made yours beat. Now tell me, *convince* me, your world is better for knowing this one thing about her that she'd rather you never found out?'

There wasn't a single sentiment in there I could argue with, and he knew it. None of it was made better by knowing what Morven had done thirty-six years ago. She'd been a different person, quite literally. I mean if I look at Poppy now and try to think about her in close to thirty-six-years' time, there's no way I'm stupid enough to think any of the girl she is right now survives into the woman she's going to be then. Nothing on a surface level, at least. The rest of it, the shit your parents do to fuck you up, sure that'll be lurking under the surface, but if by some miracle of quantum physics I was able to sit across from her in a restaurant tomorrow, only she'd be her mother's age, and I'd only be one day older, and she'd got to live through all of those sliding doors moments in between, shaping her into whoever she'd eventually grow into being, I don't think I'd recognise a thing about her. Why would I?

So how could I look at the girl in those headlines and let her change the way I felt about the woman who was absolutely the better part of me?

I didn't waste my breath trying to convince Mac, because we both knew he was on the money.

He pulled up across from the house, letting the engine idle.

'No offence, then, mate, but hopefully I won't hear from you for a while. Let the police do their job. And give that wife of yours a bloody huge hug from me when you get her home.'

I nodded, reaching for the door handle.

'You know I'm not going to stop, don't you?'

'I know you're not going to stop,' Mac echoed. 'Call me if you need me.'

I nodded again and clambered out of the car.

I crossed the street and walked down the short path to the house. A few grains of glass that had been too small to see ground under my foot.

I opened the door, hoping that I'd find Morven with her feet up having a nice cuppa in front of the box, but knowing that Olivia's would be the next voice I heard. Hearing it was a sucker-punch even though I was expecting it.

The television entertained itself.

'Everything go okay at work?' She called through from the kitchen.

'All good,' I shouted back.

Music was playing on the speaker, not loudly, but enough to fill the house with life. I didn't recognise it, but that's the disconnect of age. Olivia was considerably younger than me and each generation has their own go-to tracks. I kicked my shoes off and went upstairs to take care of my arm before I went through to join her. Morven is organised. We've got a fully stocked first aid kit in the bathroom, bandages, disinfectant and all. It took a couple of minutes to dress the wound. I pulled the shirt sleeve down over the bandage then headed downstairs again to join Olivia.

She was making herself at home. There was a dirty cup on the counter, and the wrapping paper and clear cellophane wrap that had come with a bunch of flowers open on the table along with some cut stems. I went over to the sink as my FLO put the flowers into a vase, arranging and rearranging them with that magic that women seem to possess innately.

I started making myself a coffee without even thinking about it, so ingrained was the routine.

'You want one?'

'Just had one,' she assured me, nodding towards the empty cup. The stain on the rim suggested a liberal interpretation of just.

'Nice flowers,' I said.

They were, and although I didn't know it at the time, there was a message in those flowers: lavender bittersweets, a single pink carnation, a white chrysanthemum, two heads of purple hyacinth, and double-headed zinnia arranged around a bunching of Black-eyed Susan in the middle. The card, in very neat script with a slight flourish to it, said: *With sympathy in these trying times.*

I was shaking as I set the little card aside.

'Who sent these?' I asked Olivia.

Outside of this room there was only a handful of people who knew what was going on: Nora, and Malcolm Mason, Ellie Underwood and Josh Morris, who'd been here when Nora and

Mason had shredded every last piece of my world as I thought I knew it, and then there was Mac. Five people. There would be others of course, inside the Protected Persons Unit and the Missing Persons Unit, but they weren't going to send flowers. It was a tight-knit circle of people who needed to know, tighter because of her vulnerable status and protected identity.

I checked the card. There was nothing to say where it had come from, no florist sticker, no Interflora identifier or tracking number to link the bouquet back to an order.

'Doesn't it say?'

I pushed the card towards her. She read it, not seeming to understand the significance of the message for a moment. There was silence in the room, louder than the music, as the track changed. And then her mind went to exactly where mine was.

There was a fundamental flaw in my thinking, of course. There were three others who knew, two of which we could discount immediately because Morven wouldn't be sending me flowers and there was no way in hell Susan Hall was, either. Which left the same person who had been sending those threatening texts.

They were playing with us.

'It was a white van. There were no markings on it. The delivery guy was in a regular uniform, baseball cap pulled down lowish, but not so low I couldn't see his eyes. I had to sign for delivery . . . there was a name on the receipt . . . what was it . . .'

'Did he give you a copy?'

She shook her head.

'Shit . . . That was him, wasn't it? The guy who's been sending those messages . . . he was on my fucking doorstep.'

I didn't stop to think about it; I ran down the hall and out into the street, looking around frantically, up and down the street, standing either side of the white line looking for the van. Because he'd sent those flowers for a reason, hadn't he? He wanted to get a reaction. I didn't know much about him, but I knew this much:

he was the kind of sick bastard who was going to stick around to see if his message had the desired effect. Otherwise why bother sending it?

I heard an engine turning over.

NINETEEN

I started to run, not caring about any other cars coming down the middle of the road as I tore along the dotted line, arms and legs pumping furiously. And for about ten metres I would have matched Linford Christie stride for stride, I was moving that fast, but by twenty metres my legs were already beginning to tie up.

The sides of the white panel van were filthy with caked on grime and mud.

The glass was dark, not tinted, and it had some sort of solarised film over it.

A combination of mud and my angle of vision meant I couldn't read the plates properly.

I forced myself to run faster, straight at the van as if I could somehow stop it in its tracks, wheels spinning, rubber burning, and me like Superman in the middle of the road, the immovable object.

At least in my mind.

The muscles in my thighs burned before I'd covered thirty metres.

He gunned the engine, making that exhaust howl.

Breathing hard, I reached out desperately for the door handle, stumbling as I threw myself in front of the white van as it angled its way out into traffic.

He drove into me, but I didn't feel the impact; the adrenalin pulsing through my system was out of control. Even as I spun away, I grabbed a hold of the handle and refused to let go. I was determined to drag the driver out, but the damned door wouldn't give no matter how frantically I yanked at it.

There was a moment that lasted maybe five awkward footsteps where I was clinging onto the handle, trying to skip-run sideways as the van accelerated, my free hand slapping against the side of the van as I wrenched at the handle, trying to pull the door open, and then I lost him.

But there was a second when he was on top of me that I could see him, or at least part of his face, with the baseball cap throwing the rest of it into shadow. We were in that weird position where I was looking up at him on his elevated seat inside the van.

He didn't look like a monster, no matter how much I wanted him to.

He looked . . . average. Like a normal guy. Unshaven. A few pockmarks on his cheeks, blackhead holes on his nose – but how I could have seen them in the depths of the van's interior I couldn't tell you. It was one of those details that lodged in my brain but might not have actually been there to see in the first place. He had dark hair. That much I was sure about. There were flecks of grey in the stubble, a little extra padding to his cheeks, like he was carrying baby fat that he'd replaced with beer fat, and weathered skin, like he worked outside a lot, in the sun and wind all day. That was it, the sum of what I saw in those few steps before I lost my grip.

He accelerated down my street, leaving me on my knees in the middle of the road.

Like the front, the back plate was plastered with dirt, but I could make out the first two letters – NO – which felt like they were deliberately taunting me. I couldn't make out the other letters, but the numbers might have been sixty something, or fifty something, the mud made it difficult to tell. Not that it was going to make a difference, there are probably a couple of million white vans in the UK.

My head dropped.

I wanted to scream.

When I looked up again, Olivia Mendes was walking towards me, phone to her ear, barking out a description of the white van and everything else that had just happened.

I was still on my knees when she reached me.

'That was him. That was the bastard who's been threatening Morven.'

'Did you get the plates?'

I shook my head. 'No.' Then corrected myself to make sure she understood, 'First two letters, NO. I couldn't see the rest. They were covered in mud.'

'Confirmed, the suspect is driving east in the direction of Boxpark and the High Street in a white panel van, partial number plate, November Oscar, the rest is illegible.'

She helped me to stand.

Behind us, a car horn blared, the driver unimpressed. I resisted the temptation to turn around and tell him to fuck off.

Part of me wanted to run down the street after the van, but it was long gone, and this place was such a labyrinth that with a couple of twists and turns, it was going to be unfindable without an eye-in-the-sky tracking it.

I let Olivia guide me back into the house, convinced more than ever that there had to be a message in the flowers, because those few words – *with sympathy in these trying times* – weren't enough. They didn't ram it home. And this guy wasn't about subtle or subliminal, he was in your face with the taunting.

I walked back through to the kitchen, going through the paper and cellophane wrap, but it was all clean. I double and triple checked the card, but the message hadn't changed. No new secret had been revealed. Which only left the flowers.

But what sort of message could they hide?

'The language of flowers,' I said.

Olivia grasped my meaning.

'It's something Morven was into once, for some project she was doing with Poppy. We've got an old Farmer's Almanac upstairs somewhere. Each flower has a meaning. There's flowers in this bunch I've never seen before and I have no idea what they're called, but . . .'

She was with me. 'But if they're deliberately chosen, then there's every chance there's another message in here . . . Go get the book. I'll try and work out what flowers we've got here.'

And that's how we worked out that they were lavender bittersweets, a single pink carnation, a white chrysanthemum, two heads of purple hyacinth, and double-headed zinnia arranged around a bunching of Black-eyed Susan in the middle. The only ones I'd ever heard of were the chrysanths and the hyacinths.

'So, what do they mean?'

I thumbed through the Farmer's Almanac, decoding the secret language one petal at a time. The lavender bittersweets represented the *truth*, whereas the pink carnation seemed to be a more tender *I'll never forget you*. The white chrysanthemum echoed the *truth* again, while the purple hyacinth was two for *sorrow*, and the zinnia was a none-too-subtle *thinking of absent friends*. The last flower in the bunch was pivotal to the whole message, the grouping of the Black-eyed Susans. *Justice*.

Was there some significance to the two truths?

Surely there had to be, because nothing about this arrangement felt unplanned.

As I read off the meaning of each one, Olivia's face darkened. She started out by making notes on each but stopped as the heart of the message revealed itself. Olivia hadn't been with us at the farmhouse, so didn't know about Morven's other life as Lucy, or what had happened down by the lake. She didn't know that we were looking at a promise of retribution. Justice for the dead kids. The threat of never forgetting, no matter how far Morven ran, no matter what she called herself, was chilling to the bone. Even so, there was threat enough in the message for her to be worried.

Did I tell her?

I should, but. . .

Even the fact that there was a but was enough to stop me from sharing. For now.

I realised that Siri had shuffled up a twisted anything-but-love song where Michael Stipe offered spiteful and sarcastic turns of phrase to the one he absolutely didn't love.

I felt sick.

But I wasn't about to let that stop me from using my head. 'How common are these flowers? I mean are they in season? Would they be carried by a normal florist or are they the kind of things that would need to be specially sourced? There could be a lead here, couldn't there? Even if we don't have a receipt or delivery slip, he had to buy them somewhere. If they're even a little bit rare maybe they'll help us find him?'

'Maybe,' Olivia agreed, but she didn't sound quite as enthusiastic about the prospect as I'd have hoped. Quick, clutch this straw. At least that's what it felt like.

I disappeared up to the office, intending to resort to the infinite well of all knowledge, Google.

It didn't take long to find this stuff and realise that they were all fairly common May blooms, with the exception of the hyacinth which was an early bloomer alongside the daffs, and the chrysanthemum, which shouldn't be blooming for another couple of months. But that didn't tell us much, really, when cultivators were manipulating the climate to mimic seasons within their greenhouses and cheat the natural order of things. The problem was most of these things could be picked in the wild. The lavender bittersweets, for instance, were, in the main, hedgerow flowers.

I came back downstairs thinking that there was precious little to be gained from knowing that two common flowers were out of season, but it was something and that made it better than nothing. I shared my findings with Olivia.

I expected her to nod along, humour me, maybe, say that's really good, that's helpful, but she didn't. Instead, she looked at me and said, 'Want to tell me where you were today?'

TWENTY

I made a decision. I didn't see the point in lying.

'I found out the truth about my wife.'

Olivia's eyes gave nothing away.

'And that explains the bandage, I assume?' A pointed look towards my arm.

I nodded. 'Man versus glass.'

'And man lost.'

'That's usually the way,' I agreed, but she wasn't laughing along with me.

I'd assumed they were all in on it, and I was the only one who didn't know why Morven had been given a new identity, but of course the whole idea behind protected persons was that people *didn't* know who she'd originally been, and the more who did, the weaker the new identity became.

I had a choice to make. It wasn't as difficult as it might have been. I needed to trust someone, because I was spinning, and I needed an anchor. So, I walked her through it, from ditching Nora at the Fleet Services to finding the footage of Susan Hall rooting through the rubbish bin and tracking her back to her car, calling in the one favour I had left with Mac – without naming him – and visiting her farmhouse, only to end up with a shotgun in my face and a truth I wasn't ready to handle.

'I keep trying to tell myself she's still the same person she always was, you know?'

Olivia nodded. 'That's what you need to hold onto, Alex. People change. They really do. And just because she did something truly horrible as a child doesn't mean she's a monster, no matter how seductive that line of thinking is. It means she did something truly horrible once. She's earned the right to live her best life, and that's you and Poppy.'

'It's difficult,' I admitted.

'Of course it is.'

'I almost wish I didn't know.'

'But you do.'

'I do. But what happens when we find her? When I look her in the eye for the first time and tell her I know her secret?'

'Do you need to tell her?'

I didn't have to think about it. 'No secrets.' That was the promise we made to each other, even if she'd already broken it. 'I wouldn't be able to live a lie, pretending I didn't know. Morven's a lot of things, but she's not an idiot. She'll know something is different between us. And she doesn't deserve that.'

'Then you've answered your own question.'

I blew out my cheeks. 'Ever thought of a career in the Mother Confessor business? You're a natural.'

Olivia's cheek twitched as her lips almost managed a smile.

'I've got my work cut out dealing with people like you.' It wasn't said unkindly, but there was a definite sense of rebuke to it.

'That's me, born trouble.'

Before we could get into more of it, the chimes of the doorbell interrupted us. A smooth-sided pebble of fear formed in my throat like bile and sank to the pit of my stomach. I forced myself to go and see who was at the door. My heart felt like it was trying to force its way out through the cage of bones and leave me dead on the doorstep.

I opened the door.

'Alright, guv?' A man in blue coveralls said, dangling Morven's keyring in front of my face. 'Brought your car back,' he nodded to indicate the Golf up the ramp of his tow truck. 'Where'd you want it?'

'Anywhere there's a space is fine.'

'I'm not driving up and down the street for an hour, mate.' He tossed the keys to me. 'I'll lower the wheels and uncouple the tow hook, then you can knock yourself out.'

I followed him down the path to his truck and waited as he clambered up into the cab and turned the engine over. The rattle of chains slipping through the couplings was incredibly loud in the street as the winches lowered the Golf's front wheels to the road. As I climbed into the front seat, he walked around to the pull the chains clear of the wheels and released the heavy coupling that joined us at the radiator grille. With a salute, he was on his way, and I was crawling the curbs looking for a parking spot.

It took fifteen minutes, and meant I ended up walking back from close to Poppy's school.

There was a wonderful new piece of graffiti up on one of the walls, a Big Brother-like TV screen with white nose projecting the message: *In the future everyone will be anonymous for fifteen minutes.* I thought Warhol would approve of the sentiment.

When I got home, Olivia was on the phone, no doubt relaying my confession.

I finished up making the cup of coffee I'd started to make before I realised the flowers were a threat. I made one for Olivia without asking. She nodded her thanks as I put it under her nose.

I felt like I was at a turning point – the smart thing to do was just give up and trust the police to do their thing and bring Morven home. I'd confessed what I knew, so it wasn't like they were behind me. The dumb thing to do was to dive right back into the hunt and try to find her and find bring her home. The really fucking dumb thing to do was turn things on their head and go on the hunt for the man making her life hell.

So, riddle me this, what is a boy to do?

I sipped at the steaming hot coffee, already making excuses in my head for doing something really fucking stupid.

'What are you thinking?'

'Honestly?'

'If you can manage it.'

I half-chuckled, which wasn't much more than my shoulders lifting an inch and the corner of my lips matching them. 'I've got no idea.'

'Does that mean you're going to be a good boy from now on?'

'In the spirit of total honesty? It's unlikely. The problem is I don't know what I *can* do. I mean, a partial license plate is only going to get you so far; me it gets nowhere. There's a reason people like this use white vans—'

'Two and a half million of them,' Olivia said, correcting my earlier guess of about two million.

'Exactly. And I could chase the flowers, but where would I start? Looking for growers? Walking to the flower market and asking around? I'd look like an idiot, and without a badge it's not like people have an incentive to help me.'

'And what if you did find him? What then?'

That was an entirely different question, and one I'd been fantasising about. But none of what I'd imagined was for police ears. 'Bish bash bosh,' I said, trying to smile it away as a joke, but the problem was the undercurrent was all too real. And that's exactly what she was worried about. No one wanted a *Death Wish* thing playing out. Not that I was much of a Charles Bronson, or Bruce Willis. That kind of vigilante-justice fantasy was best served as just that, a fantasy.

'You know that's not a good idea, right?'

'I do,' I said.

'But you're thinking about it, aren't you?'

'I really shouldn't answer that.'

'Which is answer enough.'

'Thinking and doing are different things. We both know that.'

'You'd be surprised how easy it is for thought to turn into action in the heat of the moment. Imagine you come face to face with the guy, there's no one around but the two of you, your brain lies to you and whispers *who's to know?* No cameras. No evidence. Why not do it and bury him in the woods. No one would miss the bastard. And resisting that little voice is going to be harder than you can imagine with all that rage and adrenalin and fear surging through your system. Stupid things happen, even to smart people. I don't want to find myself investigating you instead of helping you.'

I held my hands up, part resignation, part surrender, and a lot of understanding. She was right. A big part of those fantasies involved finding the bastard in some dark alley and taking a crowbar to his skull. But the line between doing and fantasising wasn't the kind of Rubicon you crossed by mistake, no matter how pumped up you were.

'Believe me, that's the last thing I want, as well.' I wasn't about to let on that I'd had my Road to Damascus moment on the motorway back from Susan's farmhouse. Instead of chasing the guy threatening my wife, I needed to be looking for her. Let the police hunt him. I needed to find Morven. It was as simple as that. I couldn't accept that she'd just disappear without a way for me to find her. There's no way she'd just walk away from Poppy like that, even if she could walk away from me. The problem was I couldn't start looking with Olivia around.

'Do you want my unasked-for advice?' She didn't wait to hear if I did or didn't. 'It's still early enough for you to go and pick up your daughter, spend the rest of the afternoon with her. If I was you, I'd just try to be normal for a few hours.'

I nodded. She was right again. We were in London, there were a million and one things we could do on a Saturday afternoon.

I was already reaching for my jacket again and heading for the door. There were still a couple of hours until the aquarium closed, and as long as we were there an hour before closing time they'd let us in and we could at least pretend this was a normal Saturday, then go and grab some burgers or something. 'Will you be here when I get back?'

'I think I'm going to head into the station, put my head together with the others, get briefed on what's going on, and let them know what you've told me. But I'll check in with you later. I know it's hard but try not to worry. We've got good people on this.'

'I trust you. I really do. I know you'll find the guy.'

'I'm really pleased to hear you say that, Alex. Now go, have fun with that beautiful little girl of yours. I'll talk to you later.'

TWENTY-ONE

I think everyone has their own version of a happy place. Wandering through the ice blue glass-tank tunnels looking at the hypnotic dance of the fish, the way a school could seem to ripple and break apart, mimicking the ever-decreasing circles left behind when a stone sinks, was always fascinating for Poppy. But it didn't come close to the thrill of watching a majestic shark glide up close to the glass and swim alongside us as we walked through its domain.

The underwater world they'd built here was amazing.

Poppy held my hand, pulling me towards the wall where a huge flat fish was pressed up against the glass like an *Alien* face hugger while all sorts of see-through jellyfish rose and fell behind it. But that wasn't what fascinated her, it was all the little fish behind them that she loved. Especially the sea horses. She could stand and point at them for hours.

With it getting closer and closer to closing time, the tunnels were beginning to empty. The tourists taking their selfies in front of the sea lions were gone, as were the young lovers staring at the future of their relationships in the curved glass, and before long there was only us stragglers left.

And yet I couldn't shake the feeling I was being watched – and not just by the giant sea turtle gliding across the front of its tank.

I was conscious not to make a thing of it, but kept trying to use the angles of the glass walls and the curves of the glass ceilings to try and catch a glimpse of anyone lurking back there, 100 per cent sure I was jumping at shadows. It didn't matter if I crouched, if I half-turned, if I pointed something out to Poppy and craned my neck on some weird angle pretending to look, there was no one back there.

But that didn't stop the fine hairs along the nape of my neck prickling.

I held onto Poppy's hand that little bit tighter as we made our way towards the gift shop. We had a deal whenever we came to a place like this, one treat to go home, not more than ten pounds. She was pretty good at keeping the budget down, and sometimes tried to wangle two treats at a fiver each, arguing the economics of her present, but rules are rules, no matter how creatively you try to apply them.

I let her loose in the gift shop with the warning, 'They're closing in five minutes. Try not to get us locked in,' which earned a chuckle from the assistant restocking the shelves after the locust horde of tourists had spent the afternoon stripping them.

'I'm sure we can give you a few minutes extra if you're really stuck.'

'Don't encourage her or we'll be here all night,' I said, with a smile. 'Okay madam, I'm just going to nip to the loo. Don't go getting into any trouble when I'm gone.'

'Would I?' Poppy said with that butter-wouldn't-melt smile and the assistant burst out laughing.

I left with the assistant's 'Oh, you're good, kiddo. I almost believed that,' in my ears.

I was only in there two minutes.

When I came out, Poppy was clutching a stuffed turtle that was well over her ten-pound threshold. 'Not today, kiddo,' I told her.

The next few seconds dropped a trapdoor out from under my world.

'It's all paid for.'

'You really don't have to do that,' I told the assistant, assuming

139

she'd been taken in by my daughter's irresistible charms. 'She's got her allowance. One treat at a time.'

'Oh, it wasn't me. Believe me, I wish they paid me enough that I could buy random cute kids plushies,' she busied herself behind the till, beginning to cash up.

'Okay . . . if not you, then who?'

'Oh, a guy came through a couple of seconds after you went to the toilet. He saw her looking at it and took pity on her. I told him you were just in the loo.'

'What did he look like?'

'Umm . . . average height, kinda normal. You know, not remarkable at all.' She mimed scratching her chin, like there should have been stubble there.

'What was he wearing?' I pressed, sick to the craw.

'Umm . . . jeans, he had a baseball cap . . . He only left a minute ago. If you run, you can probably catch him.'

I was half a heartbeat from tearing out of there and down the steps onto the embankment, but stopped myself, realising the bastard might just have made a mistake.

'How did he pay?' It wasn't really a question, no one paid by cash anymore. It was all plastic.

'Card.'

I tried to hide my excitement. If she was able to remember the name on the card, I might just have him. 'Brilliant. You understand I can't let her accept presents from a stranger,' the young girl nodded. 'I mean, it's very generous, of course it is, but it's a really bad precedent to set.'

'I can't refund the transaction without his card to run through the machine.'

'Oh no, I understand that, but if you could just tell me his name, then I can try my luck, and if I can find him, I can repay the kindness of strangers.'

'Even if I could remember it, I'm not sure I can tell you.'

You don't need to be sure, you just need to do it, I thought, but there was no way I was saying that out loud.

'Please,' I said, instead. 'It's just a name, it's not like I'm asking for the actual receipt, or any of his credit card details.' The inference being what harm could it do?

Poppy sidled up beside me with a carefully chosen pink dolphin, which I'm pretty sure didn't exist in real life. She popped it onto the counter, then looked up at me, those big eyes in play and said, 'Just because someone else bought me the turtle doesn't mean I've used up *my* one thing. Rules are rules.'

'She's got you there,' the assistant said.

'She's our little lawyer in training,' I agreed. 'Okay then, I guess the pink dolphin is coming home with us.'

The assistant rang it up, and took the 8.99 off my card, then, with a quick sideways glance to make sure no one was watching, wrote two words in pencil on the back of my credit card receipt.

'You're a star,' I told her.

'Me? I did nothing. I hope you find him.'

'Me too,' I agreed.

It didn't occur to me that he might have made sure she saw his name on the card because he wanted to be found.

TWENTY-TWO

Even so, as we stepped out into the light, I couldn't stop myself from scanning all the faces along the embankment, all the way along to the little fun fair beneath the London Eye. We walked as far as the temporary book stall under the bridge by the South Bank Centre, but I didn't see any suspicious watcher in a baseball cap lurking on the periphery. Poppy skipped along beside me, anticipating the greasy treat we were about to have from Honest Burgers.

Olivia was right. I'd needed this. With all the craziness of the last few days, walking hand in hand with my little Popsicle clutching her new plushies was the kind of soul restorative money couldn't buy.

She picked a burger that, when it arrived, was nearly as big as her face. And most of it ended up on it. But that was part of the fun, all of the lip-smacking and finger-licking, and that big gulp of Diet Coke to wash it down. It was a rare indulgence, and that made it easy to resist checking the receipt in my pocket. The name could wait. It wasn't like he was going anywhere.

I didn't see anyone watching us. But that didn't mean he wasn't there. Anyone who could time it so perfectly as to buy that sea turtle and make a present of it and be gone without me seeing them in the two minutes before I got out of the toilets had to be keeping pretty close tabs on us, didn't he?

That didn't feel great. But I wasn't going to let myself obsess over it. I had him now, he just didn't know it.

I took a minute to enjoy a young mum in tee-shirt and jeans doing a little dance that mainly involved sticking her tongue out at the toddler in the pushchair beside her table. It was such a mum thing, and a lovely reminder that we really didn't need to worry about the world watching when the only thing that mattered was the two of us. That was a good life lesson to remember.

'Ice cream?'

A sharp nod, halfway between *of course* and *are you stupid?*

A particularly sloppy sundae was polished off with sticky-fingered abandon.

When Poppy was finally done, the sun had begun to set, and we walked the short distance back to the car for the drive home. Normally we'd have got the Tube down from Shoreditch, but given everything I didn't feel like cramming into a hot sticky train with all the football fans, tourists and everyone else out on a Saturday afternoon. Besides, there was a freedom that came with the car. If I'd changed my mind or needed to get somewhere fast because Mac called, I could adapt. I couldn't if I was bound to public transport.

There was a note folded over and pinned beneath the windscreen wiper. I assumed someone had dinged us and left an apology and a number to call.

I checked the note.

You're welcome.

That was all it said, but there was no doubting what I was meant to be welcome for.

'What's it say?'

'Nothing.'

I stuffed the note into my pocket.

'Why'd they stick a piece of paper under the wiper if it doesn't have anything written on it?'

'Because people are strange, kiddo,' I grinned, and gurned a ludicrously un-scary face that had Poppy in fits of giggles as she climbed into the passenger seat.

I was beyond angry, but I couldn't let it show. This guy was worming his way into every inch of our lives and making sure we knew he was there. He wanted me to know there were no safe places left.

'How many hours is it until mum's back?'

It was a common enough question, she liked to know stuff in terms of hours and needed things all very precise, but this time it was like a knife to the heart.

'Forty-eight,' I said, without thinking. Teatime Monday. That was the answer she'd be expecting, not the truthful *I don't know* that was the alternative.

Deep breath. Check the mirrors. No cars coming, no watcher staring at us from the side of the road. We joined the snake of traffic to slither across the river on the long drive home.

It was a slow drive with everyone else in the city doing a similar version of it. It gave me plenty of time to think. Like it or not, whatever I did, the guy seemed to be one step ahead. There was no legitimate way he could have known we'd be making an impromptu visit to the aquarium for the last hour and a half of the day, and yet there he was, paying for Poppy's stuffed turtle and gone back out into the city within a two-minute window.

That meant he had to be watching. But how could he be, without me seeing him?

Because it felt like he was *everywhere*.

Outside my house in his white van.

Flowers on my kitchen table.

Texts to Morven and to her mother.

Dictating the action at the motorway service station.

At the aquarium just now.

Like some great manipulator, making us dance for his amusement.

So, assuming he couldn't literally have eyes on us at all times, it had to be something else. Something that enabled him to wait a safe distance away, no risk of being seen as he followed us. Five years ago, this might have taken some sort of tradecraft of technical know-how that today was reduced to pet trackers, AirTags, and Tiles and other stuff easily available over the counter of dozens of stores in the city. All you needed to do was stick the Tag on the car and follow it on the app on your phone. GPS and Apple Magic took care of the rest of it for you.

I parked in an empty spot closer to the house than I'd left and sent Poppy running on ahead while I checked the wheel arches and other obvious hiding places for the tell-tale tracker.

I would have been disappointed if I'd found it straight away, probably more so than if I hadn't found it at all.

I resisted the temptation to check the name written on the back of my receipt. I didn't want it up front in my mind when I talked to Olivia. What I didn't know, I couldn't tell.

There had been a bunch of stories in the news over the last year or so about stalkers using Tags to follow their victims, the hand-off technology meaning they didn't need to be close to them because any iPhone signal would wake the Tag and send its location back to the stalker without their victim ever knowing. It had taken a couple of serious assaults before Apple had set up an alert function so any phone being used to transmit the signal on would know, but I assumed he'd found some way to work around that and keep his Tag hidden.

I found a fake AirTag stuck magnetically to the inner rust rim of the back well, pavement side. I almost missed it. I left it there. If he was watching his app and saw the little GPS device suddenly wander inside my house, whatever advantage we might have been able to get from its discovery would be lost. This needed to be played properly. We weren't going to get that many chances to shape the way the hunt unfolded, so I wasn't about to waste this one. I assumed the benefit of the cheap Chinese knock-off AirTag was that it circumvented Apple's new security features.

Poppy was kicking her heels by the garden gate as I caught up with her.

I let us into the house, calling out for anyone home, just in case Olivia was still in there, and hoping against hope Morven would answer, 'In here.'

'Go pick yourself a movie, I'll be with you in a second and we can watch it together.'

'Anything?'

Which was her way of asking if we could watch the latest Disney for the two hundredth time.

'Within reason,' I agreed, which was my way of saying anything but that. We had our own secret language. 'I need to make a call first.'

She didn't need any more encouragement than that.

I retreated to the office, and dialled Olivia Mendes's number. She answered on the first ring. 'You guys have fun this afternoon?'

'We did indeed. You were right. A little Poppy time was exactly what the doctor ordered.'

'Good. That's really good to hear, Alex.'

'You asked me to trust you,' I said, setting up the not-quite free flow of information.

'What happened?'

'He was there.'

'What?'

I explained how he'd bought the stuffed turtle for Poppy while I was in the bathroom and gave her a moment to ponder how he could have pulled it off before I told her. 'I found one of those Apple AirTags on the car, inside the rear wheel arch, kerb side. I left it there. If he's using it to track the Golf we don't want him knowing we know he's watching.'

'That's good, Alex. Thank you. I'll get someone from tech down there to examine it, maybe there's a way we can reverse it, or follow the signal back to his phone?'

'Maybe,' I said, 'I'm not sure how the technology works. But I'm thinking more old school, he must have handled it, maybe there's a print on the device, and if not the device, on the stuffed turtle. Maybe some sort of DNA transfer or something.'

'I wouldn't get your hopes up. Those gift shop toys are pawed over all day every day. Chances of getting a good print off one is probably next to impossible, but that's not your problem. Or mine. We'll let SOCO worry about it, eh? Better still, though, there will be CCTV footage in a place like that. We should finally get a good look at his face. And assuming he didn't steal it, we ought to get a name to go with that face. That's a game changer. You did good, Alex.'

I did better than good, I thought to myself. *I got the name already.* So, for a little while at least, I was a couple of steps ahead.

I was going to need Mac to help if I wanted to keep it that way.

'Give me an hour or so to get things together here, then I'll be over.'

'It's okay, you can sleep in your own bed tonight.'

'I know I can but make up the spare room.'

'Okay.'

TWENTY-THREE

But first I needed to be a dad, and that meant going up and watching a couple of hours of Disney with Poppy.

I poked my head around the door. She'd got her toys all lined up and was in the middle of seemingly re-enacting something I didn't quite understand, giving a couple of the stuffed bears a stern telling off. I always loved these little moments, the few seconds before she saw me while she was still in her own world.

'All set?'

Poppy looked up and flashed me the most infectious smile before she patted the side of her bed. I joined her.

We spent the next couple of hours watching impossibly bright colours, up-beat music, and some mildly amusing double entendres, and loving every minute of it.

After the credits rolled, I sent Poppy to clean her teeth and get ready for bed.

I'm a simple man.

The greatest pleasure of my life for nearly ten years was reading to my little girl before she fell asleep, introducing her to the worlds I'd fallen in love with when I was younger. She had her favourites, of course, and they were hardly ever my favourites, and that really didn't matter. It wasn't so long ago she'd have been begging to go to bed just for story time.

But things change, meaning kids grow up, and one by one break the ties that bind us. It had broken my heart the first time

Poppy said she wanted to read to herself rather than have me tell her a story.

It hadn't been any easier the second or the third or the fourth time, but I'd grown used to it, even if it hurt every single time. Eventually I'd stopped offering because I didn't want to hear her say no.

It had been six months since I'd read to Poppy.

'Tell me a story,' she said, coming back in her pyjamas.

'You want me to read to you?'

She shook her head. 'No. I want you to *tell* me a story.'

I smiled then, and made myself comfortable beside her, fluffing up the pillow so that I could lean against the headboard without performing human origami on my spine.

Downstairs, I heard the key in the lock. Olivia letting herself in with the spare I'd given her. She shouted up, 'Only me.' And we shouted back down, 'Only us!' And for a moment it was the most natural thing in the world. I could follow her by sound only as she took her shoes off, dumped her bag at the bottom of the stairs and went through to the kitchen. Now would have been the perfect time to explain away the stranger in our house and how she had her own key. But what was I supposed to say? Again, she was nine, not stupid. I wasn't ready to tell her the truth, so I stuck with the lie that we were working on a new film idea, and Olivia was helping me out with my research like Uncle Mac had. Poppy accepted everything at face value. Of course she did, she was my kid, how could she even imagine a world where her dad would lie to her, even with a good reason?

Lie told, I turned all of my attention back to Poppy. 'Okay, how about I tell you the story of the deaf girl who saved the world from the great shrieking monster only she couldn't hear?' I said, offering up the first strangeness that sprang to mind.

Poppy shook her head. 'I don't want made up stuff. I want you

149

to tell me something real. Tell me a story about us. About you, me and mum. Our story.'

I nodded, understanding that this was more about the uncertainty she could feel around her, and the fact Morven wasn't home, than it was about any real desire to find out some secret history of us. I'll be honest, right then, I probably needed it as much as she did, so I asked her, 'Have I ever told you about what really happened the day your nan lost you at the seaside?'

She grinned. 'You mean when the donkey ran away with me? I like that story.'

I nodded. 'That's the one, only that's not what really happened, at least not all of it.'

'No?'

'Nope. You want to know?'

'Yeah.'

'Are you sure? I mean are you grown up enough to handle it?'

'I lived it, didn't I?' Poppy said, and I burst out laughing. That kind of logic was hard to beat.

'It's a scary story,' I said, hamming it up for a second and earning an elbow in the ribs. 'Okay then, well, it was a hot day, really hot, so we decided we were all going to get ice creams, and while we were in the queue you saw the donkey rides and kept on pulling and pulling at nan's arm until she relented and took you over to the donkeys while we waited for the ice cream man to do two scoops all round.' She nodded; this stuff was all familiar. It was a well-established part of family legend. 'Only, see, what we've never told you was that it wasn't at the seaside.'

'But—'

'Trust me. It was a summer fair, in the grounds of a hospital near nan's house. You got on that donkey and kicked it so hard it started to run, and no one was stopping it. That old donkey had to go.' Poppy giggled. She always liked this part of the story. 'Your poor old nan chased after you, yelling that the donkey was kidnapping her granddaughter, and then it started pooping as it ran, with your nan yelling at it to stop pooping because it was disgusting, and that was her granddaughter up there, which had everyone else laughing, and you were howling with delight, kicking the donkey to go faster, faster, as nan slipped in that big pile of donkey poop.'

'But you've told me all this before,' Poppy said, still grinning at the thought of her great escape on the pooping donkey.

'But I *haven't* told you how you were rescued.'

That threw her. She sat up in her bed, shaking her head. 'I needed to be rescued?'

'Oh yes. When we found the donkey you were nowhere to be seen,' I said, shaking my head at the memory of the sheer panic that had followed that moment, juxtaposed so wonderfully with my mother caked in donkey shit yelling Poppy's name over and over, and dad just leaning over and saying, 'I think you mean poopy.' It was his finest hour.

She looked at me then, and I could tell she wasn't sure whether she should believe me or not. 'Where was I?'

I smiled. It was funny now, but it wasn't back then. Back then it had been absolutely terrifying. 'One of the psychiatric patients had found you wandering on the donkey and you'd told them you were lost, so they decided to be helpful and take you to their room so you could live there with them, because you were a little girl and you couldn't be left out there all alone. And obviously no one loved you because we'd let you wander off. We looked everywhere. All over the grounds, through the fair, the rides, the stalls. We had everyone looking for you.'

'You didn't.'

'We did. The police were there. We looked everywhere. After nearly an hour, a nurse found you in the patient's room. She opened the door and you shouted, *Help, help! I don't want to be kidsnapped!*'

'You really lost me?'

'We did, but we found you again,' I said. 'That's what's important.' And that, I realised, was something that I'd needed to remember.

'You're making this up.'

'I could be, but haven't you always wondered why your mum always makes that joke about not wandering off because she doesn't want you kidnapped?'

'I thought she was just weird.'

'She is, but the two things are not mutually exclusive,' I kissed my little girl on the top of the head. 'You're lucky. When I was your age, if I went out to play with my friends your granddad would call the police to report me as missing if I was late coming home for dinner.' She laughed but it wasn't a joke. He called the police at least twice a month to say his son had disappeared. There was a full-on manhunt once, when I was two hours late because we'd been playing on a building site; it was the middle of summer so the sun pretty much never set and none of us had our watches on. The policeman had torn me a new one that evening. I hadn't thought about that night in forever. 'Okay you, story time's over, you get yourself some sleep.'

'Like I'm going to be able to do that,' Poppy said accusingly. 'I'm going to have nightmares.'

'You lived it, remember?' I grinned, ruffling her hair. 'Just think happy thoughts, like nan covered in poop yelling at that donkey.'

'I can't believe you let me get kidnapped.'

'Never again,' I promised and kissed Poppy on the top of the head.

I turned the light out as I left the bedroom door open a crack behind me and went through to the study to call Mac before I went down to join Olivia.

TWENTY-FOUR

'What do you want me to do with this?' Mac asked, down the phone.

Poppy was in bed, though I doubt very much she was asleep. We've trained her well; little pocket torch under the covers to sneak a few extra minutes of reading before she finally gives in to sleep. She loves it, because she thinks she's being clever and stealing a few more minutes after bedtime, we love it because she's reading of her own volition.

I had the music on. Not to listen to, to drown out my words.

Propaganda were busy assuring me the first cut wouldn't hurt at all, but by the third I'd be on my knees, bleeding. I figured we were up around cut two and a half right now. Not on my knees, but not happy about life.

It was a moral dilemma. I'd given Mac the name of Morven's tormentor and the first couple of letters of his white van's registration. That ought to be enough to get an address, even though it was a fairly common name. I was wrestling with just how far I wanted him to go with this. Was I asking Mac to pay him a visit? Lean on him a little, help him see the error of his ways? Was I asking him to dig up dirt, and find something I could use to put the guy back in his box?

Or was it darker?

Because, I'll admit, my instinct was to go dark. I wanted to hurt the guy, see who ended up on their knees fastest.

I was damned if it was going to be me.

But whatever else he was, Mac was still a cop. He was still bound by the letter of the law, even if I'd flouted it so casually with my little B&E stunt at Susan Hall's farmhouse. He couldn't just turn up at the guy's address with a baseball bat and shatter a couple of kneecaps.

'I don't know,' I admitted. 'I was kinda hoping you'd just volunteer and I'd follow your lead.'

'Right up to the gates of hell.'

'If necessary.'

'I love you like a brother, Alex. But this isn't you.'

'It's easy for you to say that,' I countered, shaking my head even though there was no one around to see my denial. 'I don't know who I am right now, Mac. I just want Morven home.'

'Of course you do. So, ask yourself this, does going after this guy bring you closer to her coming home?'

'No,' I said. 'But if he's out of the picture . . . maybe she feels safe enough to come home?'

'Do you really think that?'

'No. Maybe. I don't know.'

'Let's just say I turn up on this guy's doorstep and tell him I'm a friend of Morven's and this stops here, and he tells me no, and I believe him. And looking him in the eye, I realise it won't stop until he's got exactly what he wants which is to destroy her life. That means I have a choice, I can walk away and let him get on with it, and just hope the police catch him before he does any serious harm, or I can do some serious harm of my own. What do you want me to do?'

It felt like a test.

It felt like being honest would have Mac putting the phone down and telling me to trust Olivia and the process, put my faith in the system.

It felt like I was going to fail the test because I was only ever going to give him one answer.

154

'Do serious harm.'

There was a moment's silence punctuated only by breathing. 'I think this is a mistake, mate. Want to know why? Let's just say I take this name and put it into the PNC, get an address that I cross reference with that partial plate, I'm committing a crime. It might not seem like much of one, but what happens if I turn up at his door in the dead of night and bring down the pain? I mean I really go to town on him. He isn't walking away from this beating. This comes right back to me in thirty seconds. We've got checks and balances with the PNC searches. It's all about public safety. As much as we might like to think otherwise, these detectives aren't idiots.'

'I didn't say they are,' it was a pretty weak sounding objection.

'And if I don't go down there to play righteous fury and hammer of god shit on his skull? What if I just tell you, and you go there and can't control yourself? Depends how it plays out, you think, maybe you ask some questions, no harm done, even if you tip your hand that we are onto him. But what if, God forbid, you kill him? Maybe not deliberately, or maybe absolutely cold bloodedly, how do you think it looks when the detectives turn up and the first thing they do his run the vic's name in the system and see that a day, a week, even a month earlier, he was run through the PNC by yours truly? It paints a target on our backs that we don't need, Alex. I told you before, I love you like a brother, mate, and that means telling you when you're in danger of fucking up. And you're in danger of fucking up.'

'What choice do I have?'

'Give Olivia the name.'

'They'll have it in a few hours anyway.'

'Those extra few hours might make all the difference.'

I didn't need to ask what sort of difference he meant. We were talking worst case scenarios. The body in the woods option.

'I don't know why you insist on hunting this guy,' Mac went

155

on. 'You need to ask yourself what's important, and if the answer is bringing Morven home, then that should be the be all and end all. Every ounce of your efforts should be directed towards finding her. Let the police deal with this guy.'

I'd already come to that realisation. The problem was knowing something and being in a position to do something about it were two very different things. I knew this guy's name. I had it in black and white on the receipt for a stuffed turtle he'd bought to taunt me – and the more I thought about it, the more it felt like there was a threat in that, too, that he could reach my little girl that easily, in the seconds when my back was turned, and that there wasn't a thing I could do about it – all I had to do was tell Olivia and the full force of the law would come crashing down on his head in a matter of minutes. It was the smart move. The right move.

But.

Always that fucking but.

I didn't want to let him go, and that's what turning him over felt like. It felt like throwing a fish back into the sea when I had it on the hook.

Of course, it wasn't so hard to figure out the reason I felt like this. It was helplessness. I didn't know where Morven had gone after she'd left that service station food court. She could be quite literally anywhere by now, and I didn't have the first clue how to follow her there. That was the top and bottom of it. Going after him felt like I was doing something, whereas trying to find Morven was reduced to making lists of friends she might contact and places that maybe meant something to her and wracking my brain for any thread I could pull on that might, just might, unravel, spooling out far enough that it eventually revealed her waiting at the end of it.

It was wishful thinking.

'I know you're right, but that doesn't mean I have to like it.'

'No, but admitting that is a step in the right direction, brother.'

'I still want you to find out where that bastard lives. I'm sorry. I can't help it.'

'Which is exactly why I shouldn't,' Mac said, ending the call.

I went down to tell Olivia I'd forgotten to change the sheets, and show her where the airing cupboard was in case she wanted to.

TWENTY-FIVE

David Dodds.

I'd seen the name before.

It had been under one of those class photos in the clutter of Susan Hall's shrine to the life she'd lost in that one dreadful day.

David Dodds.

I couldn't remember which one he'd been. There were eleven boys in that class photograph, all of them in 1980s' cagoules. They all had the same sort of mop top mess of hair, mostly dirty blond and brown, skin too smooth for the zits that would come a year or so later. I remembered the photo. It had been at some sort of salmon farm or something. One of the kids had been crouched down with a huge net, while a couple of the others pointed at shadows in the water. Not that you could really see any of this stuff in the fuzzy grain of the faded newspaper print.

His name stood out because of the alliteration, and the fact it felt like the kind of name I always imagined a bully would have. Look, I've never hid my prejudices. I'm a simple man like that. I'm also quite capable of making unreasonable decisions about someone based on nothing more than their name. We're not even talking first impressions. David Dodds. I could imagine him now, a tattooed grease money, bald or maybe a skinhead under that baseball cap. The sickly-sweet aroma of sweat because he wasn't a friend of deodorant. It was an easy picture to paint. David Dodds didn't sound like some sort of lay pastor. He sounded like a man who worked with his hands. No real education.

That was the kind of bastard who would make Morven's life hell.

I knew it.

David Dodds.

All I needed was an address.

And given just how easy it was on the internet, I was pretty sure I could find it myself, and rock up unexpectedly on his doorstep in the middle of the night to see how he handled a grown man. Two vulnerable women was one thing; I like to think that I was something completely different.

Suddenly I had nothing to do.

It was the first time in forty-eight hours where I was at a complete loss.

I checked in on Poppy, who was flat out, the pages of her book creased where it had fallen out of the bed. I tucked her in properly, kissed her lightly on the top of her head, and took the stuffed sea turtle downstairs with me. I saw a sliver of light beneath the door to the spare room.

I knocked softly.

Olivia told me to come in.

She wasn't in bed, but on top of it, with the laptop beside her on the duvet. She was in a pair of jogging bottoms and a tee-shirt.

'Need anything?'

'All good,' she assured me.

'Okay. See you in the morning.'

'Sleep tight.'

'We both know that's not going to happen.'

'Try anyway.'

I offered her a crooked smile and closed the door.

I headed downstairs and got myself a beer out of the fridge and took a hardback down from the bookshelf, cracked open the can and the spine, and settled in to try and lose myself in a good book for a while.

Which was all good in theory, but a dead loss in reality.

I kept reading the same few lines over and over, the lines of text bleeding into each other. I gave up. Instead, I ran my fingers along the narrow spines of the thousands of vinyl records I'd picked up over the last few years, rebuying all the records I'd sold or trashed when I embraced CDs, and others I'd never owned, and settled on something ripe for listening to in the dark, *Portishead Live at Roseland, NYC*. There weren't many more haunting songs than 'Glory Box' and 'Sour Times'.

Putting my ridiculously expensive over-ear headphones on, I sank back into my chair and closed my eyes, letting the music own me.

Music sounds better in the dark.

But the problem with this darkness was that I wasn't alone in it. It was filled with thoughts of David Dodds.

I couldn't help but put myself into the story I was making up in my head, remembering my own torments at the hands of bullies, being chased home and terrorised for shits and giggles. And I knew none of this stuff was really down to him, but he became the personification of all of it.

After the side came to an end, the needle skipping along the groove over and over rather than lifting, I switched the record out for an old favourite, *August and Everything After* by Counting Crows. It was one of those albums I just returned to again and again. Tonight I turned to it as a place of refuge.

I fell asleep listening to it, only for the incessant vibration of my phone against my leg to wake me in the middle of the night. I scrambled about, heart in mouth.

I almost dropped the phone in my haste, then saw Mac's name on the screen.

'Mac.'

'Meet me here in two hours.' He gave me an address. I didn't need to ask whose it was. 'You owe me, shithead. If this goes tits up, I'll kill you.'

He hung up.

Without leaving my seat, I put the address into Google, which reckoned on the full two hours plus some to get there, assuming I adhered to speed limits. And there was no way that was happening. We both knew that, hence Mac saying two hours.

I padded bare foot through to the kitchen, splashed water on my face to wake myself up even though the adrenalin was doing a good job of that, and grabbed the Golf's keys from the counter.

I was halfway out the door before conscience got the better of me and I went back to write a note for Olivia – telling her I was fine, that I'd be back soon, not to worry, without telling her what I'd gone out to do.

I closed the door behind me so softly the tongue of the lock barely clicked back into the hasp.

There was no one out there to see what I looked like as I walked bare foot down the drive, shoes in hand.

A couple of minutes later, shoes on, I was driving towards the address Mac had given me, knowing it was a bad idea. I just had no idea how bad until I was within a couple of hundred yards of the house.

I didn't even think about the AirTag that told him I was coming.

Everything about the place defied my expectations. It wasn't some housing estate hell hole with rusted bikes strewn across the yard and a bricked up thirty-year-old Escort blocking the garage door.

It was nice.

Respectable.

Detached. Given the location, up in the Black Country, it was nowhere near as expensive as it might have been back in Shoreditch where it would probably have run a not-so-small fortune. Here, maybe three hundred thousand. Three fifty.

I'd wanted David Dodds to be struggling.

I know that's incredibly petty, but that's my deep dark secret soul talking. I can be as petty as the best of them.

The voice of the GPS assured me my destination was two hundred metres away, on the right. I wasn't in the wrong place. But I knew that anyway. Mac's car was across the street from it.

I couldn't see him.

I drove closer, looking for a decent place to park.

The house was far enough away from neighbours that I didn't need to worry about unwanted eyes and twitching curtains, even though it was barely dawn. I'd passed a paperboy on his route a few minutes back, peddling with fury between houses in his rush to be done.

There were lights on inside.

Both the glass porch door and the wooden front door behind it were wide open.

Mac was already inside. My bad habits were rubbing off on him.

Well, I could hardly leave him in there alone with Dodds, whatever he'd asked. I killed the engine and got out.

The air was crisp. Early morning air. I always imagined it tasted different this early in the day, like it hadn't been polluted for hours and was still heady with oxygen. I breathed it in.

This really could have been anywhere in about a one-hundred-mile radius. Everything was green. Hedgerows were neat. Flowerbeds were competing for the Britain in Bloom awards. There were no cars parked along the kerbs because there were no kerbs, which was a marked difference from my own slice of this Sceptred Isle. And the trees were well established, with the oaks and sycamores too thick for me to wrap my arms around the trunks. There was a short-spired baroque church with a well out front, and a farmhouse off down a dip.

The sign claimed *Honiley, Population 62*.

I could imagine this was a great place to grow up. But then, that's why it sounded so idyllic – a magic dragon might frolic in the autumn mist.

'Puff the Magic Dragon' was one of those songs, like 'Two Little Boys', that I'd loved as a kid, which made me cry my eyes out as an adult. There's something so harrowing about the idea of dragons living forever and not so little girls and boys. Even now, just thinking about it, and about my own little dragon tamer back home in bed, I felt the tears welling up behind my eyes. Growing out of that magic age sucks. There's no other way of putting it. I wish we could all just carry on believing in magic, sneaking off to visit our imaginary dragons and having wild adventures. The world would be a much kinder place.

Maybe there would be fewer David Dodds in it?

I walked towards the house, trying to think what I was going to say to him when I finally came to face-to-face with the man who had been making my wife's life hell. I allowed myself a few seconds to imagine storming in there now, all rage and furious noise, hitting him while he was confused and disoriented, like some Stasi hit team come to end him. There was absolutely nothing kind about the things I was imagining as I walked up the long dry-stone path to the open porch door. Nothing.

All of that pent up anger, trapped inside me for so long, threatened to tear out of my skin and set the place ablaze, it was so hot.

I needed to calm down before I faced Dodds.

I walked along the steppingstones that lead up to his little gingerbread cottage of rural bliss. The flower beds were lined with some of the brightest, angriest, roses.

Somewhere in the distance I heard the deep resonant chime of a church bell tolling the hour.

I saw a single black bird, a jackdaw, perched on a fence post, watching me.

I stood on the threshold for a full minute, blowing out my

cheeks, afraid to set foot inside. I heard voices. Low. Muted. Deeper in the house. I assumed it was Mac interrogating Dodds, but I couldn't make out anything that was being said.

I went in.

Inside, it looked like something one of those couples on *Escape to the Country* would reject; it was dated, the wallpaper faded, curling at the skirting boards, the white paint yellowed from nicotine, but there had been thought to the original design. I could easily imagine the hand of a good woman guiding stuff, but she was gone, replaced by the smell of cigarettes that was ingrained in the bricks. The carpet was some expensive and stupidly light shag pile that had been ruined by years of dirty shoes traipsing across it because there was no one around to enforce the 'take your shoes off at the door' rule.

The voices were deeper in the house.

I called out, 'Mac?'

No answer.

The voices didn't break off. It took me a second to realise I recognised one of them, and it wasn't Mac's. It was Mr T. A late-night re-run of *The A Team* playing away to an empty room, I realised, as I reached the first door. I stuck my head around the corner. The room was a juxtaposition of tasteful wallpaper and oak bookcases that had been custom built, though they were all but empty now, stripped of the nick-nacks and colourful spines and the tea lights, with whatever had been there replaced now with ugly cheap leather furniture with pillowed arm rests that had worn down so far it was obvious the 'leather' had never been in contact with a living breathing animal. The glass coffee table was covered with petrol-head magazines. I didn't waste my time digging around. I contented myself thinking of David Dodds as a man whose life had fallen apart. That was something.

The kitchen was more of the same.

The mud room on the other side of the kitchen had a couple of dog bowls, but there was no sign of food or water in either, so I assumed the dog had moved out with the ex.

'Mac?' I called again, moving back through to the hall.

I thought I heard something upstairs.

I went up.

Halfway up, the risers groaned under my weight. Loose boards. 'You up here?'

I got my answer as soon as I came around the landing. There were five doors. Four of them were closed. The fifth was open. Through it, I saw Mac slumped against the wall, blood down the front of his shirt. His hands were down at his side, useless. The blood was spilling out of a deep cut in his neck. It was a mercy that it had missed the jugular, but that wasn't going to matter soon. There was so much blood. I stood there for half a second, not really processing what I was seeing, separating fear and panic from everything else and trying to think. Seeing me, he tried to talk. His lips moved. Barely. Nothing came out of his mouth.

You learn a lot about yourself in a few brutal seconds like this.

My body's natural response was pure panic. Not fight, not flight. I couldn't move. There was no self-preservation instinct that had me looking over my shoulder to see if Dodds was behind me. The reality was, in that moment, I couldn't put one foot in front of the other.

I looked into the face of my friend, and all I saw was fear.

I ran towards him.

I know I talked to him, but I've got no idea what words came out of my mouth.

Reaching out, I clamped my left hand against his throat as I scrambled about with my right, on my knees, trying to get my phone out of my pocket. I didn't bother trying to dial, I needed my hands. On speaker I told Siri to call an ambulance. She told me she was calling, and a moment later the Emergency Services operator was asking me, 'What service do you require?'

'Ambulance.' There was a beat, a change of operator, and I was through, interrupting them with, 'My friend's been stabbed. He's bleeding badly,' the words came out in a rush.

'Can you tell me where you are?'

'No,' I said, my mind a blank, before I remembered the sign in the street. 'Honiley. Population sixty-two,' I told her, not that the amount of people living here made a blind bit of difference to anyone. 'In the house by the church. The door's wide open. Please. He needs help. Fast.'

'I'm dispatching paramedics to your location now, sir. Can you tell me your name?'

'Alex,' I said. 'Alex Kerr. My friend is Mac.'

'Okay, I need you to stay with Mac until the paramedics get there. If you've got a towel or something you can use to help staunch the blood, that would be good. Can you do that?' I nodded, but I wasn't leaving the room to go and look for a towel. I pulled my tee-shirt up over my head with my free hand, wriggling it down along my arm without taking my hand away from Mac's throat. 'Okay, the ambulance is on the way, Alex. They'll be with you in five to seven minutes. I need you to keep pressure on the wound. Everything you are doing for Mac now is about buying time for the paramedics to get to him.'

'I will,' I promised, already feeling the blood beginning to soak through the thin cotton.

'I want you to stay on the line, Alex, keep talking to me.'

'I'm not going anywhere,' I told her.

I pulled Mac towards me, then, still pressing the tee shirt against the wound, worked my way around behind him. I sat with my back pressed against the wall, clutching Mac to my chest, my right hand clamped over the gash in his throat, trying to stem the weakening pulses of blood with nothing more than my bare hands and a ruined tee-shirt.

I refused to believe that my obsession with David Dodds had killed my one real friend in all of this.

Dodds couldn't be far away – I hadn't passed another car on the road into Honiley, and Mac couldn't have been bleeding for more than a minute or two before I found him, meaning Dodds could walk in at any second, intending to finish what he had started. I held Mac, and together we waited for the paramedics or death, which ever won the race to reach us first.

TWENTY-SIX

'Up here!' I yelled.

Booted feet rushed up the stairs. A few seconds later two paramedics were crouching over us, one trying to peel away the bloody tee-shirt, but I wasn't letting go, even if I wanted to – my hand wouldn't obey me, it was clamped on to Mac's neck for dear life – while the other was on his knees beside us, already beginning to prep dressings to pack the wound.

'I need you to let go, Alex,' the paramedic said. He knew my name. That threw me for a second, until I realised the operator would have told him what he was walking into.

I let him lift my hand away.

More blood spilled out of the wound.

I couldn't tell if Mac was conscious or not, but he was cold in my arms and that couldn't be good.

I kept my left hand wrapped around Mac's midriff, holding him tight as the paramedic worked on him. I needed him to know I was there. That he wasn't alone. The paramedic smeared something across the wound that looked like superglue. That stemmed the blood loss and allowed his partner to pack the wound and dress it.

I wasn't letting go of Mac until they prised him from my grasp.

I kept mumbling over and over, 'Stay with me . . . stay with me . . .' the same plea over and over and trying to answer their questions while they worked on him. Not that I could tell them anything. I think they were just trying to keep me talking to fend off panic a few seconds longer.

I focussed on the room.

It was a glimpse at the inner workings of David Dodds's life. It was some sort of study, but interestingly, unlike the rest of the house, it was fitted out with some high-end looking electronics, including a quad monitor set-up on a metal spider of arms that must have cost a small fortune. There was a speaker array, scanner set up, expensive mic on an audio boom, what looked like a network storage drive, and all sorts of other tech.

Beside the monitors, old school, there were dozens of post-its stuck to the wall. The writing on them was too small for me to make out from the floor.

Finally, they eased Mac out of my arms and lifted him onto the stretcher they'd brought up with them.

I didn't move. Without the wall I think I'd have just collapsed. The initial adrenalin spike had washed away, and I was running on empty. They worked around me, bracing Mac's head and neck so that it wouldn't move under transportation.

How quickly things turn on their head; a few minutes earlier I'd expected to walk in on Dodds, on his knees, begging for mercy and been ready to hurt him. Instead, I'd walked in on Mac bleeding out. It was nothing short of a miracle that he wasn't dead already.

'Do you know his blood type?'

'No ... but he's a cop ... it'll be in his records somewhere, won't it?'

The paramedic nodded. 'Good. That's good. And his name's Mac?'

'Dylan Mackenzie.'

Turning his back to me, his partner radioed through to dispatch to request a blood match for Mac. He stepped out of the room to do it, but I could still hear it all.

'Let's get him back to Uni,' he said, returning.

'Got a match?'

'O negative.'

'Okay, we've got blood in the ambo. We'll transfuse on the way.'

Together they lifted the hard stretcher, careful not to spill Mac as they angled their way out of the cramped study.

The lead paramedic caught the edge of the desk with his hip and must have jarred the mouse, because a couple of seconds later, the monitors woke.

'You want to come with us?'

I would have said yes if not for that slight bump.

'No . . . it's okay.' I was the only one in the room who could see the screens. And I couldn't take my eyes off them. There's a moment when you rationalise what you're about to do, a choice you're about to make, even the worst, most heinous act, you just make it make sense. Looking at the images on those four screens, seeing different angles of my own house, from the inside, I knew that I was going to have to kill David Dodds. That was the only way I was going to stop him. I believed myself when I rationalised it. It was the only way. I heard sirens outside. Police arriving. I needed to get a look at what was on those hard drives and get out of there before they stopped me. 'I've got my own car outside. I'll follow.'

'Okay, we're taking him to University Hospital. Ask for him at the triage desk and they'll tell you where he is.'

'Will do,' I said, not daring to move from the floor until they were on their way downstairs. Then I pushed myself up and moved closer to the screens. One showed our bedroom, our bed in the middle of it, from a high angle, looking down. Another focussed on the chair I'd fallen asleep in what felt like a lifetime ago already. The third showed Olivia busying about the kitchen. I couldn't take my eyes off the fourth and final one, though, watching Poppy, still in her pyjamas cleaning her teeth. She rinsed and spat soundlessly. They weren't live images, they were recordings. These were the last images he'd been looking at before he left this place. That he'd chosen to focus on my little girl in all of this was beyond chilling. Worse than the fact that Dodds had eyes in our house and had been watching us, enjoying the torment his torture caused.

Outside, I heard a car door slam.

I saw familiar place names on the post-it notes beside the monitor, the address of Poppy's school, my mum's place, and more, along with comings and goings noted on them. He'd been watching us for almost a month; from before he'd first made contact, sending that first threatening text telling Morven he knew who she was. The detail was chilling. His surveillance had been methodical and thorough. I recognised dozens of excursions we'd taken as a family, and several more Morven must have taken alone.

What stopped me cold though was when I began putting together the through-line that ran through his voyeurism and realised that Dodds had been watching us on the school run, morning and afternoon, for two weeks and somehow, I hadn't seen him. I started to wonder if he'd sat across from me in Maggs's Jamaican café with the pushchair mafia, or did the head-dip hello with me in the street as we both went on in our different directions. I wouldn't recognise him because I wouldn't have been trying to recognise him, and he was ordinary enough that seeing him three or four times in a couple of days wouldn't register like some sort of glitch in the Matrix.

I heard voices outside.

The police talking to the paramedics, getting a situation report.

I had to be fast, but I couldn't look away from the screens. With grim fascination, I rolled the mouse over to the command line and searched through the root directories in the network drives, instantly seeing hundreds of video files, just like the few that had been cued up, with times and dates stamped into their names alongside the camera number.

It didn't demand any great expertise to dig around.

They were listed in a 'last opened' order, and it only took a couple of seconds to look at each one. The next on the list, after Poppy brushing her teeth, was of our bedroom from the morning of Morven's disappearance. I don't know how many times he'd watched that last hour of normal life, with us in bed together, before we got up and our world was ripped apart. But even once was too many times for me to deal with. I picked a couple at random and saw Poppy doing her homework on the kitchen table in one, and Morven stepping out of the shower in another. I watched as she wrote a message in the mirror and felt sick.

Worse, in another one I watched as Dodds wrote a message on the same mirror, mocking the intimacy of our little secret messages.

I didn't need to see any more.

I'd wasted enough time as it was.

Red rage burned in my brain. I wanted to slam my fists through the quad screens, to rip them off their spider arms and hurl them out through the window. I wanted to pick up the chair and smash its legs through the images of the inside of my house and rip out every cable from his home invasion and wrap them around his neck until I choked the life out of him.

But more than anything, I just wanted my life back.

Smashing the screens wouldn't achieve anything.

Ripping the cables out wouldn't make a blind bit of difference.

If he was savvy enough to get into and out of our house, hiding cameras for his twisted little movie nights, he was savvy enough to store the stuff on some off-site drives, maybe in the cloud – though that really just meant another computer somewhere else – so even if I ripped the network drive out of the wall and carried it out of there with me, he'd still have access to backups of his voyeuristic porn if that was what he wanted. And if he didn't, he'd got what he needed out of those cameras.

Knowing that didn't stop me from grabbing the drive, which was barely the size of my hand, yanking its cables out of the computer and the wall, and running out of there with it in my back pocket. The closest thing I got to logic in that moment was knowing I needed to take those files to Olivia. This stuff was ammo. Mac was right, it was up to them to use it to put David Dodds down.

I stopped on the landing, bloody tee-shirt in my hands. I could still hear them talking outside. My thoughts were a mess. I needed to get out of there before the cops came inside, go to the hospital, but I couldn't drive out of there like this, covered in Mac's blood, so, moving fast, I tried the first door – which opened into the bathroom – and the second, which was the bedroom. I went through his drawers, looking for a shirt to steal. We were about the same size. Looking in his mirror I didn't recognise myself.

I rushed down the stairs and went out the back door, not closing it behind me as I ran for my car.

TWENTY-SEVEN

I drove in a haze, following the voice of the phone around a string of roundabouts to the glass doors of the accident and emergency department. The façade was strange, like the crown of Lady Liberty, but here in the heartland. I couldn't park out front, so needed to find somewhere to leave the car. That took another few minutes and ended with me hitting the ticket machine in frustration as it refused to print out my permission slip. Someone tried to tell me it was all done by app now, but I wasn't listening. There wasn't room in my head to hear them. I'd take the ticket. Wandering in, I must have looked like a victim, with shock flooding my system, looking everywhere, at everything, and not really seeing any of it. I was confronted by a shopping mall rather than gurneys and whatever else an A&E should have in it.

A nurse saw me and took pity on me.

I tried to explain where I needed to be, what had happened to Mac, only for her to tell me I couldn't have been more wrong. Rather than send me off following signposts, she walked with me, talking to me all the time. I couldn't really focus on what she was saying but followed the sound of her voice like my own personal pied piper. We took turn after turn, through double doors, up stairs and down endless corridors to a reception area.

She saw my bandages, and Mac's blood, dry on the side of my neck and said, 'You should get yourself checked out while you're here. There are no prizes for being a hero.'

The sign on the wall said Major Trauma. That was hard to argue with.

'I'm hardly that,' I said, as she led me up to a desk. 'I'm fine. Just a scratch.'

'Uh hunh, just a flesh wound, eh?' she said, not believing me for a second. 'He's looking for his friend,' she told the nurse behind the desk.

'Dylan Mackenzie,' I said.

She checked the computer, before telling me, 'He's in surgery right now. You can wait over there, we'll let you know as soon as he's out.'

'How is he?'

'He's in good hands,' the nurse said, completely not answering my question, but how could she? They don't make promises in places like this.

She steered me towards the seats and asked if I was going to be alright. 'I will be,' I assured her before she left me. I stared at my hands for a bit, and at my phone for a while longer, but at my feet for the longest time, saying prayers and making promises to the universe I couldn't hope to keep.

People came by in every direction, a constant flow of life. There was such hope and such fear in each of them. I saw myself reflected in more than half of the people drawn to the reception. Occasionally, I'd hear a buzzer and see a light summoning one of the nurses to a room along their ward, but more often I'd see them prepping meds, including morphine injections and other stuff, to salve their patients' pains. After a while the pill trays were replaced by food trays. It was all routines. Everything timed. I was an oasis of stillness in the constant, controlled, chaos.

Every time someone slowed in front of me, I looked up, hoping they'd deliver good news, terrified they'd tell me he hadn't made it.

I had one missed call. The Caller-ID said Mac. He'd left a message.

'Alex,' hearing his voice was like a sledgehammer to the heart. I willed him to make it, yet again. It was a constant prayer. 'Where are you? Scratch that, if you've got half a brain you've stayed at home and done the sensible thing for once in your life. Look, I've been doing some digging on our friend Dodds, and he's a nasty piece of work. We've got four calls in the last eighteen months relating to domestic abuse, and that's barely scratching the surface. The guy's comfortable with violence. I think we need to be very careful how we do this. I'm going in to dig around, see what I can find.' That was it. I didn't need to play it twice. He'd learned the hard way just how comfortable Dodds was with violence. He needed to pull through. I wasn't having these be his last words to me.

More than once I started to call Olivia, to tell her what I'd found, but it felt like a face-to-face confession, and I just didn't have it in me to deal with her barrage of *I told you so*'s. Not yet.

So, instead, I just sat there.

I don't know how much time passed before a doctor emerged to tell me it went as well as could be hoped, which meant Mac wasn't dead, but was far from out of the woods.

'Your friend is a very lucky young man. It could have been a lot worse, believe me, but he's done the hard part, now it's just a case of wait and see, but there's reason to be hopeful, which is more than there was a couple of hours ago,' but I'd stopped listening after the lucky young man.

Mac was alive.

Through the glass doors I caught a glimpse of a man in a baseball cap, turning away from me before I could get a decent look at him, and I realised I'd seen him before, here, more than once, while I was waiting. He'd been watching me. I pushed the doctor out of the way, apologising and running before he could finish delivering Mac's prognosis.

I hit the glass doors hard, shoving through them, and started yelling, 'Dodds!' as I chased the man who'd been making my life a misery down the corridor.

People were looking at me.

I didn't give a shit.

I chased him down, fixated on that fucking baseball cap as he wove a path through the walking wounded and their loved ones, forcing my way through gaps that weren't really there, until I had him. I grabbed the back of his collar, damned near choking him as I yanked him back on his heels. I yelled. I don't know what words came out of my mouth. My brain was on fire. It was all in there, Mac, Morven, the spy cameras, the texts, the flowers and threats, spots of pain and fear burning everything else out into a searing black nothingness.

And God help me, they were right, in the heat of this moment the all-consuming need to make David Dodds hurt came roaring out of that black void. If we hadn't been surrounded by so many people, there was no 'might' about it, I would have done something beyond stupid.

I grabbed at his head, knocking the cap from it as I tried to dig my fingers into a fistful of hair and haul him back. My heart was out of beat, everything was so bright, so loud. People were screaming. At me. People were screaming at *me*.

Those people and the security cameras saved me every bit as much as they saved the man in the baseball cap, because before I could start beating at his face with my fists, I realised it wasn't him. It wasn't David Dodds. It was just some guy in a baseball cap, and I was left saying, 'Sorry . . . sorry . . . shit . . . sorry,' over and over, robbed of who I had always thought I was.

I pushed him away, shaking my head.

I couldn't believe what I'd almost done.

I was shaking.

I needed to get out of there.

I couldn't trust my eyes. Not anymore. Not when I'd be seeing him under every baseball cap, in every stranger. That was how thoroughly he had invaded our lives, how deep he'd got under my skin. He was living inside my head now.

I stumbled away from him, looking round frantically for the fastest way out of there.

No one tried to stop me.

TWENTY-EIGHT

I thought about not going home.

Inside me, that gnawing dread that the next time I saw Olivia she'd be telling me they'd found Morven's body, festered, getting more toxic with each passing day.

There was nothing to be gained by sitting in the carpark waiting for Mac to wake up. My being there didn't help him, and it didn't help Morven.

I needed to get the network drives to Olivia, and get the police to Dodds's house, confess about our being there and the attack, and explain about Mac.

But then what?

Turning the key in the lock I allowed myself a few seconds to imagine yet again that it would be different, that Morven would be in the kitchen, not my FLO busying about, or in the lounge with her feet up reading some trashy romance novel and howling with laughter as page after page turned compulsively.

I closed the door behind me and just stood in the hallway, breathing deeply, each breath slow, forcing myself to be calm before I faced Olivia. The problem was, when I closed my eyes, Mac was there, bleeding in my arms. The first thing I wanted to do was take a shower to get the stench of death off my skin but wasn't stupid enough to think Olivia would let me disappear upstairs before I'd explained myself. I couldn't remember the last time I'd take a shower. Thursday night? That couldn't be right. I must reek.

I leaned back against the door and didn't move for the longest time. It would have been even longer, but Olivia emerged from the kitchen, with a face like thunder. 'Where the hell have you been, Alex? I've been worried sick and trying not to frighten Poppy.'

I held up the stolen network storage drive like that was an answer.

'Where is she?'

'Upstairs. So, am I supposed to know the significance of that?'

'It's Dodds's'. He's been spying on us, filming us in here.'

She didn't ask how I knew his name even though she hadn't told me. We were beyond that now. 'I'm going to swear at you, a lot, in a few minutes, but first you are going to tell me just what the fuck you are playing at, and how you got your hands on what I assume are his 'home movies' of this place.' She was angry, understandably. But it was more than that. She was frustrated, and it was all bubbling up to the surface now she was finally facing me. 'It feels like you've been lying to me, Alex. A lot. I can't pretend that I like it. I think it's time for a few home truths. We are all trying to bring Morven home. This isn't about you. You aren't our primary concern. Morven is. I told you before, I really don't want to be investigating *you*, but that doesn't mean I'm just going to turn a blind eye while you do stupid shit, even if we want the same thing. You stole those films. That's a problem for us. It's illegally obtained evidence.'

'Can you still use it? Because that's all that matters.'

'Maybe, but if you had trusted me, if you'd let me do my job, and we could have done this properly, we'd have him now. You understand that don't you? You might have a smoking gun in your hand, but if you'd just trusted us, this could have been over already.'

I didn't waste my breath with apologies.

Instead, I told her, 'It's too late for regrets.'

I sounded calmer than I might have done even yesterday. Colder. But then so much had changed in twenty-four hours. The new me was being forged in this crucible and I'm not sure I liked how he was being tempered. We like to think we'll be better, but the world had shown me I wasn't. I tried and I failed, I gave in to the anger Olivia had been frightened I wouldn't be able to resist. I did the stupid thing and now Mac was fighting for his life. 'Right now, I want to rip the damned cameras out of the walls and I want to wash my friend's blood off me.'

'What?'

'Mac. Dylan Mackenzie. My friend. He used the stuff I got him to get David Dodds's address.'

'How?'

One-word questions.

'He's a cop. He ran the partial plate and the name from the credit card receipt from the aquarium through the national computer. He got the address. He told me to turn it over to you. He told me to trust you.'

'Smart man.'

'Not smart enough. When I got there, I found him bleeding to death.'

'Jesus Christ, Alex.'

'He's in hospital. That's where I was.'

'Is there anything else you're not telling me?'

'You know everything I do,' I said, which wasn't a lie. It was just wriggling between the lines of the truth in a way I wasn't exactly proud of – and frankly wasn't even sure was smart anymore. A huge part of me just wanted to let it all spill out in a desperate rush.

'Are you sure about that?' Olivia asked, not happy.

I nodded. 'Yeah. I mean, there's details, but you know the big stuff. I went to the service station with Nora, you know that. What I didn't tell anyone was that I saw security footage of Morven putting a package into a bin there, and an old woman collect it.'

'The missing money?'

'It was supposed to be, but Morven didn't pay up. She put together a package of things to prove she wasn't who they thought she was.'

'But obviously she is. So, do I want to know how you know what was in that package?'

'Probably not.'

'Tell me anyway.'

So, I did. I told her it all. Or almost all. 'The woman was Susan Hall . . . She had been Susan Galvin . . . Morven's mother. We went to her house.'

'You've ignored every single thing I've told you, haven't you? You didn't just compromise Morven's new identity, going back to her birth mother, you absolutely shattered it. There's a reason there's no contact between them, Alex. There's a reason that woman has no idea who her daughter became.'

I told her about the shrine to Lucy Galvin and the dead kids, and the class photos. Olivia was a cop; she'd ask the same questions and get to the same inevitable conclusion as I had if she did. I told her what Mac's digging had turned up about David Dodds's history of violence and domestic abuse.

She just listened.

'I wish you had trusted us earlier, Alex.'

'I couldn't,' I said. 'Not when there was the risk that someone inside the system was behind everything . . . All I could think was who else had the ability to breach her new identity? I know . . . I wasn't thinking straight. The only thing I knew was I couldn't trust anyone who turned up on my doorstep.'

'And yet you trusted Mac.'

'Because he wasn't part of it.'

'But he could have been, just as easily as anyone else. Especially if he had a personal relationship with Morven. He might have recognised her. You have no way of knowing. But you chose to trust him, the same way you chose not to trust me.'

'I can't explain it any better than that. I'm sorry.'

'But you've told me everything now?' I nodded. 'We're going to need you to come in. We'll need a statement about the stabbing. Everything you can remember.'

'Dodds knew we were coming. Worse, he *wanted* us to come. He was listening to my side of our conversation as Mac gave me his address. He watched it all. If I'd got there a few minutes earlier, it could have been me.' *Not could, should. It should have been me.* This wasn't some lightning bolt from the sky realisation. It was one of the reasons I'd struggled to sleep. The breadcrumbs had been laid out nice and neatly in a tantalising trail with a single purpose: to lead me all the way to the gingerbread cottage's front door.

And I knew why. I'd worked it out. David Dodds wanted me dead because it was the easiest way to deliver the same kind of crushing hurt to Morven that she'd inflicted on the Langs.

Just because he'd failed once didn't mean he wouldn't try again.

'Now, are you going to help me get these fucking cameras, because the idea of that bastard watching us for even a minute longer makes me sick.'

'I need to call all this stuff in.'

'Fine. You do that.'

I walked away from her, into the lounge, trying to fix the camera angles as I remembered them in my mind's eye, and work my way back from there to the hidden surveillance device.

I would never have found it if I didn't know it was there.

It was smaller than I imagined possible, barely half the size of a cigarette, hidden on top of the kitchen cabinets and wired into the up-lighting on top of the units, meaning that it wasn't dependent upon any sort of battery that would eventually fail. I ripped the wiring out and dumped the spy-cam on the kitchen counter, realising it was still relaying its images back to Dodds, and would keep on doing so until I smashed it.

Before I could, Olivia took the choice out of my hands. She put the spy-cam inside one of the leftovers boxes on the drainer and closed the plastic lid on it, effectively blinding it.

'There are more, in the bedroom, the bathroom, and the last one's in Poppy's room.'

Even knowing where to look for them, it took us half an hour to find the other cameras. I told Poppy to go play downstairs while we searched her room. She didn't object.

'How did he get in here to do this?'

It was a good question. I'd thought about it on the drive home. There was an obvious answer, of course. That first broken window by the door, nearly a month ago. He'd been watching us for that long. It made my skin crawl.

'You're not forgiven, Alex.'

'I'm not looking for forgiveness. He watched us in bed together. He watched my daughter cleaning her teeth in the morning. He watched it all. Hundreds of hours of my family, like some fucking pervert. I'm not the one who needs absolution here, Olivia.'

'We've had another text message to Morven's phone today.'

'What did it say?'

I could tell that she was thinking about it before she finally told me, 'You should have brought the money.'

'That sounds like a threat.'

She nodded. 'It's getting to him. He doesn't feel in control anymore. He's spiralling. This is when he starts to make mistakes.'

But at what cost? I thought, knowing it wouldn't be Olivia who paid the price when it came due.

TWENTY-NINE

Confession is good for the soul, even if no one hears it but God, right?

Oliva had gone to get take-outs – Poppy's choice. Poppy had gone with her. They'd be gone an hour or so. I sank into the same chair I'd been sitting in when Mac had called in the middle of the night. The same record sleeve was leaning against the unit. Everything about the room was the same.

I couldn't move for the longest time.

It was as though all the events of the last few days came crashing down on me, the weight of them pressing me down into the seat. It wasn't so much exhaustion as it was will. I just couldn't face moving. I couldn't summon the energy to even lift my arm or kick off my shoes.

The empty house was a killer.

It made everything feel real.

Not that it hadn't felt real before, but it felt like the first time I'd been properly alone since Morven had disappeared, alone meaning no one to turn to for help, and I hated it.

By the time I was under the piping hot stream of the shower, it felt like I was never going to be able to scrub the stain of Mac's blood from my skin. I did a whole Lady Macbeth thing under the spray, working lather after lather up and rinsing it off, only to work up more until we were out of shower gel, and I was standing under water that had long since gone cold.

I stayed in the cold shower until I couldn't stand it anymore, and clambered out, shivering as I wrapped a towel around my waist and draped another across my shoulders.

The mirrors were steamed up.

There was writing on the glass, but it wasn't the heart with an arrow through that Morven had left on Friday morning.

Sick dread filled me. He'd been in here after she'd gone, which explained the second brick through the window on Friday.

The three little words weren't 'I love you' this time.

Nowhere to run.

Seeing them stopped my heart.

I remembered the image of Dodds I'd seen on his screens, writing on the mirror. He'd transformed our secret little shorthand language of love into a threat delivered right into the heart of what should have been our one safe place in this world.

I felt sick.

I padded barefoot across the floor and reached for the towel to wipe the letters away but stopped myself. I tried to think like Olivia and Mac. This was evidence, but it was ephemeral. It would fade away to nothing. It needed to be recorded before that could happen, so with the towel wrapped around my waist, I went downstairs to get my phone to take a photograph.

I left wet foot prints all the down to the kitchen, but they dried up long before the return journey was finished.

I took photos of the mirror writing with the light on and off, not sure which would show up better. If I hadn't used up all the hot water in the shower I'd have run it now to get more steam going, but the threat was still legible.

Where did you go when there was nowhere left to run?

Solve that, I found Morven.

The flipside of that was what if Dodds solved it first . . .?

I couldn't let myself think like that.

We had a name, the police had leads that would take them right to him once they panned out. If I could somehow put everything else out of my mind, then it was good. For the first time in three days, it was good. The problem was I couldn't put everything else out of my mind, no matter how hard I tried.

I'd noticed something. Even after finding out her real name I couldn't think of her as anyone other than Morven.

She wasn't a Lucy.

I heard the door downstairs, Olivia and Poppy returning weighed down with enough food to feed the five thousand.

'Down in a minute,' I shouted in answer to their, 'Food's here!'

They were getting on well, the pair of them. I didn't feel bad about lying to Poppy about who Olivia was. The truth wouldn't have helped.

I couldn't look away from his three-word message.

I stared at it as I cleaned my teeth, rinsing my mouth out with a stinging mouthwash that scoured any last lingering germs and left my tastebuds concussed, then finally stopped looking at his words as the condensation lost its hold on the mirror and took them away with it.

I went through to sort out some clean clothes before I went down to join the others.

I'm a man of a certain age. That means I've got a uniform. Sure, it's over three decades since I was moaning about being forced to wear that blue- and red-striped blazer at school and getting grass stains all over the knees of the grey trousers every lunchtime, protesting loudly how once I was out of that hellhole I'd never wear a uniform again, but all I did, like every other man of a certain age, was swap it for another one. In my case it was jeans, a cotton shirt, checked, because every shirt in the world seems to be checked these days, with a plain black tee shirt underneath. It takes the whole thought process out of getting dressed, like Steve Jobs and his black roll-neck jumpers.

Today it was a battered old Martin Stephenson concert tee-shirt – without the Daintees logo that would have been there a few years before and a few years after – that was so moth-eaten it had a third armhole, but I couldn't bear to bin because it had been our first concert together way back when.

It made me feel close to Morven.

Dressed, I went down to share the honey and sweet chili chicken Poppy had picked.

I was starving.

'I found something,' I confessed, after we'd gorged ourselves on the takeaways and Poppy had disappeared back up to her room, reclaiming the space from our earlier invasion.

'When?' Meaning how long had I been holding out on her again.

'When you were out getting food. I couldn't show you when Poppy was around.'

She nodded. That was reasonable.

'Okay, what did you find?'

I took my phone out of my pocket to show her the photo of Dodds's mirror writing.

'Nowhere to run,' she said, reading it back to me. She didn't need to ask who'd written it. We'd just spent hours ripping out his spycams.

'Another threat.'

'And too close to home.'

She nodded. 'You need to tell them all of this when you go in to give your statement, Alex. All of it. Don't leave a single thing out. This is the kind of stuff that will see him put away for years.'

THIRTY

I slept like the damned.

Mac was dying in my dreams and I couldn't get to him in time.

Morven was screaming for help without making a sound. Drowning.

Waking up, it felt like losing them all over again.

I wasn't doing well.

Olivia had gone home after we'd eaten, telling me in no uncertain terms I needed to sleep. She'd made me promise to go into the station first thing Monday morning and go through everything I'd told her, making an official statement. I told her I'd meet her for ten. I looked at the clock, and realised I'd only been out for five hours. It took another second to realise why I'd woken up. The phone was ringing downstairs. The landline.

I stumbled out of bed and went downstairs.

I didn't reach it in time. Whoever it was had hung up when it went through to the machine. Normally, my first instinct is always *if it's important they'll call back*. But this time it was different. No one uses the landline anymore. My natural response was panic. What if it was Morven trying to reach me? We're so used to mobile phone life we don't have to think about someone else's phone number. It's just there, in the contacts list. But I still remember my home phone number from back when I lived with mum and dad off by heart. It's not just committed to memory, it is absolutely burned in.

And that meant it was the one number Morven had almost certainly burned into her brain – despite the fact we hadn't really used it for years.

I snatched the phone up and punched in the numbers 1471 to get the number of the last call only to be told it was blocked. I slammed the handset down again like it burned. She wouldn't be able to get through if the line was busy.

I tried to tell myself it couldn't be her, that it was some cold caller trying to sell me solar panels or explain how I'd been falsely sold PPI. Those were the only calls that ever came through.

But. But. But.

There was no rationality to it. The moment the ringing had dragged me out of sleep a surety had come alive inside me: Morven would try to contact me. She wouldn't just leave me hanging, not knowing if she was alive or dead.

Whoever it was didn't call back.

The silence left me feeling lost in a way it hadn't before.

I needed to occupy my mind to stop it from spiralling. What if she wasn't calling back because she couldn't? What if he had her? What if he'd solved the riddle of where you went when there was nowhere left to run first and she'd been bound and gagged in some secret under-the-floorboards basement hatch in the middle of nowhere, and she'd managed to wriggle free just long enough to call me, and when I hadn't answered he'd come back and found her and now he was punishing her?

I didn't know what else to do but go back to the beginning – and maybe that was his mirror message mocking me, I had nowhere left to go – and sat down with that list of significant places I'd started making for the police when I'd first realised Morven wasn't coming home.

It's hard to dissect your life into significant moments – and to actually work out if something significant to you is just as import-ant to someone else, even if they shared it with you. I mean, one of

190

the absolute first and best memories I've got of our being together was when we used to visit this basement record store – Pet Sounds – it smelled of damp and old paper on the edge of mildew, but it was a treasure trove of impossible wealth. The guy who owned it used to get all of the record company promos, the radio cuts, and everything else, and he'd just dump them in the cheap racks at the front of the store, no order to it, just this beautiful chaos of stuff you'd never actually get to hear on the radio because the DJ had been too lazy to listen to it and decided to cash in on a few hundred at a time for a free meal.

Morven and I used to have this competition. We'd set a limit, sometimes it was 10p, sometimes it was 50p and every now and then if we were feeling rich it would be a pound. We'd have an hour to wander the shelves, flick through the bargain racks, and delve into the bins, and have to pick one CD or record blind, take them home where we'd sit cross-legged on the floor eating a take-away and listening to the two albums, and whoever discovered the best won whatever joke prize we'd come up with.

We only ever had the cover art, song titles, and if we were really lucky, a lyric sheet to go on, which led to some interesting discoveries, and some utterly forgettable experiences, but at pennies for an evening's entertainment it was cheap fun, and it made for some good memories, not least because we were barely out of university and living on the dole. That meant the prizes were more often than not sex of some description, like the chance to get to live out one fantasy or other. Shower sex. That was my prize for unearthing possibly the best offering of the entire competition, a promo import of a band neither of us had heard of, with the most innocuous black-and-white photo for a cover – at first glance it looked like a farmhouse in the dust bowl, then you saw the axe, and the farmer with his head down and the chicken he was holding on the wooden chopping block.

It wasn't like she could go back to the record store to hide, or our old flat from back then.

But, thinking about that game, I went across to the rack and picked out the 10p CD that had stayed with us all this time because it really was just a brilliant album and hands down the best 10p I've ever spent in my life.

I sat at the kitchen table listening to it and forcing myself to remember everything, everywhere we'd been, every good and bad moment, trying to find the one.

The one.

Such an impossible concept.

Whether it's the one we're meant to love forever or the one we can't live without, the one we want to share with the world, the one we want to see the world with, the one we need to find because she's being hunted by a fucking psychopath who just cut the throat of my friend. . .

I might as well have sat there with a map and just stuck random pins in it.

But at least it felt like I was doing something.

So, I wrote down the names of places we'd been that I thought meant something, places where I'd felt happiest and where I thought she'd felt most connected, and they weren't always the obvious ones. There was a lot of beauty on the list, places like High Force, Ullswater and Harter Fell, Corfe Castle, and along the Jurassic Coast, Durdle Door and Old Harry's Rock. But then there was a completely different kind of beauty we were surrounded with every day in London, with the majesty of Christopher Wren, John Nash and Charles Barry to the modern spectacles of Renzo Piano and Norman Foster.

London might have been the most obvious choice for her to hide, too. I mean, where better to become invisible than surrounded by nine million others? There were so many places of shared significance here, from first kisses to life-changing ones, but it wasn't like she was going to take refuge in the hospital where Poppy came into our world, or the hotel where we think she was conceived. Or maybe that was exactly the kind of place she would hide.

None of them felt right.

None of them felt like the one.

So, what was I doing wrong?

It didn't matter if I fixated on landmarks, like where I'd first told Morven I loved her, or where I'd asked her to marry me, they didn't have obvious places alongside them where she could hide. But what if she wasn't trying to hide? I mean, in all the time I'd known her I don't remember Morven ever running away from any problem. She was more of a stare it in the face, kick it in the teeth, kind of problem solver. It was one of the many things I appreciated about the force of nature that was my wife.

As the tracks changed, I thought about why I'd given up with the list in the first place. Frustration. And the root of that? The fact there was this whole secret life I didn't know; this life as Lucy Galvin, that she had this effective Year Zero just a couple of years before we met, where Lucy ceased to be, and Morven took shape.

But the hours in her mother's shrine to Lucy had changed that, hadn't it? I'd read parts of hundreds of pieces about her, with the gossip magazines and red tops dissecting every aspect of her childhood in the search of what made her a monster. It was the key to her past. I'd seen photographs of her classmates, including David Dodds back when he'd just been the lanky, awkward, nasty-looking kid in that group. I'd seen stuff about that fateful school trip, including maps. I knew the youth hostel where they'd stayed, which had been an old keep built by King John as a hunting lodge. I knew the places they'd visited that day, including the crannog at Llangorse Lake where Chrissy Lang and her brother Scott had drowned. I knew the clothes she wore. I knew what had happened to her dad in the wake of the trial.

I wouldn't begin to claim there were no secrets now, but I had a better idea of what places might have been significant to her.

Significant didn't have to mean happy, did it? And I couldn't think of a single more significant place in Morven's life than where Lucy effectively died along with those two kids.

The more I thought about it, the more it made sense.

It was a place that linked her to David Dodds.

He was one of the few people who had lived it. He'd been there at the time, by that lakeside. He'd experienced the tragedy in a way only a few others had. Of course it had scarred him. How could it not? Somewhere over the last few minutes I made a decision; I wanted a few hours head start getting out to the Wye Valley. I was going back to where it all began. That was the answer. I knew I was right.

THIRTY-ONE

'Come on, trouble, let's go give nan a surprise, shall we?'

Poppy hadn't said much since breakfast, when I couldn't tell her how many hours were left until her mum came home, but she hadn't protested when, instead of telling her to get ready to go to school, I'd decided she was spending the day with my mum.

Instead of the usual half-skip half-run up the garden path, Poppy was glued to my side, walking in lockstep.

Halfway up the path, I crouched down beside her and stroked the side of her face.

She looked at me, all big eyes, and nodded with so much need to believe me when I said it was all going to be alright that it broke my heart.

I kissed her on the forehead.

'I need you to promise me you'll be extra good for nan today. No skipping off in a hurry if you go for a walk, just doing everything she tells you. Can you do that for me?'

She nodded again, suddenly grave as she swore, 'Promise omiss.' That was something she'd picked up from her mum. There were promises, and then there were promise omisses, which were unbreakable.

God, I loved my little girl right then. More than the world. And I ached that her mum wasn't here with us. I wasn't going to be able to handle doing this alone. That wasn't even an option. Morven *was* coming home.

We knocked on the door together, and when my mum

appeared, confused but full of smiles at the sight of us on the doorstep, I did my now familiar disappearing act without giving much of anything away. She ushered Poppy inside with a promise of biscuits in the conservatory.

'Hold your horses, son,' she called at my back. I stopped mid-getaway. 'Not that it isn't always lovely to see my favourite little person, but this becoming a bit of a habit. You'd tell me if something was wrong, wouldn't you?'

I took a couple of steps back towards the door.

'Does something need to be wrong to spend time with your granddaughter?'

'Don't be funny, Alex. It doesn't suit you. What's going on?'

I rubbed at my chin. I had two choices, lie or tell the truth. No, there was a third choice, of course, tell shades of the truth, just try and do it in such a way as not to create all out panic and make things ten times worse than they already are. Three was always going to be easier than two and I hated lying to my mother, so I said, 'I just need to keep her out of the house while the police are there. It's easier.'

'Police?'

People of a certain age all react identically to that word; it's a mixture of fear and respect and utterly unlike anything that comes from my own generation when we hear the word.

'Okay, mum, I need you to remember that Poppy's in the other room and has big ears for a little person. Morven's missing. She didn't turn up at the work thing. No one's heard from her since Friday morning.'

'Oh Jesus, Jesus . . .' The Son of God Squared. We were in serious imprecation territory here.

'I need you to keep her occupied and try not to worry, mum. If you're worried, she'll pick up on it. She needs to think everything is normal. Promise me. Normal.'

'Which is easier said than done.' Then she saw the car behind me and seemed to realise the conundrum its presence presented. If the Golf was here, and Morven wasn't, how did I get it back?

I filled in the missing pieces.

'They found it abandoned on the motorway,' I told her, and could see the fear come to life behind her eyes. I wanted to reassure her, but what could I say, really? I know she's alive because I have seen a video of her? That was the only thing I could say that was remotely reassuring, but opened up a whole slew of new questions I didn't have the strength to explain.

And then mum asked the question I should have been asking all along. 'Are they looking for her, or are they looking for her body?'

'Her,' I said, needing that to be true. 'I need to get home, mum. I promise you; I'll tell you as soon as there's anything to tell.'

She nodded, and then with all the love in the world, said, 'Go bring your girl home, son. We'll keep Poppy safe.'

'I'm going to bring her home,' I swore.

Mum nodded. She didn't stop me when I walked away a second time.

The clouds looked as though someone had taken a razorblade to the sky and slashed seven straight cuts across its face. There was some serious symbolism going on up there. Still looking out into the road, watching as the cars crawled by, I went back to the Golf and set off on the long drive for Wales and the lakeside where it all began, knowing even as I did that the AirTag was still attached to the inside of the wheel arch. I could have tossed it anywhere along the road, but part of me wanted Dodds to know I was coming for him.

I wanted him to be afraid.

I was in Streatham before I realised I'd left my phone charging on the side. I thought about not going back to get it, trying to weigh up the time wasted going back against what it would be like trying to operate without it, and honestly, the fact that Olivia wouldn't be able to yell at me for breaking yet another promise was tempting – I'd left the AirTag in place, so she could track me anyway, phone or no phone – but I decided the phone was worth more than the inconvenience, so drove back, wasting almost an hour in total, before I was accelerating towards the suspension bridge across the Severn with the phone charging through the dashboard.

I could only pray I wouldn't regret that hour.

I put the music on, loud. I didn't care what I listened to. I just wanted to lose myself in the noise for a while. I wasn't sure where I was going to sleep at the other end, though the obvious choice was the same hostel that Morven had stayed at all those years ago. Back to the beginning.

I drove into the afternoon, thinking about my life.

I caught myself remembering another silly little thing I hadn't thought about in forever. We'd gone to a party, not long after we first got together. We were still close enough to student days that parties were pretty crowded and particularly seedy affairs that involved pretentious conversations espousing Kant and Durkheim or some other 'thinker' we barely understood, arguing about sex, death and religion and pretending to be oh-so-grown-up, when Morven had leaned over to me, and in the most serious voice imaginable – made all the more so for the fat joint she inhaled and passed across – asked what I thought was the most sensual part of the human body.

Our conversations in those days leading up to that first time sleeping together flirted around that kind of dangerous territory, sounding each other out for what we might want from each other when the time finally came. I'm not sure what she'd been expecting me to answer, but I remember touching her ankle, in the hollow behind the bone, and saying 'Here,' and then touching the bay at the base of her throat and saying, 'And here.'

I think that threw her.

But rather than go for some cheap answer, like touching her lips, or saying it was all in the eyes, I went for honesty. The narrowing of a woman's ankle, the musculature and shape of the tendons, had become something that fascinated me. I don't really remember when I'd first realised it, but I know that was the first time I'd admitted it, and a week later, when we finally slept together for the first time, I remember her asking me to kiss her ankles and later drink the sweat from the bay at the base of her throat.

She listened.

You know what embarrasses me?

I didn't.

I couldn't for the life of me remember what her answer to the same question was.

THIRTY-TWO

I followed the narrow road up the incline to a small car park in the shadow of two towers that served as the entrance to the keep with its narrow slits for windows and a stone drawbridge that had no moat to span. There were occasional signs of crumbled curtain wall and other relics of another age, but the keep itself looked as though it could have been built in the last century, including the chimney pots that looked out of place perched on top of the gatehouse towers.

It was a curious place. I could understand why it would fascinate a bunch of school kids of a certain age.

I killed the engine and got out of the car, crossing the drawbridge to the imposing gatehouse. One side of the wooden gates were open, the other closed.

The English Heritage sign on the wall offered a two-hundred-word glimpse at its long history as a forest prison; another beneath it listed room rates for the youth hostel.

I ventured in, walking through the long tunnel into the courtyard and imagining the other life this place must have had once upon a time.

In another world Morven would be home already.

I felt like death as I clambered out of the car into the breeze that pretended today was a day like any other. I went to see if I could find someone in the reception. I could hear kids shouting inside. I couldn't really hear what they were complaining about, but it was obvious they were aggrieved about something. It wasn't that much of a stretch to imagine this was exactly what it would have been like back on that day Lucy Galvin broke.

I went through the red door, phone in hand ready to show the first person I saw a photo of Morven and do the whole *have you seen her* thing.

The interior was all wooden panels and wainscoting.

I was hit by the smell of food.

The kids were raising hell in the dining room. Best guess, there'd been some sort of mock trial, no doubt some sort of re-enactment of the keep's past life as a prison, and they were moaning because their teacher had avoided the oubliette on a technicality. I smiled to myself, thinking some things never change.

There was a young woman working the desk, or more accurately buzzing around it, tidying things away, sorting out the array of leaflets promising day trips and culturally important landmarks.

She smiled when she saw me, mistaking me for a guest. It was hardly surprising, the nature of the hostel meant fifty or sixty different faces a day for her to memorise. 'Hi there,' she said through that Colgate smile. 'Food's through there, very much a help your-self affair. Good luck with it.'

I chuckled a little, knowing exactly what she meant. The con-fines of the dining room and the press of kids promised a healthy bout of tinnitus before the scrambled eggs hit the toast.

'Hi,' I said, as I crossed the flagstone floor to her desk. 'I'm not actually staying here.'

'Ah, I'm not sure if we've got a room, there's a couple of school groups in, they've pretty much taken over the place.'

'It's fine, I'm not really looking for a room. I'm trying to find my wife,' I held out my phone, the screen alive between us. 'I don't suppose you've seen her?'

There was something going on behind her eyes, a recalibra-tion. It took the silence between heartbeats for me to grasp what the shift meant. She was immediately suspicious, putting distance between us without actually moving.

I got it.

A man asking questions about a woman who could quite easily not want to be found. It wasn't a position she wanted to be in. If she had seen Morven and told Dodds instead of me, it could easily be the death of her, so as frustrated as I was, part of me was pleased she didn't immediately sell my wife out at the first question. But it still felt strange, being looked at, and the first instinct of the person doing the looking was to see a man capable of . . . what? Domestic abuse? Of battering the woman I loved? It made my skin crawl to be looked at that way.

But I got it. I understood. And I knew it was necessary. But that didn't help me.

'I'm sorry, we're not allowed to give out any information on guests.'

I nodded. 'I understand,' I said, knowing that it would only make things worse if I pushed it.

I had no way of knowing how many abusive husbands turned up looking for runaway wives. How many times a woman like her had faced a man like me across the illusion of safety that was the reception desk and been the last line of defence for the terrified woman who'd risked everything to break the cycle of abuse.

I got it.

There was a whole world of toxic statistics that were living breathing people who had lived the worst of that, the sustained physical and mental abuse of a loved one.

'It's okay,' I couldn't help myself though, I felt like I was saying *not all men*, a toxic phrase all of its own, but I needed to say, 'It's not what you think.'

The woman behind the desk half-smiled and I didn't need any sixth sense to know what she was thinking.

'You don't have to explain yourself to me.'

This time it was my turn to nod, 'But I'm going to anyway,' I said, and shrugged, knowing that I was doing exactly what an abuser would do.

'Really, it's okay. You look like a kind man, but I can't help you.'

'I think she's in trouble,' I didn't really know what I was going to say until it was tumbling out of my mouth to this stranger. 'There's someone who wants to hurt her. She's missing and I'm frightened he's found her. We've got a little girl at home who misses her mum. All I want to do is bring her home.'

'I'm sorry,' the woman said, 'I really am, but you're not listening to me. Even if I wanted to, I couldn't help you.'

'I know,' I said, and realised I was crying. Not gut-wrenching sobs. A single tear that broke and ran down my cheek. I wiped it away without thinking about it.

'Look,' she said, 'We're not that big a place, if she's come here, she'll be easy enough to find. There are only a handful of places she could be staying. She'd have to eat, there's only a few places to buy food, it's just a case of going from one to the next and hoping someone's seen her. If she really is in trouble, I hope you find her.'

'She is,' I said.

Behind me, a gaggle of kids exploded out of the dining room in a tumult of noise, arguing wildly about something that made absolutely zero sense to anyone not involved in the argument.

I laughed. Not loud. Not long, either. But there was something just so *normal* about it that it pierced the knot of tension that twisted inside me. Only for a second, and only a needlepoint, but that single point of normality was all I needed to feel just as normal, if only for a few seconds.

'Please look at the picture. If you see her, please tell her Alex is trying to find her. Tell her . . .' Tell her what? 'Tell her I know. Tell her stay safe.'

'You look like you need a bite to eat and freshen up. You're welcome to use the shower rooms in the male dorm and then go through for a bite to eat, on me.'

The kindness of strangers.

I closed my eyes and nodded.

THIRTY-THREE

The shower was not as painful an experience as it might have been if thirty young boys had been vying for the hot water. I stripped and folded my clothes up on a stool that was provided and bought a sachet of shampoo from a vending machine on the wall. I hadn't seen one of those since the '80s, and last time it had been dispensing Day-Glo condoms ribbed for her comfort and amusingly branded Virgin.

I stood under the water as long as I could bear, with it never really getting hot, and sudsed up, then realised I didn't have a towel, so, skimming the worst of the water off my skin with my hands, I lingered in the showers letting the air dry my skin, then dressed and went down for food.

The first bite of pie and mash was good but had my stomach cramping as the hunger pangs hit. I kept on eating. I sat at a corner table, half-hoping but knowing that Morven wouldn't come down for dinner. Done, I went to help myself to a cup of thick black coffee from the thermos on the Welsh dresser. There was milk that had gone warm beside it.

I poured out a mug and went back to my table.

I sat there with my hands cupped around the mug, staring off into space, trying to think where I went from here while two by two the kids filed out to join their teachers in the courtyard. Finally, peace. The silence felt profound in their absence, deeper than the normal quiet of the world because of the thick old stone walls. Those walls meant the dining room verged on being cold despite the heat of the day outside.

Back in London it had seemed like the most obvious thing in the world to do, come here, back to where it all began for Morven, and just dig around until I found her. But crossing the Severn, with the bridge slowly swaying beneath my wheels, and following the twists and turns of ever narrowing roads to this little town tucked away in the Forest of Dean, I was forced to confront the sheer empty expanse outside the castle walls. There was miles and miles of rolling countryside out there with little pockets of housing, sometimes as little as eight or nine houses tucked into a cleft in a valley side, then there were the hunting lodges and the campsites.

My line of thinking was fairly flimsy in terms of logic: either she'd use this place as a base of operations because it was where they'd stayed as kids, or she'd try to stay as close to Llangorse Lake as possible.

The lake was an hour from here.

It came down to her state of mind, whether it was about hiding, or hunting. If she was hiding, then it was highly unlikely she'd put herself in the self-same spots. It was more likely she'd look to find somewhere in their shadows, close but not the obvious places. But if she was hunting that was exactly what she'd do. She'd want to be found and use herself as bait to draw David Dodds out.

So, which was it?

Hunter or hunted?

'I thought these might be helpful,' the young woman from reception said, offering me a handful of tourist brochures. 'They've got maps, ideas of where people might stay in relation to the landmarks, that sort of thing. It gives you a place to start looking.' She laid them out on the table in a fan. I saw pictures of Offa's Dyke, Tintern Abbey, Goodrich Castle, Clearwell Caves, Kingswood Abbey, Puzzlewood, Symonds Yat, and Kymin Hill. I knew she wasn't going to be at any of them because I didn't recognise them from those newspaper reports and magazine features in Susan Hall's shrine.

'Thanks,' I said, knowing she meant well.

I flipped the first one over and saw a number of red dots marking places of interest in relation to each other, and relative distances. It didn't stretch far enough into the Brecon Beacons to show the lake. Neither did the second one, but the third did, the constellation of red dots around it like a halo, and at the centre, the crannog.

The receptionist lingered a second or two longer, to the point that it almost became uncomfortable before she said, 'You can always try the letting agent in the village, they might know something. Even if she used the internet she'd have had to pick up the keys from somewhere.'

'Thank you,' I said again, the words anything but adequate.

'I hope you find her.'

'Me too.'

I took a sip of my coffee, which still hadn't cooled down enough to be drinkable, and started to thumb through the brochures, looking for anything that caught my eye. The problem was that a lot of these were new experiences that hadn't been around back when Morven's school trip had descended, even if the landmarks themselves were as old as the hills.

I found myself reading some of the descriptions and thinking how much Poppy would have loved this stuff.

And thinking about her, I called back to mum to make sure everything was okay with them and let her know how I was doing – which is to say tell her there was nothing new to report. The phone rang off the hook. No machine. Mum wasn't part of the modern world. I gave up after ten rings.

I needed to stretch my legs, so I finished my coffee off and decided to walk down to the village to see if I could find this letting agent.

THIRTY-FOUR

The keep was built on a limestone plateau that loomed over the surrounding countryside, with the ground dropping off sharply towards the River Wye. Signposts promised walking paths through the Forest of Dean to local landmarks including the peak of Symonds Yat and the relic of an old free mine. Behind me, one of the teachers was trying to explain how there were still traditional forester families living in the area and they had the rights to graze pigs on the land. I left him to do his enlightening.

On any other day I might have enjoyed the gentle stroll down into the village. It was picture postcard stuff. There was a pub, a nice-looking little corner shop that seemed to be the heart of civilisation, a couple of churches and a small school, without there being much else.

Bell ringers had the quarter to the hour chimes rolling from one of the Gothic Revival towers as I crossed the street towards the shop and set a much smaller bell jangling as it announced my entry. There was a heady fusion of farm fresh aromas, local produce and farmers' market stuff in the chillers, including paper-wrapped cured hams and strong cheeses. Newspapers lined up on the counter, more red tops than broadsheets. Behind the counter there were shelves of those wonderful old pick-and-mix glass jars of sweets I hadn't seen since I was a kid asking for a 20p mix up. Feeling like I'd stepped back in time, I couldn't help but smile as I walked towards the old guy working the counter.

'Afternoon,' he said, in the most perfectly thick Welsh accent. It could have been almost any word in the language.

'Hey there,' I said.

'What can I do you for?'

I took my phone out of my pocket and woke it up on the photo of Morven. 'I don't suppose you've seen my wife, have you?'

Unlike the young woman in the youth hostel, the old man didn't immediately leap to conclusions. He leaned over the counter, squinting at the screen. 'Can't say as I have,' he said after a moment, 'But I wasn't working over the weekend. You'd need to talk to my boy, Evan.'

I didn't want to get my hopes up, but it was hard not to as he leaned through to the back room and yelled up a short flight of stairs for his son to come down. After shouting, 'What?' And being told to 'Get your arse down here, sunshine!' Evan stomped down the stairs with all the grace of a pachyderm. A Pinhead tee-shirt and lank hair came around the corner, no smiles. 'What?' He said again.

I couldn't help but smile at the family dynamic as I showed him Morven's photo. 'I don't suppose you saw her over the weekend?'

He barely looked at it. I expected him to say no and stomp off back up the stairs. He didn't. He twisted his mouth, like he was chewing on the words before he let them out, then said, 'Yeah, she was in here on Saturday morning, looking at the cards in the window.'

'Do you know which one?' I asked.

He shrugged. 'One of the holiday cottages, maybe? That or she was looking to join Olwyn's band. Is she any good on the bass?'

'Don't be a smart arse, son,' the old man said, but I was grinning. I didn't care. It was my first positive sighting since the service station restaurant, he could be as smart as his arse desired as far as I was concerned.

'She can thump out a mean riff,' I said. 'But she's more of a drummer.'

'Ah, bit mad then?'

'All the best ones are,' I said. 'I don't suppose you know if she took down any of the details?'

This time he did shake his head. 'Sorry, man. Bunch of kids from the castle came in, I had my hands full making sure they didn't nick anything. She was gone by the time I'd finished sorting them out.'

'That's fine. Can I ask, is there a bus that gets you out towards Llangorse Lake?'

'From here? Nah, you'd need to go into Ross and change. Fair old journey, mind,' his father said. 'Nothing much to see there, anyway, you're better off staying local, walk along the valley to the Yat, go canoeing, check out the free mine, maybe head to the Abbey ruin.'

'Not everyone loves it round here, da,' Evan said, shaking his head. 'Sometimes, I swear, he forgets there's a whole world outside this valley.'

'Ah, but it's a beautiful valley, son. When you get to my age, you'll learn to appreciate beauty.'

I got the feeling this was a conversation they'd had on more than one occasion.

'I appreciate beauty, father. That's why I'm in a band.'

I burst out laughing at that. The kid had pretty much nailed the reason every great band was formed as succinctly as I'd ever heard it done. 'The lady at the youth hostel said there was a letting agency around here? I didn't notice it on the main road as I was walking down.'

'Letting agency? That's a grand way of putting it,' the old man said. 'It's over on Castle Crescent. You missed it by about fifty yards.'

'Ah, thanks.'

'No trouble.'

I left the father and son double act. Outside, I stopped to look at the cards in the window, skimming the details. I didn't see anything immediately obvious but took a photo of them just in case one led to Morven.

I walked back towards the turn into Castle Crescent and saw the window of the letting agency. It had been on the back angle, behind me as I'd walked down the hill, so I'd missed it. I crossed over the street. There were a dozen pictures of idyllic cottages in the window with bright red 'DATES AVAILABLE' stickers on them.

I went inside.

More hellos, more can I help yous, more have you seen my wife, but this time it all ended rather abruptly when I said, 'It would have been Saturday morning.'

'Ah, that explains it,' the woman at the metal and glass desk said, all smiles. Her name badge called her Bethany. 'We're only open Monday to Friday. Not much foot traffic, you see. Most of our business is done online these days.'

I nodded. 'So, the only places she'd have seen would have been in the window?'

'That's right. Unless she'd booked online via the website.'

'She didn't have her phone with her,' I said.

'They've got the internet up at the castle, she could have used that,' Bethany suggested, which was more than reasonable. There were an infinite variety of ways to get online these days, including buying a burner phone with some of that five grand she'd withdrawn from the joint account. I couldn't keep thinking of her as being helpless out here. She was smart. More than smart. She could run rings around me if she wanted to. She'd have found a way to make all this work, no question, but she wouldn't have booked online, I was sure of it, because online meant a paper trail, credit card confirmations and stuff the police would have been able to check two days ago. Staying beneath their radar meant cash transactions, which meant face-to-face, which, in turn meant that I had a chance of finding her if I followed in her footsteps. That was what I was clinging to. That chance.

'Don't suppose you could check if you've got a booking in her name?'

And then we circled back to the whole privacy thing, with Bethany not willing to give out confidential information and me assuring her I understood, because as much as I wanted her to check the system, I wanted to know she wouldn't just offer up Morven's whereabouts if David Dodds came asking.

'It's fine . . . can I ask, do you do stuff close to, or at least easy distance, from Llangorse Lake?'

'That's a bit of a trek, love,' she said. 'Not really our catchment area. There's places closer that'd handle lettings, I'm sure. We're more Coldharbour, Trellech, Brockweir, New Mills, places like that. We do lots of stuff in the forest itself. There's always walkers looking for a base of operations, that's our stock in trade rather than holiday makers. You want to be looking for somewhere more like Crickhowell or Talgarth, I reckon.'

I nodded. 'Can I ask you something else? Has anyone else come asking about her?'

'Not today, love, no.'

'Thanks.' I tried not to breathe a sigh of relief. 'Can I give you my number and if anyone does, will you give me a call?'

Bethany looked dubious, but she didn't say no immediately.

'If you are uncomfortable, that's fine. There's someone else looking for my wife, and I really don't want them finding her.'

'That sounds . . .' yeah, what did it sound like? Not mysterious, that's for sure, but not a normal request, either. I could understand why Bethany was baulking at agreeing. I had a choice, tell her more, and hope to get her onside, or gamble that Dodds wouldn't come this way.

Of course, if Morven was the hunter and not the hunted, she'd invite him out to the lake, wouldn't she, not just hide and hope he went away?

I opted for the less confessional of the alternatives and scratched out my number on one of the business cards on her desk, saying, 'Just in case', as I handed it back. No expectation, no explanation. It was safer that way. I'm not stupid, this was a small place. It would start up at the keep, and by lunchtime the whispers would have spread, there'd be talk of the nosy man and his questions in the village shops, and soon everyone would know about Morven. That was the joy and the curse of tight communities like this.

'I hope you find her,' Bethany said, as I left to walk back up to the castle car park.

I felt like I'd wasted time here, but I hadn't really. And the few hours I'd spent had been worth it, because they'd rewarded me with a confirmed sighting that meant I was on the right path.

And that was priceless.

I drove out of St Briavels feeling more positive than I'd felt since I found the texts on Morven's phone.

THIRTY-FIVE

The infinite summer shades of green all around me would have been enough to make a believer of even the staunchest atheist. There was beauty here that goes beyond my ability to capture with words. Every shade imaginable, countless more that aren't, rolling hills climbing towards the black slate roofs of the white cottages scattered throughout the valleys, and the looming shadows of the Black Mountains in the distance. Trees and banks of shrubberies replaced drystone walls to divide the fields. Farms, cattle grids and wooden stiles. It was another world.

At one point, the road forded a river that the constant sun over the last few weeks had drained to the point where I could see the cracked clay of the riverbanks. Even so, a mile down the road that same drained river fell away in a waterfall that was nothing short of spectacular as the white caps raged, tumbling over the drop.

I saw signs for Talgarth up ahead, and another pointing out the hospital, which, as I drove past, I saw was boarded up. The place was creepy, to be honest. A huge sprawling maze of crumbling buildings, the walls covered in moss and all the ground floor windows replaced by wood and graffiti. I saw slime on the walls, and as the road swept me around the bend, the broken glass roof of what I assumed was some sort of conservatory or orangery. The weathervane on the main tower spun like something out of a cheap horror movie. It wasn't a stretch to imagine what kind of hospital this abandoned complex had been back in another life, but even without any imagination, another sign gave the game away; it was an old Victorian lunatic asylum. There was no way that place wasn't haunted.

I drove down into the town proper, looking for somewhere to park, before I went in search of more newsagent windows to check for cards advertising potential lets and, from there, see if I could find a way to wherever Morven was staying.

According to Google Maps I was eleven minutes from the lake and there was a direct bus. That meant this was almost certainly the closest town and, in all likelihood, where Morven was staying. And if she wasn't sleeping here, she had to eat. Coming into town made sense.

I found myself looking at every face in the fading daylight, trying to see her, but of course it was never going to be as easy as that.

Talgarth was on a hill. There was a main square that challenged the definition of geometry, a village hall, a bakery, a tourist centre and country market in what had probably been a church hall twenty years ago. Right in the heart of it all, I saw an estate agent with a window full of possible places Morven might be staying. Across the way, there was a church with a kissing gate that served as its entry.

I found a spot near the hotel, which looked more like a pub, with its hanging baskets swinging in the breeze. Some of the other cars in the small car park cost serious money, including a sports car that would have taken me three- or four-years' full time work to afford, and even then I'd have had to forego eating.

I had no intention of sleeping in the car, so figured I better check to see if there were any rooms at the inn before I did anything else, even if it felt like the day was getting away from me. Locking the car, I crossed the tarmac to the door. The chalk boards outside promised food was served all day.

There was a room, and the rate was reasonable, so assuming a worst-case scenario of not finding Morven in the next few hours,

I paid for the night in advance and took the oversized room key, but didn't go up.

The receptionist, Charlie, hadn't seen my wife, either.

I tried the tourist centre first, looking for a map of the walks around the lake and other places of interest in the vicinity. Unlike the inn, the two women working here had seen Morven on Saturday morning when she'd come in asking for the same map.

I wanted to kiss them.

'Was she interested in anything particular? Do you remember?'

'We did what we always do, didn't we sis?'

'That we did, sis, that we did,' the younger of the two said, with a half-grin and a slight shrug of the shoulders.

'And what might that have been?' I asked, enjoying another local double act.

'Well, we marked a couple of walks on the map for her, highlighting nice viewing places. We like to be helpful.'

'There's a lot of lovely places. If folks don't know what to look for, they miss them.'

'Besides, it's what we're paid for.'

And that earned a bigger grin from both of them.

'Could you?' I asked, opening my map up.

They had their highlighters in hand before I'd spread it out on the counter.

When I left there were half a dozen spots of interest marked on the map as well as a couple of snaking lines that showed different routes to and around the lake itself.

I tried the estate agents next.

I was beginning to think that I was going about this the wrong way. A place like this would have wanted references, bank accounts, Visa cards, it wouldn't have been doing cash-in-hand, no-questions-asked lets. That's what I needed to focus my attention on. And that meant cards in windows and word of mouth.

Even so, it didn't hurt to ask, so I went in with my phone in hand and went through it all again. I could only imagine how it must have felt to do this day after day after day, looking for some lost loved one, and how it must grind you down and down and down until your bones were dust.

They didn't remember seeing Morven on Saturday morning. They closed at noon, so it was possible they were already closed before she arrived in town.

'Can you check if you've let any places close to the lake in the last few days?'

'I can check,' the agent said, blowing his fringe out of his face and he hunched over the computer to check the most recent lets. 'Nope, nothing in the last couple of days,' he said, confirming my suspicions.

'And, just say I didn't want to go through you, is there somewhere that handles private lets?'

'You mean like another agency?'

'No, I'm thinking more old school, like cards in the newsagent's windows, that kind of thing?'

'Oh, sure, you've got the notice board in the country market, there's another one in the mini-market down the hill, and there's the little place on the corner, the bookshop that's a cafe, too. They have a few local interest ads.'

'You're a star.'

'You know what to do then, hit that five-star review button on all your favourite apps,' he said, grinning. 'And say Aiden was just the best ever.'

'You can count on it,' I promised.

We both knew I wasn't going to follow through.

Outside, I had three choices, each one a little further down the hill than the one before. Taking them in order, I started with the country market.

I was hit by the smell of fresh bread as I walked through the iron gates and into the hall. There were a dozen sourdough and farmhouse loaves piled up on a table just inside the doorway, and all around me there was food, food and more food. Wicker baskets of fruit and veg lined the walls and spilled out into the centre of the stone floor in Mondrian blocks of bright colours. A chalk board nailed to a wooden beam listed prices by the weight. There were a couple of fridges with frozen foods, and tins and bottles filled the shelves deeper into the place. There were a couple of people moving through the maze of food with baskets in hand, feeling out the freshness of the produce before taking the prime pickings. A young lad in a dirty apron wrestled with new potatoes, while behind the counter a woman sorted through what looked like fancy dog treats.

I saw the notice board. There was a flyer for a local choir, another one for an open-air aerobics class, a lost cat and an oboe for sale, and scattered between them, a couple of holiday lets. I took down the details, thinking I'd make a couple of calls and swing by to see for myself who was staying there after I was done here.

Plastering on my best smile, I went over to the woman who was almost finished sorting out the clear cellophane bags of dog treats, tying them off with tartan lace bows before arranging them beside the till. 'Can I help you, love?'

'I hope so,' I said.

'Well then, let's give it a go, shall we?'

'I'm looking for someone,' I showed her the photo on the phone again. 'I think she's rented a herder's cottage out near the lake?'

'Has she now? Very nice,' the woman said. She peered at Morven's photo and shook her head. 'Sorry love, haven't seen her. But there are plenty of other shops round here. I'm sure someone will have.'

I nodded.

'Can I help you with anything else? Hate to see someone leave disappointed.' It was said kindly enough that I smiled as I told her it was okay. 'You sure I can't tempt you?' She held up one of the bone-shaped biscuits. 'They're really good.'

'More of a cat man, sorry,' I said, earning an amused tsk from her.

I was out the door and halfway towards the bookshop-cum-cafe on the corner when the kid in the apron caught up with me. He was breathing hard, the hundred metres taking it out of him. Grinning, he planted his hands on his knees and said, 'I couldn't help overhearing . . . I do the deliveries for mum. Picked up a couple of new ones this week. Want me to look at the photo?'

'Sure,' I said, getting my phone out to show him. I had to dismiss the low power warning in the middle of the screen. It was down to sub 5 per cent.

He cupped a hand over the screen to cut out the glare and nodded. 'Yeah, I took some stuff out to her this morning. Paid cash. Nice lady.'

My heart lurched arithmetically, a beat missed. This wasn't a two-day-old sighting. We were talking hours. More than that, it wasn't some glimpse caught in a crowd, it was meeting on her doorstep, planting an X very firmly on the map that said: *here she is.*

'Can you remember where she's staying?'

'Yeah, we only do a couple of deliveries most days, helping the older folks or dropping off stuff to the tourists who've been here a little bit longer. They find us on their first trip into town, then they take deliveries for later in their stay, so they don't waste the holiday shopping.'

'Makes sense,' I said.

'She's in the old Pearse place down by the lake. Nice place. You can't miss it. The road runs out nearly a mile from the house, but there's a track, you just keep walking until the land runs out. Nearly killed myself dragging those bags.'

'Hope she gave you a good tip,' I said.

He laughed. 'Women are the best tippers.'

'So, how do I get to the Pearse house from here?'

'If you follow the road out of town, towards Llangorse, it's a series of right, left, right, lefts, four turns, as you get to the old vicarage. They'll take you past a caravan park and eventually you'll end up at a gravel car park with a picnic place and a view of the water. There's a track that dead ends in a paddock and beyond that, a farmhouse to the right, and a smaller footpath that skirts the paddock and leads around to the old Pearse place. A lot of the land down there is flooded out, even in the summer so you're going to need better shoes,' he said, looking down at my trainers. 'Some proper hiking boots wouldn't hurt.'

'I'll have to take your word for that.'

'You'll see a little jetty down there. There's normally four or five row boats you can hire if you want to go out to the crannog.'

'Thanks,' I said. 'Will you do me a favour?'

'Sure.'

'If anyone else comes asking, can you send them somewhere else? Doesn't matter where. Just so long as they go the wrong way.'

The lad laughed. 'I'm sure I can manage that,' and held out his hand, waiting for it to be crossed with silver.

I took a twenty out of my pocket, knowing that in his place all it would have taken to buy my loyalty after I'd pocketed that twenty would have been forty from David Dodds.

THIRTY-SIX

Walking back to the car I spotted a hardware shop on the corner, opposite the mini-market and thought about buying some sort of makeshift weapon, maybe a crowbar or something like that, but I remembered something Mac had said to a group of kids when we'd been shooting on that first day: *Whatever you bring you better be prepared for it to be used against you.*

Olivia was right, he was a smart man.

Crossing the road, I had the weirdest sense of being watched, but as I turned and turned about, shading my eyes, the only person I saw was the woman standing in the doorway of the country market. She raised a hand in greeting. I waved back, wondering if her boy had told her that he'd seen Morven and she was coming out to watch, or if it was just coincidence that she was watching me walk back to the car.

I opened the door, and got in.

I could see her through the rear-view mirror, still in the doorway, arms folded. She watched me all the way down the hill, until I was following the road down towards the lake itself.

I don't know, something about that last lingering exchange shook me.

It's hard to explain, and after everything else, it ought to have been so inconsequential, but it just got under my skin.

I did my best to put it out of my mind, focussing on the right, left, right, left combination of turns I'd been told to look out for as I reached the old vicarage.

By the time I reached the first turn I was the only car on the road. The hedgerows encroached on the tarmac, one grown so large it spilled beyond the edge, giving a good sense of how little traffic there was down here. I passed signs for the caravan park, promising there were pitches available.

Over the next half mile it felt like I left civilisation far behind.

With the fields rolling away from me down towards the water, I could see what I thought was the house. There were farm buildings and hedges that formed walls around what I assumed were the paddocks.

I was barely driving five miles an hour as I crawled past the visitor centre, a dull cinder block affair, and turned into the car park – which in itself was a laughable description. There was space for five cars in a single line, that was it.

There were no cars.

I killed the engine. Before I clambered out, I took my phone out of my pocket only to see the list of missed call notifications. I must have knocked it onto silent somewhere back there. There were at least a dozen, all from Olivia. The sheer number of them frightened me. I went to unlock the phone to call her back but the damned thing died in my hand. I tossed it onto the passenger seat. I didn't have time to worry about it.

The air hit me. I know it sounds stupid, given I was only a few miles on down the road, but it was so fresh here, sharp in the lungs, and heavy with so many fragrances it would have sent a hay fever sufferer into traumatic rhinitis.

Up above, there was a storm brewing. There was a steel grey to the low-lying clouds that only served to hurry along the last of the day, eager for the dark to follow.

You can tell when there's a storm in the air; it takes on an entirely different quality, thickening, the humidity in it almost too heavy to breathe.

There was a piebald pony in the field.

I saw the four flatbed rowing boats at the end of the jetty, and was struck by the grandiose nature of that word. The jetty was little more than a dozen planks of wood nailed together with the algae green water lapping up around their sides.

It was impossible to miss the crannog out in the water.

The lake was larger than I'd expected, over a mile long, and probably three or four miles around. There were ripples across the surface. I couldn't tell if they were down to voles or pike moving beneath the surface, or the breeze working across the top of it. Algae was thick around the shoreline, giving the illusion that the land reached out into the water. Tall reeds grew close to the shore. There was a conical roofed building – a roundhouse – which I assumed was something to do with the crannog's 'visitor experience'. As I stood there a huge damselfly settled on the wooden post beside me. It looked utterly alien with its vibrant blue tail.

There was another longer and considerably more substantial jetty on the crannog itself, though there were no boats tied up against it.

I stared out over the water and all I could think was: *so this was where Scott and Chrissy Lang drowned.*

I couldn't turn away for the longest time.

But finally, I couldn't put it off any longer. I walked towards the paddock and the farmhouse on the other side where, if I was right, Morven was waiting.

I'd been thinking about this moment for so long I'd actually stopped imagining what it might be like. A couple of days ago it had been all about being swept up in tight embraces and hugging each other like the world was ending around us, then it had changed, becoming more tentative, the truth of what had happened here coming between us, and in all the hours between then and now it had gone through a hundred variations on a theme, and none of them had felt natural.

Walking the last hundred metres or so to the house, I kept

telling myself: *She's still my wife, whatever else she was, she's still the same person she was on Friday morning. She's still my Morven.*

It was an unassuming building. Two storeys high, with grimy net curtains at the windows. The chalk white walls wept where the weather had undermined them. There were dark stains around the foundations where damp had got hold of the stones.

I saw light inside.

There was so much junk in the yard, including the wire frame of an old bed and a mouldy mattress. There was a bike without a front wheel. There were two odd shoes, one a canvas sneaker, the other a wellie. A large green barrel collected the runoff from the roof, though it had long since overflowed and now the rainfall soaked into the dirt – or would, if it ever rained again.

The chips of stone crunched beneath my feet as I walked the final few steps up to the door.

It opened before I could knock.

And my heart stopped in that moment and every doubt I had flailed away to nothing.

I hadn't thought about what I was going to say. In the end it didn't matter. I told her the truth.

She looked at me.

That smile . . .

It broke me.

I wanted to reach out.

I wanted to hold her.

But I couldn't move.

'I know,' I told her.

Two words that made her cry.

THIRTY-SEVEN

Morven hesitated, then reached out.

I stepped into her arms.

I felt the sobs wrack her body next to mine.

I reached up, cupping the back of her head with my hand, and tried to say, 'It's okay, it's alright,' but the words wouldn't come out right. It took me a moment to realise why; I was crying along with her.

I don't know how long we stood there, long enough for it to stop feeling natural, but I didn't want to break the embrace before she was ready to let go and if that meant holding on for a minute or an hour or a whole day then I would hold on.

Eventually, she let go, and looked up at me, red-eyed, tears and snot running down her face. She'd never looked more beautiful to me than in that moment, as she wiped the back of her hand across her eyes. Her hair fell into her eyes. It was hard to believe that she'd only been gone for four days. It was an insane realisation. Four days.

'You came . . .'

'Of course I did.'

'I wasn't sure you would . . .'

It didn't hurt that she'd doubted me. I'm not sure I would have been certain of her coming if the roles were reversed. We like to think our loved ones would walk through fire for us, but until the mettle is tested there's no way of knowing for sure. And that's not saying I'm more in love or somehow better, just that I had absolutely no choice, I was always coming here, and I think she'd have done exactly the same if I was the one in trouble.

'Never in doubt.'

'So, what happens now?'

'I haven't thought that far ahead,' I admitted. 'I got to the *you and me against the world* part of the plan and figured that was as much as I needed to know.' Again, I tried to offer that smile I know she needed to see.

She closed the door behind me, and we went through to the kitchen. We've always been kitchen people. I'm not sure why, but all of our important conversations have always end up happening in kitchens, not bedrooms or lounges. She rattled about in the cupboard for a few seconds, getting cups out. I saw the glass jar of instant coffee beside the kettle.

I filled the kettle from the tap.

It was an easy routine. Something to trust in these first few minutes back together as we looked to re-establish some sort of equilibrium.

Cups clattered, water ran, the kettle steamed, and eventually we had to talk.

Morven cradled her chipped mug in both hands as she leaned against the sink.

I leaned against the table.

Behind her, the lake looked like a pastoral postcard painted on the glass.

'How's Poppy?'

'She's fine. She's at mum's. She's got no idea what's going on. We went to the aquarium on Saturday. David Dodds bought her a stuffed sea turtle.'

'Jesus Christ . . . what happened?'

'It was his one mistake. It got me his name. That got me to you.'

'But Poppy?'

'She's fine. She had no idea. She just thought some nice man had taken pity on her and given her the stuffed toy she wanted.'

'We need to have serious words with our girl when we get home,' Morven said. 'No more sweets from a stranger.'

I appreciated the Squeeze reference. My wife knew me and every obscure and forgotten record I loved.

'Damn right. She's far too trusting.'

'Takes after her father,' Morven said, and I knew there was an undercurrent to the comparison, rippling away just beneath the words. I'd trusted her. That's what she was saying. But of course I had. I loved her.

Love her.

'Okay, I guess one of us needs to acknowledge the elephant in the room.'

She nodded. She didn't look happy about it, but there was no way we could get through this without having the conversation.

'I met your mum,' I said.

'What was that like?'

'She's got a shrine to you upstairs.'

'I very much doubt that. She hates me.'

'I don't think she does . . . the box room is full of old magazines, newspaper cuttings . . . I guess everything that was ever written about what happened is in that room.'

'You can say it. Everything about the murders,' Morven said. She wasn't being deliberately confrontational. She was telling me she was done hiding from her past. 'I've come to terms with what I did. And why I did it. I'm not a monster, Alex, whatever you may think right now. I didn't just drown two kids because I wanted to know what it would be like to feel the life go out of them. I'm still me. Lucy Galvin is gone. She's every bit as dead as those two kids.'

I nodded. I didn't really know what to say to that. I make my living from words. I like to think that I know how to use them, that I'm particularly skilled when it comes to conveying what I want to in any given turn of phrase, but I had nothing.

Through the kitchen window, I saw a swan out on the water and was struck by the symbolism of it. I'd read somewhere that swans mated for life. My gaze drifted back from the water to the woman in the kitchen with me. I understood that total commitment, one swan to another. Morven was my swan.

'You don't have to do this. You don't owe me any explanation. You've only ever been Morven to me. You'll only ever be Morven to me. Like you said, Lucy Galvin is dead. She doesn't exist.' She nodded. I could see the gratitude in her eyes. 'Nora told me you had wanted to tell me years ago.'

'You met Nora?'

'I've met everybody,' I said, wryly. 'Including David Dodds.' She waited for me to elaborate, so I told her about the encounter outside the house, him in his white panel van, me clinging to the door handle as he drove away. I told her about coming home to the broken window and about being at his house, finding the cameras and how he'd been spying on us for a month. I thought twice about telling her what had happened to Mac, not sure that she needed that added weight on her soul. But told her anyway, no more secrets. That was important.

She listened without interrupting me, even though I could see the desire to explain something, to clarify something or push for more detail about something she didn't quite understand or where she could tell I was hiding something.

At the end of it, I simply said, 'You could have told me, you know . . . last week . . . you didn't have to go through this alone. If it was about the money . . . we could have solved it.'

Morven looked down. Not in shame. At least I didn't think so. She was hiding something, or rather trying to work out if she could tell me whatever it was, or if she had to hide it. Her right hand was clenched so tight her knuckles had turned white and the fine bones stood out on the back of her hand, adding these stark ridges to the topography of her flesh.

I didn't say anything.

Whatever it was she was deciding, she needed to do so without my encouragement.

Finally, she looked up.

She shook her head, and I thought she'd decided against taking me into her confidence, but even as her head was saying no, she reached out for my hand, like she wanted to lead me to the truth.

I took her hand and let her steer me up the narrow wooden stairs to where she'd been sleeping.

The place smelled damp: like it wasn't used to people living in it. It was probably empty two hundred days of the year. That kind of abandonment seeped into a building and took up ownership of the stones.

The bed looked like it was something out of the 1950s, covered with many throws and blankets and topped with a crocheted spider's web of colour. The curtains didn't match anything else in the room. The chest of draws beside the wall was almost as tall as Morven. The top was covered in Olympic rings of stains where candles and water had eaten into the lacquer. There were a pair of shoes, polished to within an inch of their lives, on the rug beside the wardrobe and a lace dress hanging on the back of the door. There was a mirror on one wall. Even from the doorway I could see the silvering beneath the glass had begun to flake, giving the illusion of decay to my reflection.

It was a peculiar room, trapped in time.

There were lace doilies on the bedside tables, with little trinkets on them. I don't remember seeing a lace doily in twenty years.

Morven crossed the Chinese rug to the bed and took something from beneath the pillow.

I couldn't see what it was at first, but as I stepped into the room, I saw her lay a small cloth-wrapped bundle on the bed.

She peeled away the cloth one corner at a time, each edge

lifted with infinite care. It was reverential. Like she was unwrapping precious gems and didn't dare risk one of the tiny fragments of diamond falling away and getting lost between the cracks in the floorboards.

I knew what it was before the final triangle of cloth was peeled away.

A gun.

I'm not a gun fetishist. I couldn't tell you the difference between a Smith and Wesson, a Browning, a Walther PPK, a Heckler and Koch or a Desert Eagle. I only know the names because of films. What I did know was that this thing was made with a single purpose.

'You wanted to know what our money bought. This.'

'Where did you get it?'

'I picked it up on Friday, from a place in Soho.'

'After you abandoned the car?'

She nodded. 'I got the train back into London after I dropped the envelope in the trash like Dodds wanted. Bet that surprised him, expecting a nice little payoff and instead he gets a bunch of photocopies about our life.'

It was my turn to nod. 'It wasn't Dodds who picked it up, it was your mum.'

That threw her for a second.

'They're in this together?' She paused a beat, trying to wrap her head around the implications of the two of them being in it together. 'I always knew she was a bitch . . . but . . . she's something else.'

'I don't think she is . . . I think he was taunting her, looking to make her hurt, and use you to do it. You should have seen her, Morven, she looked . . . hollow. I can't believe you bought a gun,' I told her, changing mental gears. 'I mean, what are you planning on doing with it?'

'Making number three,' she said, and for a second I didn't follow. And then I did, and I felt sick.

'You're not serious.'

'I am. He's not going to stop. He's going to keep coming and coming, and I'm not prepared to uproot my life and start all over again, again. I'm doing this for us. For you, me and Poppy. You don't have to be a part of it if you don't want to. But I have to do it.'

I'd known this was the endgame from the moment David Dodds came into our lives. It wasn't going to be enough for the police to go and lean on Dodds and tell him to let things go. Once her new identity had been compromised there were only ever two ways this played out. And after Mac's attempted murder, only one.

Starting over was never going to be enough.

Part of me thought Dodds would just keep coming and coming and coming because he was fuelled by rage and hate and everything that had been allowed to fester in there since that day at the lake. But another part of me was pretty sure it had nothing to do with that. He'd wanted money. You didn't send those texts or arrange money drops if it wasn't about greed.

He'd recognised her, and in that moment recognised the earning potential that knowledge presented – either to sell her out to someone with reason to hate her, like the parents of the two Lang kids; or some relative looking for biblical justice because they couldn't live with the fact she'd been given a new life when Chrissy and Scott wouldn't even get to live their old ones; or to blackmail her, threatening to sell her secret new life to the tabloids.

And once she started paying, a few grand was never going to be enough. Then it was all about how much we thought her new life was worth. What price do you put on a happy family? A nice house? A decent school for your kid? A family holiday every year? Or just the peace of mind to know life gets to go on as normal day after day? Stuff you take for granted that's priceless when it gets right down to it.

And when the money ran out, he'd sell those secrets anyway. They had to be worth twenty or thirty grand to those shitrags.

I'd put my hand in my pocket.

I know I would.

Even as it was bleeding us dry.

I'd still put my hand in my pocket.

Because I love my family. I love the life we've made for ourselves. I love being able to walk Poppy to school in the morning and head around to the cafe to make some shit up or disappear down the next internet black hole of research I stumble across. I love being able to sit across the dinner table and look at my wife and think how fucking proud I am of everything she's accomplished, knowing I'm punching well above my weight and just so incredibly lucky that out of all the people in the world she chose me.

I'd put my hand in my pocket because the alternative was unthinkable.

The truth was I'd go to war for my family if that was what it took.

Looking at the gun on the bed I was in no doubt Morven was preparing to do exactly that.

She was going to war for our family. And that was different. Because for her, it was never going to be as simple as self-defence. If she killed Dodds in cold blood she was going away, no new names to hide behind. Three was never a charm when it came to killing.

Kill Dodds and she was never coming out.

I remembered that old quote: *three people can keep a secret if one of them's dead.*

Okay, the quote's actually two of them are dead, but I wasn't going anywhere, and I'd be damned if I was losing Morven now that I'd found her again.

THIRTY-EIGHT

'It's a ghost gun,' she said. 'Clean. No serial number. Nothing to link it back to us,' she was talking like someone who knew far too much about guns. I didn't have a clue what a ghost gun was. It could have been homemade for all I knew.

'Cover that thing up,' I said.

'You wanted to know what I spent the money on. I bought us a future, Alex.'

'The best money we've ever spent,' I said, the sarcasm dripping off my tongue. I resort to stupid jokes when things get too real for me. Always have done. I'm not trying to be funny, I'm doing everything I can not to be frightened.

I don't know what I'd expected. No, that's a lie. I know exactly what I'd expected. I'd thought I'd turn up on the doorstep, tell her I knew what had happened, and tell that it was okay, we could go home, he couldn't hurt us. But that was beyond naive, wasn't it? The whole male saviour thing. I looked at my wife. She didn't need saving. She'd got herself a gun and was getting ready to go hunting for the man who'd tried to ruin her family.

Just how far would she go to protect the ones she loved?

I think the gun on the bed was all the answer that question needed.

Morven refolded the wrap and put the gun back beneath the flat pillow.

'Are you hungry?' She asked.

It was such a mundane question that I almost laughed. 'Not

really. I should be. I've only had a bacon sandwich all day, but guns kill my appetite.'

I'm not sure what she was about to suggest, but we both heard it through the open window; the sound of a car coming down to the water's edge. There was nothing immediately threatening about it, this was a destination for all sorts of kids' groups and school trips and other excursions, but there was just something about the sound of the lone engine coming down the hill that sent a shiver chasing down the ladder of my spine.

It was David Dodds.

It had to be.

That was why she'd picked this place. It was remote enough to work as a flytrap.

Sickness twisted at my gut. I couldn't move. It was only two seconds of hesitation, but it was enough. Even as I asked, 'What did you do?' Her answer was to grab the gun from beneath the pillow and run down the stairs to face him, leaving me rooted to the spot.

Instead of following her, I went to the window, thinking I might be able to see Dodds' white panel van from this vantage point. Leaning on the windowsill, I pushed the window open wider and craned my neck, trying to get a better view of the car-park beyond the paddock.

I couldn't see any white vans.

What I could see was a dirty old Land Rover. It was one of the 1970s models. The last time I'd seen it, it had been bricked up.

I recognised the old woman as she hauled herself out of the driver's seat. This time, at least, she wasn't holding a shotgun.

That feeling of being watched back in the town centre made sense now; it wasn't the scrutiny of the woman in the Country Market that had made my skin crawl. It was Susan Hall. She'd been there, somewhere, staring at me.

She walked with a curious kind of waddle, with her low centre of gravity, six steps taking her out of sight.

I left the window open and headed downstairs.

I heard the sound of the door opening before I was halfway down and called, 'It's not him,' but Morven was already through the door. I was answered by her shout of, 'You!'

By the time I reached the door, she was halfway down the drive to the paddock, facing the woman as she waddled towards her.

It was the first time they'd seen each other in twenty years, mother and daughter, but it wasn't some joyous reunion. The tension in their bodies was unmistakable, even from where I was. I knew my wife. I could see the muscle and fibre lock like iron, it was in her stance. This wasn't fight or flight – it was pure fight every inch of the way.

I couldn't hear what Susan Hall said as she neared. Her words weren't pitched to reach me, but it was obvious there was some real aggression in the meeting, even without the words. It was choreographed by their bodies.

Whatever she said, it had an effect of Morven.

She seemed to buckle as her mother closed the distance. Our responses to some things, I swear, are genetically hardwired into our bodies, like how we stand up to our parents. I could see it in Morven then. She'd come out ready for a fight – worse, ready to commit murder – and instead of facing the nightmare man who'd threatened to shred her world around her, she was up against the woman who brought her into that world and was immediately her little girl all over again. The only difference between then and now was that she wasn't seeing the ally she might once have seen.

I'd been wrong about her. What I'd taken as grief and that hollowed-out sadness was anything but.

That shrine of hers wasn't a memorial to her daughter, it was an evidence room filled with reasons to hate her, and like everything in that room, her hatred had had twenty years to fester, turning toxic. The older woman was as much a victim of that day as the two kids; even as she'd kept on living and breathing, she'd been paying the cost of it every single day of her life, hounded out of her home and forced to relocate to some isolated region where she could start again, a new name, new life. She'd lost her husband to suicide because of the pressures of the public scorn piled on by the red tops that had made their little girl public enemy number one, the most hated child in England. She'd faced the hatred in the streets from all of the ugly people out there who were so righteous in their fury, and walked home with a bundle of newspapers under her arm trying to hide the headlines from her neighbours. There was a not-so-secret shame to all of it for her, and beneath that shame, genuine pain.

It had changed her. Of course it had. She wasn't the young mother she had been. That day, and the ones that followed, had changed everything for her. But Susan would have been lying to herself if she ever thought there was a happy-ever-after in her future. I know that now. Even if I didn't in that moment.

I started to walk towards them.

Finally coming into earshot, the first words I heard were, 'Aren't you going to invite me in, Lucy?'

'That's not my name.'

'It's more your name than the one you call yourself,' Susan spat. 'It was good enough for you growing up.'

'It's not who I am.'

'Yes, it is. I don't care *what* you call yourself, you are always going to be that kid. She's in you. She is you, Lucy. You can lie to yourself all you want. You can run from who you are. But you are always going to be that wretched piece of shit who killed two kids, whatever you call yourself.'

Morven didn't buckle this time. No more shrinking. It was as if those barbs galvanised her. She straightened, facing the woman. From behind I saw what Susan didn't; her grip tighten on the gun in her hand, the muscles quiver along her right side.

For one sickening second I thought she was going to lose control, goaded into it by her mother, and add another life to her debt to the universe.

But the moment passed; the tension eased, and the gun stayed at her side.

'You throw insult after insult at me and expect me to invite you in?'

'I'm entitled to. You're my daughter.'

'You don't know me. You don't know anything about who I am.'

'You keep telling yourself that, *Lucy*. I might not recognise your face, but I know your soul.'

I could have let them go at each other, each tearing strips off the other. There was a lot of anger there to burn, but something about Susan Hall's presence here felt deeply wrong. The only explanation I could come up with was that Dodds had sent her, just as he'd sent her to the motorway service station food court, but was she a willing participant or another pawn he was manipulating?

'What are you doing here?' I asked, not caring that I was putting myself in the middle of their fight.

'I've come to see my daughter,' Susan said.

'Bullshit,' I cut her off. 'How did you find us?'

That brought a smile to her face, though there was no humour behind it.

'Find you? I didn't find you, I followed you. You led me all the way to her door, Alex.'

'Why? Why come here?'

'A better question.' I saw then that she had something in her hand. It took me a moment to realise it was a phone.

The older woman held it out for Morven to take.

'It's going to ring later. You're going to want to answer.'

Morven didn't take it.

'I'm just the messenger,' the woman said. 'You don't have to thank me. I'm not doing this for you. I'm doing it for me. I want to be there the moment it sinks in. I want to see the grief and the fear on your face. I want to experience it right along with you.'

'What do you mean?'

'You'll know soon enough. I don't want to spoil the surprise. Now, why don't you invite me in, put the kettle on and let us all be civilised as we play the last few minutes of happy families, shall we?'

Morven stepped aside.

It was the closest she was going to get to an invitation.

Susan dipped her head in a nod and waddled on, lurching from side to side as she made her way to the door.

Morven turned. We exchanged a look, both of us not quite grasping what was happening here, but sure the happy families crack wasn't about the three of us walking into that herder's cottage.

I closed the door behind us, shutting out the world as best I could.

I heard Morven in the kitchen, rattling through the cupboards for another mug.

It felt strange, walking into that room. I was an intruder here. This was all about their personal grief and years of shared pain that I wasn't party to.

But as soon as that phone rang, I was going to be very much a part of it.

THIRTY-NINE

They sat across the table from each other.

From the doorway, I was struck by the similarities rather than the differences. There was a very definite set of family features they shared. Facing each other, it was like seeing some weird horror movie effect where a young face ages and crumbles before your eyes. The flakes of dry skin around Susan's chin seemed to be saying give it a few more years and all this will return to dust.

The coffees went cold on the table between them, untouched.

There wasn't much in the way of conversation, either. Not the deep heart-to-heart you might have expected after more than half a lifetime since they'd been in each other's company. Just accusations and recriminations.

Morven's face was stone.

There was no love lost between them.

'Why would you say that?' Susan asked. 'To hurt me? Because it doesn't. Nothing you can say or do could hurt more than what you've already done.'

'I've done nothing you didn't deserve, mother.'

'Deserve? You think I deserved any of this?' She hit her chest a little too hard. 'No one deserves what you did to me, girl. All I ever did was love and care for you. What did I get in return? You drove my husband to suicide. You tore my life apart. I couldn't even walk down the street.'

'It's always about you, isn't it, mother?'

'You always were a hateful child.'

Morven leaned closer, steel in her gaze. 'No child is hateful, mother. Just the same as no child is born troubled or born an old soul. That's all down to the parents and putting their kids into situations they aren't able to cope with. You did this to me. Everything I became. Everything I did. It was down to you and that rat bastard sperm donator.'

'You can't even own what you did, can you? After all this time you are still trying to blame us for what happened. Well, I've got news for you, Lucy. It wasn't me who held Chrissy Lang's head under the water until she stopped clawing at my arms, desperate to breathe. It wasn't Garry who dragged that nine-year-old boy into the water out there,' she threw a hand towards the window, reminding us just how close we were sitting to where it had happened, 'That was all you. It's about time you owned it.'

'Oh, believe me, I own it. I know exactly what I did. And I know *why* I did it.'

'Here come the lies.'

'You can cover your ears and make as much noise as you want, it won't change the truth. I did it because of him.'

Susan was having none of it. 'You can't help yourself, can you? You just open your mouth and more hateful crap spills out.' But she had my attention. Because I knew my wife. She was a lot of things, but she wasn't a liar. If anything, she was too honest; brutally so. If she said she did it because of her father, that's exactly why she did it.

A grim knot of fear twisted around my heart, dreading the next words out of her mouth.

'Why do you think I did it then? Why do you think I killed my best friend? Maybe she copied my homework? Or did she kiss the boy I loved?'

'I don't know why you do *anything*, Lucy. I never did. You're broken. You aren't right.' She tapped her temple, an old-fashioned mockery of mental illness, tap tap tap.

'I'll tell you if you really want to know. But you won't want to hear it. You never wanted to hear it before, and I tried to tell you. I know I did. I did it for you.'

That brought a bark of laughter from her mother.

'You never did anything in your life that wasn't for yourself, girl. Not once.'

'I did it for you,' she said again. 'And I did it for dad, because I loved him . . .'

Susan was shaking her head. She might as well have had her hands over her ears and been going *la la la* because she wasn't listening.

'I did it to shut her up . . . I begged her not to tell our teacher, to just stop talking. You have no idea . . . I cried for her. I offered her everything, everything I owned . . . she came to me the night before, in the dormitory . . .'

'And what could she ever say that deserved what you did to her, Lucy?'

Morven looked at her mother, no backing down now.

'She told me what he'd done to her.' There was a moment where those last few words just hung there, unanswered, a weight in the air. Then Morven delivered the hammer blows. 'That night Chrissy knelt down beside my bed and told me what my father had done to her. She described how he had *touched* her . . . she made me listen to all of it . . . even when I begged her to shut up . . . she didn't care that I called her a liar, that I promised to make everyone hate her . . .'

'You're lying.'

Morven shook her head, and I knew it wasn't anger now, or hatred, it was sadness she was sinking into, the memories taking her back there, to that place, that time, and the decision she'd made.

I shouldn't have been there for this. But I couldn't just lurk in the doorway like some emotional vampire, feeding off their pain, so I moved closer. I stood behind my wife. I put a hand on her shoulder, letting her know I was there, for all of it, no matter what. No words. Just that connection. The human touch.

She reached up and squeezed my fingers.

'I'm not lying. Chrissy knelt down beside my bed that night and asked me if he'd done it to me . . . I couldn't see her face because the lights were out, it was just her voice . . . her asking if he'd touched me like that, like he'd touched her . . .'

'Shut up.'

'That's what I said to her. Shut up. I didn't *want* to hear it . . . she made me sick . . . I *knew* she was lying . . . she *had* to be . . . she was talking about my daddy, the man who loved me more than anyone in the world . . . the man I ran to when I was frightened, who wrapped his arms around me and protected me and made me safe . . . She was scaring me then . . . because she wouldn't stop talking . . . and I couldn't stop her . . . lying there in the dark that night listening to her, I asked her why she hated me so much? Do you know what she told me? She told me she didn't hate me . . . she loved me . . . that was why she had to do it, tell people . . . to save me from him.'

'You hateful creature,' Susan Hall spat.

'You don't like the truth, do you mother? It's easier to just hate me. But that doesn't change the fact I did it to protect him. I knew that all she had to do was accuse him, it didn't matter if she was lying, it would still kill him . . . how would he be able to walk around the village? How would he be able to go to work? How would he be able to go to the pub when all of his friends *hated* him? Because they would have. That one word would have broken every relationship he had. I was old enough to be afraid *for* him, because I loved him.'

'You're lying. None of this happened. Not a word of it.'

'I'm not lying. I'm just not telling you want you want to hear.'

'You never said a word of this before.'

'Did you never ask yourself why he killed himself? He couldn't live with the guilt. He knew what I'd done for him. I *told* him. I told him what Chrissy was going to say about him. I told him why I had to shut her up. He never came back to see me after that. A few days later he was dead.'

'Every word out of your mouth is a lie. You should be the one who died, not him.'

'And that's the crux of it, isn't it, mother? That's why you hate me so much, because I'm the one who lived.'

'You horrible—' she was reaching around for a word, something truly vile to spit in her daughter's face, and struggling, a war going on inside her. Finally, two little words won out. '—little cunt,' Susan Hall shoved her chair back from the table so violently it skittered away across the stone floor, falling.

'You wanted the truth. There it is. Ugly as ever, but the truth.'

I thought Susan was going to launch herself at Morven. Her face twisted, anger blazing in her eyes, but she held back, somehow.

In that moment, the older woman looked down at the mobile phone she'd put on the table between them, and a cold smile stole over her hate-twisted features.

She didn't need to claw at her daughter's face when she could rip her heart out far more effectively.

All she had to do was answer when David Dodds called.

'What's the matter mother? You don't like the truth?'

FORTY

I don't know if the truth was worse than I'd built it up to be in my head, but it was certainly more tragic.

I knew I'd never ask any of the questions that would need to be asked to work out the ultimate truth of it, whether she was a young girl who'd killed her best friend because she was going to lie about her father, or because she was going to tell the truth about him. There was a third alternative there I didn't want to think about, too: whether she was another victim of Garry Galvin.

I didn't need to know that.

Either way, she was a victim of a terrible situation she should never have been in.

She should have been protected.

She was a child in all of this. Her mother should have protected her. Her father should have protected her. Her teachers. The whole fucking world. They should have protected her.

Instead, they failed her.

And in her child's mind, a mind of black and whites, of absolutes, the only answer she could come up with was silence. Because if Chrissy Lang couldn't say those things, then they hadn't happened. It really was as simple as that. And when she couldn't bribe her best friend into silence, or bully her into it, she'd felt like there was no other choice.

She wasn't some monster. She was a child.

I wondered if she'd confided all of this in Nora, and that was why the old woman felt so protective towards her? It would go a long way to explaining why she acted like a surrogate mother.

'It took me years to realise the worst part of all of this,' Morven said, unflinching in the face of her mother's anger. 'You knew, didn't you?'

'What are you talking about?'

'This was the man you loved. You can't tell me you didn't know what he was doing with his junior league football practices and his youth club stuff.'

'He was a good man,' Susan Hall said, like that simple denial was enough to disprove everything else.

'He was a predator, mother. And you knew it. You turned a blind eye because you didn't *want* to see what he was doing, but that doesn't mean he wasn't doing it.'

'I hate you.'

'I know you do. And I don't care. Do you know why I don't care? Because I sacrificed my childhood for him and for you and it was the worst mistake of my life. He didn't deserve my protection or yours. He was a monster right up until the end. That's why he took the coward's way out, mother, because he couldn't live with what he was. Not because of me. For a while I let myself think it was remorse, that he knew what he'd done and couldn't cope with the fact I'd sacrificed my life to protect him. But I don't think he had normal emotions like guilt. He wasn't wired that way. He had a sickness. He fought it. But it won.

'But none of that changes the truth. *You* should have been protecting me. You should have been looking out for Chrissy and Scott and all those other kids in the youth club.

'But you weren't. And that makes you as bad as him, because you enabled it. You might not have put your own hands on those kids, but he couldn't have done what he did without you. And that's the truth.'

The accusations hit home, sucker punch after sucker punch.

Susan Hall sagged under the continued onslaught, each accusation weakening her until she sank back against the kitchen sink, needing its support not to end up on the floor. 'Why are you saying these horrible things? Why are you lying about him? He never did anything to hurt you . . . he loved you.'

Morven didn't say anything for a second.

She stared her mother down, the table still between them.

Then a cruel smile began to spread across Morven's face; I only saw the corner of it, but that was enough. 'You really believe that makes a difference, don't you? Just because he didn't touch *me*, he gets a free pass? Other kids were fair game. You do know that's worse, right? That you are happy for their lives to be utterly fucked up, just so long as it doesn't impact yours. You were the Rose to his Fred West . . . you are complicit, mother. You had a hand in every single thing he did to those kids. And worse, because you knew what he was doing, you were fundamental in covering it up. You gave him *permission*.'

Before she could say anything else, the phone rang between them.

With each cycle of the ring signal Susan Hall seemed to gather strength and grow taller, as she pushed away from the kitchen sink. 'You will want to answer that. He wants to talk to you.'

Morven was shaking as she snatched the phone up, answering before it could ring through to voicemail. The anger shimmered through her one-word answer. 'What?'

Susan's smile wasn't just cruel, it was vindictive and so sickeningly sweet.

She'd known this was coming; known and was excited to see it play out in front of her. It was difficult to grasp the kind of deep-seated loathing that would make this moment enjoyable.

I couldn't hear what the man on the other end of the line was saying, but I didn't need to hear the actual words to understand what was happening. Morven's responses were enough. Her body language betrayed her immediately. She turned on her mother and rasped, 'Listen, you fucking little prick,' down the phone line. 'You lay a fucking *finger* on her and I'll rip your cock off and choke it down your throat.'

Susan actually laughed, like it was the funniest thing in the fucking world – a world that was falling away beneath my feet.

Morven was right, her mother was every bit as much a monster as her husband had been. But she was wrong, too, because this wasn't just about enabling someone who was broken, she was drawing pleasure from it. And that was so much more twisted than just letting something happen. I understood it all in that smile; the whole reason for the sit down had been about *seeing* this moment. She could have left the phone and walked back to the old Land Rover and driven off into the sunset. But she wanted to be here for this.

This had been festering in her for years.

She'd been locked away in her house with her shrine to Lucy and her dead man, nursing this black anger, dreaming of a moment where she could finally see her little girl brought down and made to hurt the way she'd been hurt.

And now it was here, she was relishing it.

I clenched my fist without thinking about it, and for the first time in my life imagined hitting a woman, hitting her so hard she buckled and fell, and hitting her again and again until I made myself sick. It was only Morven who dragged me out of that red rage haze, saying, 'No, listen to me, if you've hurt my girl, I will find you and I will kill you. Make no mistake. You might think you have the power here, but I've killed two people. I have no problem with making it three.' Her gaze went from her mother to the gun on the table. She didn't need to add: *Or four.*

'Where are you? I'll come to you. No . . . give me an address . . . Alone. Yes.'

'No,' I said, patching the instructions together in my head.

'You're not going to him,' I said, but she wasn't listening to me, only to the voice on the phone. Morven turned her back on me, putting her free hand over her other ear as if that could shut the rest of the world out.

She was making a deal to deliver herself to David Dodds and there was nothing I could do to stop her short of ripping the phone out of her hands – and if I did that, what happened to Poppy then?

FORTY-ONE

'Yes, alone. I don't need anyone else to do this, David. I never did. This is between you and me . . . The only thing I need is to know where I'm going . . . okay . . . fine . . . text me the address if that makes you feel like you're in control of this. Just know that you aren't . . . it's an illusion . . . I'm coming for you, David, and this isn't going to be some tearful reunion. I'm taking my girl back. You made a mistake taking her . . . now you are going to pay for that mistake.'

She wasn't angry. Every word was delivered with cold precision. In that moment I didn't recognise her; it was the mother-bear thing, protecting her cub, and it was terrifying. I absolutely believed she was going to kill him. But then, I'd known that from the moment she took the gun from under the pillow and showed it off like a prize.

I didn't doubt for a second that she was capable of it, either.

Morven crossed the stone floor, phone still pressed to her ear, still talking.

She turned to me and held out her hand.

I thought she was asking for the gun. She wasn't. She wanted the car keys. Of course she did. Without thinking, I took them from my pocket and tossed them to her.

Morven snatched them out of the air and was out of the room before I could react, still talking down the phone as she went to the car. Even then, I second guessed myself and lost a few precious seconds when I realised she'd left the gun on the table and tried to decide whether I should grab it and run after her, knowing that to do so would be akin to becoming the gun in her hand. But without me and that gun she was going after David Dodds with her bare hands – unless she intended to run him down with the Golf, which wasn't exactly likely.

My head was spinning.

It's hard to put into words. You want to believe you'll be calm in a raging storm, that you'll react rationally and won't monumentally fuck up, but when the panic of reality hits, you're flailing around looking for anything to cling onto while nothing makes sense.

All I knew was that I couldn't let her go alone, no matter what she promised him. Promises like that don't matter anyway. No one expects you to keep them. Dodds would know I had to come running. It was my little girl and my wife, two of the people I loved more than life itself. There was no way I could just sit on the sidelines and watch him destroy my family. No. Like fuck. He knew I was coming, even if I was trailing hours behind, even if I was walking into another trap, just like at his house, I was coming.

I couldn't bring myself to think about mum and what he must have done to her to get Poppy away from her. That way lay panic, irrational ghosts and a kind of existential fear that was utterly paralysing. Letting that into my mind would only serve to break me all the more completely.

No.

I had to trust that she was okay, or at least not dead in a ditch somewhere.

I had to focus on my family first, on Morven and Poppy, because I *knew* they needed me. Mum had Olivia Mendes and Nora and everyone else who was on the doorstep, too. My girls didn't.

The world reduced to me and a gun on the table.

I needed to get it and get out of there. I was faster than Morven, I could catch her up on the track around the paddock. In my head, we were driving out of here together to bring our daughter home.

I shoved my way past Susan and grabbed the pistol off the table.

It felt heavy in my hand. In that moment a wild thought stole in: how much does death weigh? Is it 21 grams like the soul is supposed to weigh? Is it the 10 grams of a bullet or the kilo of the unloaded gun? Is it the weight of the hand holding the gun or the fourteen stone of the man holding it? Or was it literally nothing, weightless and meaningless? Whatever the truth, metaphysical or moral, that gun felt like it weighed a lot more than a kilogram in my hand, as if it had taken on the weight of David Dodds's life as well as the weight of its own metal.

But I carried it out of that room.

Morven was already halfway down the path.

'He's going to kill her, you know that, don't you?' Susan Hall heckled. She stood in the doorway, blocking my way out of the house.

'What the fuck is wrong with you?'

'She deserves it,' Susan said, which was no kind of answer. 'She shouldn't just be able to start again playing happy families, not after what she did. She ruined my life . . .' and beneath that was her truth, in Susan Hall's mind the wrong person died . . . 'She should have killed herself, not her father.'

'If you don't get out of my way, you're going to join your precious fucking Garry,' I spat, waving the gun in her face.

She knew I was never going to use it.

And that knowledge was enough to keep her feet rooted firmly to the spot and make it impossible for me to get through.

'Move!'

She didn't, forcing me to shove her out of the way, but all that succeeded in doing was staggering her back a couple of steps and making her come back at me like an enraged bull, head down, ready to butt me in the chest. The old woman was ridiculously stubborn, but she wasn't an immovable object any more than I was an irresistible force. Finally, hitting her harder than I'd have ever wanted to, I bundled past her and made it out of the house – only for her to reach out a hand as she hit the ground, and pull me down with her.

I went down hard, my hands out to break my fall.

The gun went spinning out of my grasp and ended up in the dirt ten metres from where I'd fallen.

Susan tried to beat me to it, but I scrambled faster than her, snatching it up and rolling onto my back, gun levelled at her face as she loomed over me. 'Don't make me pull the fucking trigger,' I rasped, struggling to stand, and knowing all the while I was losing precious seconds as Morven ran towards the car.

'Please,' she said then, throwing me. 'Put me out of my misery.'

And the pain I saw in her eyes would have been heart-breaking if it wasn't for the fact that it was there because she wanted my wife and daughter dead.

I used my left hand to support myself as I stood, not taking my eyes off her for a second.

'You're a weak man. I don't know what my daughter ever saw in you. She's so much more of a man than you are. Look at you . . . you're pathetic.'

I didn't bother answering her. I knew what she was doing. She was trying to goad me into biting, because it would slow me down. The satisfaction of some brutal comeback would be short-lived in the wake of the Golf's exhaust fumes if I was too slow getting back to the car.

So, gritting my teeth, I ran, head down, arms and legs pumping furiously, leaving her to yell at my back.

The wind was up, churning now. It whipped at my body, bullying me back even as I lengthened my stride, eating the dirt path around the paddock's perimeter. The sky was bruise purple.

Two hundred metres, and I was breathing hard, my lungs burning brutally inside my chest as the adrenalin shot boosted my strength.

252

Spots of light sunburst across my eyes. I dug deep, somehow finding an extra kick to carry me around the corner of the paddock and out onto the short dirt stretch between it and the carpark.

I couldn't see Morven.

A split second later, the sound of the car door slamming was like a gunshot to my heart.

It felt as though I was running through treacle. My muscles knotted, each new step seemingly taking forever. My head rolled on my neck. I was screaming at her, but I have no idea what words were coming out of my mouth, or if it was just some wild incoherent noise – some primal scream.

The gap was nothing. Twenty metres. Ten.

The rough gravel shifted under my feet, betraying me.

My ankle rolled, but I wasn't going down, not with the car door so close.

Five.

I reached out.

Grasping.

The engine roared to life as I reached the passenger door and grabbed for the handle, my free hand slapping against the side of the car as Morven threw it into reverse.

I wasn't letting go.

But it wouldn't open.

And half a step later, it was wrenched out of my hand no matter how desperately I tried to cling onto it. Because of the angle, I couldn't see Morven's face in that moment, but I wasn't letting her go. I ran faster than I had ever run in my life, chasing the car. There was no way I could catch it. By the time I reached the visitor experience, she was already disappearing around the corner, leaving me with my hands on my knees, gasping for breath.

And still part of me was determined to carry on chasing her up the winding hill back up into Talgarth and wherever he was leading her beyond that.

But it was pointless. She could be twenty miles away before I even made it to the outskirts of town.

And that left me with the reality that I was cut off from everyone I needed to be connected with. My phone was on the passenger seat. I couldn't call anyone. Not mum, not Olivia, or Nora or anyone else who needed to know what was happening. All of my mistakes came home to roost at once. Every error of judgment hit me in the moment that I turned around trying to think of where to go next and left me reeling. For a minute, I didn't go anywhere. Then I started walking back towards the herder's cottage, trying to think if I'd seen a phone in there.

Susan Hall stood in the doorway, leering at me as I approached.

'She ditched you? That's got to hurt.'

'Get out of my way.'

'What? Or you'll hit me again? You're a big man.'

'I'm not in the mood for this. My daughter's out there.'

'So is mine.'

'Oh, you lost the right to think about Morven that way a long time ago,' I said.

'Doesn't change biology.'

'It's fucking convenient though, when you're looking for sympathy,' I spat, and pushed my way into the house. I hadn't seen a phone in the kitchen, and there wasn't one in the hall, so I went through to the parlour, where an old cathode ray television set stared blankly, the largest piece of furniture in the room.

There was a yellow rotary dial phone on the windowsill.

I hadn't seen a phone like that in twenty years.

Lifting the handset from the cradle, I heard the dial tone.

The problem was that reliance on contacts and mobile phones meant I didn't remember any actual numbers. I couldn't dial with the gun in my hand, so I put it on the windowsill beside the phone. I was halfway through dialling 999 when I remembered Olivia had given me a card that I'd stuffed into my wallet the first time we'd met. I dialled her mobile. She picked up on the first ring.

'Who is this?'

'Alex Kerr.'

'Alex? Where the *fuck* are you?'

I ignored her question. 'Is my mum okay?'

There was a beat.

'She's okay. I've been trying to reach you all day if you'd just answer your bloody phone, Alex.'

'She's okay?'

'She's getting checked out, but yeah, she's okay, bruised. She's a lioness, that mum of yours. She gave as good as she got, but she couldn't stop him, Alex. Dodds has got Poppy.'

'I know.'

'Where are you?'

'Wales. Morven's gone to meet Dodds. To get Poppy back. I'm drowning, Olivia. I don't know what to do. I can't think.'

Another beat, then she fell into the familiar role of Family Liaison Officer, voice calm. 'Focus on my voice. That's all that matters right now. Just you and me. You said she's gone to meet him? Where? Do you know?'

'No.' But then it hit me. I didn't need to know. Not when my phone was on the seat beside her and we had the fake AirTag on the wheel arch. 'There's the AirTag,' I blurted, mind racing. 'You can track that, can't you? Ping the signal towers or whatever it is you do? It'll take you right to her . . .'

'We can. Where are you?'

'Wales,' I said, which was met by silence. 'I know. I know I'd promised not to do anything stupid . . . to talk to you . . . but—'

'But you did it anyway.'

'That message in the bathroom mirror, it wasn't for Morven, it was for me . . . Where do you go when you have nowhere left to run?'

'Back to the beginning,' she said, following my logic.

'It made sense she'd come back here, to the lake . . . it was the beginning of everything. The lake where she drowned those two kids. That's where she's been hiding. In a herder's cottage here.'

'That's where you're calling me from?'

I nodded. 'Yeah. Her mother's here. She's been helping Dodds. He's got Poppy and he's using her as bait to lure Morven into whatever trap he's laid. It's all such a mess . . . you need to get here. I don't care how. You just need to get here . . . Fast.'

'People are already moving,' she promised me.

'He's going to kill her,' Susan Hall whispered, right up close behind me. It was like she reached down through my skin and tried to rip my bones out with those five little words. I knew her taunt had carried down the phone line when Olivia Mendes said, 'Not if I can help it. We're going to find her, Alex. I promise you that. We're going to find her.'

'You're not,' Susan told her, though how she'd been able to hear her, I have no idea. What she said next changed everything. 'But I know where he's taking her.'

FORTY-TWO

'Where?'

'That's not how it works, Alex. I'm not just going to tell you. Besides, it would be meaningless to you. Just some strange sounding name with too many syllables.'

'Tell me where he's taking her.'

'No.'

The phone hung on the wire, the earpiece on the carpet where I'd dropped it. Olivia's tiny voice came out of it in a static crackle, demanding to know what was going on. I ignored her. Susan Hall had my full attention.

'If you don't tell me, God help me, I'll do something you won't live to regret,' I said, spiralling. The gun was far too convenient for my temper. It was just there, beside the phone.

'And then you'll never see her again. Kill me, I don't care. I've been dead for twenty years. You'd be doing me a favour.'

'Where is she going?'

'I'll show you.' She reached into her pocket for the Land Rover's keys and dangled them in front of my face like a promise. I bit. I snatched them out of her hand.

'I'm driving.' I gestured towards the door with the barrel of the gun. 'Come on.'

I left Olivia hanging on the telephone.

I didn't bother closing the cottage door behind me. Susan didn't share my urgency as she waddled her way back towards the Land Rover as though we had all the time in the world. The more

I tried to hurry her, the more her gait seemed to roll and the slower she actually covered the ground. Frustrated, I stalked along beside her, trying, uselessly, to get the old woman to share our destination.

All I could think was that Morven was slipping further and further away from me. She'd been so close. *We'd* been so close. And now I felt more separated than ever.

A good fifteen minutes had passed before I was struggling to get the Land Rover started, much to my passenger's amusement. In the end she had to show me the trick to it, and we were moving, with Susan Hall telling me, 'Left, follow the road around,' which I did, trying to look everywhere at once as though I might catch a glimpse of the Golf despite the fact that in fifteen minutes Morven could easily be as many miles away.

We passed the visitor centre and Susan directed me back towards the town centre.

'He better not have hurt my mother.'

'David? I'm sure he was perfectly gentle when he attacked her. You Londoners, happy in your middle class bubble of safe streets, letting an old woman look after your daughter . . . just asking for trouble. Of course, he would have hurt her a damned sight less if she'd just given up the girl. But no, she had to fight.'

My head was spinning.

'I'm going to kill him.'

'I doubt it, dear, but it's good to have ambitions in this life.'

'Why is he doing this? You know him . . . why is he going after my family?'

'Because it's personal. Imagine being nine years old and seeing two of your friends drowned. That kind of thing changes you. Whatever life had in store for you, it's gone, forever. You're a different person. You're this new thing, a product of tragedy. Instead of your childhood being the happiest days of your life, it's this fresh hell where someone you chased around the schoolyard playing kiss chase drowns your friends.'

I couldn't imagine the impact of something like that on a group of kids. When I was thirteen the big brother of one of the kids in our parallel class, Jon, had been killed rollerblading along the side of the bypass during the summer holidays. He'd been hit by a lorry and thrown a hundred yards down the road, dead on impact. Thinking about it, I only said two words to him that first day back, *I'm sorry*, because it hadn't happened to me, and it wasn't in my world.

But put like that, playing stupid games like kiss chase with a murderer . . . that would fuck you up immeasurably, wouldn't it?

'We were all close back then. It was a small village. I had grown up with David's mum and dad. His mum was my best friend when we were Lucy's age. Inseparable. The three musketeers. Me, Garry and her. We were David's godparents. They were Lucy's.'

I didn't ask any questions. She'd talk if she wanted to talk. Nature abhorring that vacuum. It didn't take long before Susan offered, "There's been so much tragedy in his life. This, then his dad Marvin died in a car crash . . . so it was just him and his mum. It's hard to imagine how he coped with it.'

I resisted the temptation to say he obviously didn't.

'And when Julie, his mum, died of breast cancer, well, he had no one, so I took him in.'

And suddenly it all made sense.

'You infected him with your poison,' I said. It wasn't a question.

He'd replaced the 'dead' Lucy in her life, but he'd never quite been her, missing that flesh and blood link, and never quite been Garry either, the boy too young to replace the man. But there was something sick about the dynamic, the older woman making the orphan her life and forging him in the crucible of her bitterness.

He hadn't stood a chance of a normal life.

But then of course he wouldn't have been too young to replace her dead man, not for ever. I didn't want to think about what else might have happened to David Dodds, the grooming, the eventual shift in affection, but it was there, in an undercurrent to everything she said. Of course it was. And it was beyond sickening. Morven had killed Chrissy and Scott Lang because they were going to talk about the abuses of her father, and everything Morven had said back there, those accusations, what they meant about her mother and father . . . they were different aspects of the same sick beast. Susan Hall was absolutely complicit in the crimes of her man. The Rosemary to his Fred, just like Morven had said.

Once he was under her roof David Dodds hadn't stood a chance.

He was just another victim in all of this, even if I wanted to paint him as the monster.

'Poor bastard,' I said, staring at the road.

I couldn't help but think how lucky Morven was to have escaped that life, and understood why she'd never looked to re-establish contact with her mother.

Sometimes dead was better.

And Lucy was dead. I understood that now, finally. Truly. It's hard to explain the disconnect between a new identity and a dead past, but suddenly it just clicked into place in my mind, and I got it. Not just the how, either, but the why, too. Just why it was so important Lucy Galvin was dead.

'Left up ahead,' Susan said. I followed the directions without thinking. She seemed to be leading me into the heart of the mountains. The world outside the car was full of sharp cliffs and deep clefts where rivers cut through valleys and roads followed.

I tried again, 'Where's he taking her?'

But all I got was a 'You'll see, soon enough,' in return and a 'Right, here,' that came so late I almost missed the turning.

Over the next hour she led me a merry dance through the Welsh countryside, seemingly choosing turnings at random, and I swear at least three times we drove down the same stretch of road.

The problem was that everything began to look the same. The night sky overhead shifted from brooding to thunderous.

And then the first few fat drops of rain fell, splattering on the windscreen, one, two, three, like bullets from the sky.

Inside a minute it was impossible to see through the deluge. The windscreen wipers couldn't sluice the water away fast enough, and more kept coming down. It was damned near biblical in nature. The noise inside the Land Rover's cab was deafening, the rain drumming on the steel roof adding to the timpani playing on the windscreen.

A cattle grid thrummed under the wheels, sending shivers up through the steering column.

I had no choice but to slow down.

It was as though early summer had become late winter in a single stretch of country road.

'There's a turn coming up, you'll see the gate posts. You'll need to get out to open the gate,' she said.

I couldn't tell if she was taking the piss; she was enjoying the moment, though, that much was painfully obvious.

Off to the right I saw a ditch rapidly filling with run-off water, and, as she'd promised, a five-bar gate that was chained to the concrete post. I couldn't see much beyond that, with the narrow track giving no indication where this road might be going – other than nowhere.

I left the engine running as I clambered out.

Head down, one hand up over my head uselessly, I ran the ten steps to the gate and fumbled with the chain, struggling to get it unhooked with one hand and cling on to the gun with the other, before I eventually managed to haul the gate open. The bottom bar dragged across the ground. There were already a dozen little lakes forming in the potholes ahead of me.

The rain stung my eyes.

By the time I was back inside the Land Rover I was soaked

to the skin. I slammed the door, put the gun on the dashboard and drove forward with a lurch as the front right wheel dipped into a pothole the size of my head. We jounced and juddered down the country lane. I had no idea where we were going. I was sure Susan was leading me round in circles with no intention of actually taking me to where Dodds was waiting for my wife.

The rubber of the wiper dragged across the glass.

'Where the hell are you taking me?'

'Where you wanted to go. You wanted to see Lucy. This is where she is.'

'We're in the middle of fucking nowhere!'

'Not true. We're exactly where we need to be. Patience. You can kill the engine; we're not going anywhere.'

I looked at her like she was insane. Outside, there was only rain. The landscape had ceased to exist.

I heard the scrape of low-hanging branches across the top of the Land Rover's roof.

Another deep pothole had us lurch forward in our seats.

The engine whined.

The hole was deeper than we were easily climbing out of, even with the four-wheel drive. There was nothing for the tyres to bite onto but water and slick mud.

'We can walk from here,' Susan assured me, even as I revved the engine again, trying to will the damned thing out of the pothole.

I killed the engine, leaving us unbalanced.

She got out of the car, into the rain.

I grabbed the gun off the dashboard and did the same.

The rain had taken on a kind of elemental fury I wasn't used to seeing back in the city; maybe it was down to the wilderness of the location here, and how we were so utterly exposed to it. It lashed in from all sides, the wind cutting through it so it fell in razorblade tears that sliced into every inch of our skin. Steam rose from the bonnet of the Land Rover where the rain evaporated on contact with the hot metal.

I couldn't hear the ground crunch beneath our feet.

There was only the sound of the rain.

I turned my face to the fury of the storm and walked, following Susan, into it.

Huge trees bent against the elements. The rain lashed at trunk and branch. All along the fields more hedgerows made a patchwork out of the farmer's fields, their lines running perpendicular to our path. And in the distance, through the downpour, I saw the lake.

We walked down the slope, slipping and sliding on the muddy path.

I gave up trying to brush the rain out of my face. It was pointless trying to keep my hair from my eyes. It didn't matter how many times I ran my fingers through it, brushing it back, the rain kept spilling it forward, plastering it flat against my forehead.

The rain squirmed down the gap between my neck and my collar.

It turned my clothes into a semi-transparent second skin.

But none of that mattered. I walked down towards the water's edge, a single purpose burning bright enough in my mind to turn the rainwater to steam on my skin. Morven needed me. Poppy was out here somewhere – with him.

David Dodds.

I shouted, but the wind stole away my words.

I couldn't see them, or any other cars, which made me think Susan had been playing me to give Dodds whatever time he needed to make sure Morven wasn't walking away from his trap – whatever that trap entailed.

We were no more than a minute's walk down the banks to the lake itself. I had given up trying to think how the next few minutes were going to play out. To be honest, somewhere back there within the endless twists and turns and doubling back on ourselves so we weren't getting anywhere fast, I'd given up on seeing Morven again – or at least reconciled myself to the idea that I wasn't going to be her white knight, and in no small part that was because she didn't want me to be. That was tough to accept, but it wasn't like I had a whole lot of choice in the matter.

I was clinging to the slim hope that Olivia had got access to the AirTag's data and was able to ping it off the cellular towers or whatever it was they did to track the built-in locator, and was able to isolate her location quickly enough to get to Morven before she sprung Dodds's trap.

But even then, they had to get from London to Wales.

It all took time.

This, here, was about me making sure her mother couldn't be part of whatever it was that he had in mind.

Even so, out here, now, in the heart of the storm, it didn't feel *enough*.

I felt the weight of the gun in my hand, all of my grand ideas about putting a bullet between David Dodds's eyes washed away in the flood. I wasn't a killer. I wasn't much more than a frightened man. I might as well have hurled the piece into the lake.

I made my way down to the water's edge, wrestling with Morven's confession. It was difficult to imagine how she could have kept all that locked up within herself all these years we'd been together, all of those eye-to-eye moments and midnight promises where we'd sworn to love forever and never leave each other, all of those intimacies where we'd been so vulnerable with each other, and somehow, she'd held this entire hell of another life back, compartmentalising life before and life after and keeping me out of it. I knew that she'd done it for my own good, and not just because she didn't want it to change how I looked at her, or how I loved her. It genuinely was as though she'd been born again when she cast off Lucy and became Morven, and it didn't matter why she'd done that, only that she had.

Even so, strangely, it made me feel better to know she wasn't a monster – to hear it from her own mouth, even though I'd known it in my heart, hearing that she had been a kid unable to see another way out, trying to protect her parents who were the real monsters here. It just reminded me of the remarkable woman she'd grown up to be.

The rain washed away my tears as I reached the water.

There were lights on the other shore.

No, not on the shore, spearing down onto the shore.

I tried to peer up at the sky, looking for their source, but the rain blinded me.

I heard the *dub-dub-dub* of rotor blades though, and realised there was a helicopter up there, battling the worst of the elements as they tried to find Morven with their searchlight.

There were sirens, too, but every time I thought I heard them they were snatched away by the wind.

Olivia was good to her word.

They were here.

Morven had a chance.

Susan Hall came up to stand beside me, a hand shielding her eyes as she tried to see what was happening on the other shore.

The light shone down. In it, I saw the unmistakable conical roof of the crannog and realised what I'd already suspected – we'd driven round in circles for a couple of hours before Susan had steered me back towards Llangorse Lake, but on the far shore, away from the jetty, the rowboats and everything else, giving Dodds time to arrive and keeping us apart at the same time.

I still couldn't see her, but I was in no doubt she was out there somewhere, Dodds with her, and Poppy.

And Susan Hall knew full well how helpless I had to be feeling, because it was how she'd felt from the moment her daughter had drowned two kids a few hundred yards away from where we stood.

There was a symmetry to it.

I knew with sick certainty what Dodds intended to do. He was going to drown our daughter and make Morven watch, the circle of death complete.

The searchlight roved across the other bank, lurching violently through the sky. The rain looked like scars in the light.

I stood rooted to the spot, watching the sky helplessly as the light scoured every nook and cranny of the landscape until it found her.

She stood on the jetty.

I couldn't see him at first. But then the angle of the searchlight shifted, and I caught sight of the dark shadow of a rowboat bobbing in the churning waters, anchored up on the crannog itself. There was no telling how long he'd been there, but the defensive nature of the location made sense; she couldn't just rush him with a span of thirty or forty foot of water between them. I couldn't see him from where I was, but I was in no doubt that he was there, hidden within the trees, watching her.

The beam of light speared down, roving across the surface of the lake and along the wooden jetty, before it picked him out.

He appeared deformed over the distance because of Poppy, who he held in front of himself like a shield, one arm wrapped around her neck. I couldn't tell, but I imagined she was fighting him, putting up a struggle that meant he needed to use all of his strength to hold her. But how could a kid, even a scrappy one like Poppy, put up any sort of real resistance against a grown man? Not strength pitted against strength. Not a prayer.

I couldn't see clearly, because of the distance and the rain, but for a moment I believed Susan when she said, 'He's got a knife to her throat, that bitch of a daughter of mine makes the wrong move, he cuts it and it's all over for your girl.'

'Why are you doing this?'

'You know why, but more importantly, *she* knows why.'

'You heard her . . . she was trying to protect you . . . protect him.'

'And she's a dirty stinking liar. She hated him. She always did.'

I heard it in her then, the pain of a lost future. In so many ways that sting had to be worse than the loss of what you'd had, because you'd had it. This was the loss of something that never existed. It was her happily ever after. I understood it. No more than six hundred metres away, across the lake, mine was in jeopardy.

Susan Hall had my hand. She wasn't holding it in any sort of affectionate way. She was holding me back, as though she expected me to plunge into the lake and wade across to the other side.

The constant chop of the helicopter's blades was damned near deafening, despite the distance.

I saw another dozen headlights streaming down the hillside towards the lake.

Everything seemed to be so far away from where it needed to be, right there on that crannog with Poppy.

Morven was thinking the same thing, because she had started walking towards one of the rowing boats moored alongside the jetty.

'I don't get it . . .' I shook my head, not realising I was talking aloud as the first part of the thought found my lips. 'How does he think he can get away from here?' There was one road. There was a helicopter in the sky. I could hear the sirens of more cops coming. 'He's trapped.'

Beside me, Susan laughed, and it was the bitterest sound of the night.

'You're assuming he *wants* to get away from here. You know what they say about assumptions making an ass out of you. Dear sweet David has no intention of walking away from here. This is his sacrifice to me. His offering in return for the years of love I gave him. He knows what's waiting for him now. You don't gut a pig and get to live happily ever after, Alex. You know that. Not in the real world. No, this, all of it, this is for *me*. He's making sure I get the one thing I've truly wanted ever since they told me my Lucy was dead, my happy ending. He's giving me a grave to visit. Not that I intend to grieve for that murderous little bitch.'

'You can't think you're going to walk away from this? This is on you. You're not walking away from this.'

'I've made my peace with that, too. All that matters is that she doesn't.'

FORTY-THREE

I reacted without thinking. One foot forward, then another, and in a couple of seconds the water was up around my knees.

My girls were on the other side of the water.

I had to get to them.

I wrenched my hand free of Susan's grasp as she tried to hold me back, and even then I stumbled, the soft mud under my feet giving way as I twisted my body. I hit my knees hard as I went down, the jagged edge of some submerged boulder cutting into my shin through the thick denim of my jeans. I couldn't see the blood in the water as I stood, it was too dark around me. The storm had effectively made it into a black midnight.

The rain pelted down, transforming the water's surface into the skin of a drum.

I waded out into the water, Susan Hall yelling at my back.

This was her moment.

She was yelling so much shit at me, about Morven, about her precious David and Garry, about justice and right and retribution and pissing on graves.

It didn't matter.

I was done listening to her.

I stared out across the water, trying to see through the rain, but it was difficult.

A low-lying mist clung to the water, giving the whole place an ethereal quality.

Under normal conditions I figured I could swim the six

hundred metres to the crannog in five or six minutes. But these were hardly normal conditions, with the elements raging and fear coursing through my veins. So much could happen in those extra sixty seconds I could only pray that it was closer to the five, but even as I waded deeper into the lake, I started to panic that it could be closer to seven or even eight, fighting the wind and the rain.

I waded in, not even thinking about the gun in my hand. I could hardly swim clutching it, but I wasn't about to leave it behind. I pushed it into the waistband of my jeans.

Two more steps, deeper into the lake, until the water was up around my waist. The cold swallowed me as I threw myself forward, launching into the first strokes, my hands cutting through the water as I kicked off, powering towards the crannog in the distance.

I'm an okay swimmer. Duke of Edinburgh Awards, all that stuff as a kid who went to a posh school. Morven used to take the piss out of my survival skills when we went for walks with Poppy through Epping Forest or some other inner-city wilderness. Right now, I was glad for every hour of it. Even so, it didn't take long before each new stroke burned the muscles of my shoulders, and I wasn't even a hundred metres out. It felt like I was clawing at the water, trying to haul myself forward as the weight of my clothes dragged me down.

I'd forgotten what it was like trying to swim in anything but trunks. It had been about thirty-five years since I'd tried. I hadn't factored in the sheer weight the soaked denim and heavy cotton added to my body, and its determination to drag me down slowly but surely.

Suddenly six hundred metres felt like a marathon.

I swallowed water with every other turn of the head, spitting out the thick algae that coated the surface.

The rain hammered at me, kicking up water in my eyes as I forced myself to swim.

My heart hammered, my head swam, and I felt like I was going to be violently sick, but I couldn't stop. Not for anything. I tried not to think about what I couldn't see – what I knew was happening across the lake, and worse, what I *imagined* was happening there. Even so, every time I turned my head to one side, swallowing down a gasp of air, I heard the chop of the rotors holding their position in the sky and knew that I had absolutely no control over the next few minutes of my life. The only thing I could allow myself to think was: *swim*. That was it, the be all and end all of my existence.

Once, as my body salmoned through the icy water, the searchlight blinded me – meaning for whatever reason the pilot was searching the water for something.

My blood ran cold, ice in my veins.

I arched my back, half-rising out of the water just long enough to see that Morven was no longer on the jetty.

I fucking *hate* water.

I'll hate it for the rest of my life.

The jetty was still so far away, and it felt like I'd been swimming for an hour.

I splashed down hard, swallowing a huge lungful of air to give my body as much natural buoyancy as I could as I struggled to counter the weight of my clothes trying to pull me under.

And with every stroke I could feel my strength draining, but I was damned if I was going to give in to exhaustion.

One stroke at a time. That was the only way to think of it. Not three hundred metres or four hundred. One stroke at a time. I could do that. One. And the next. And the next.

But I couldn't.

With my arms blazing and my lungs burning right along with them, I had no choice but to tread water for thirty seconds to catch my breath before I pushed on again. I used the brief respite to try and see them, I scanned the crannog for any sign of David Dodds, Poppy or Morven.

The searchlight roved across the landscape, picking out a small boat bobbing in the surf. It was empty. I twisted, trying to see beyond the boat to the island where I'd seen Dodds a few minutes ago, but it was impossible to see anything through the tears and rain.

I wanted to scream.

Instead, I swam towards the light.

FORTY-FOUR

Morven faced him.

There was no more than ten feet between them. He was in the water, still clutching Poppy to his chest. The water was up around her chest.

I couldn't see any of their faces properly.

I was too far away to do anything, even with the gun. Christ, I was more likely to hit the conical roof of the crannog or the bloody helicopter than I was to put a bullet in David Dodds if I pulled the trigger.

The water was thick with reeds that were impossible to swim through.

They were still maybe two hundred metres away when he plunged Poppy under the water.

Morven's screams ripped through the rain, meeting mine halfway.

She started to wade through the water, frantic.

I hurled myself forwards, tearing at the lake in my desperation to get to the other side.

And then she was on him, clawing at his face, and he was struggling to fight her off.

I felt something brush up against my skin, and as I saw the slick fur panicked, lashing out frantically.

I reeled and the vole went splashing.

Breathing hard, I plunged on, fighting through the tall marsh reeds towards the boat as Morven and Dodds fought wildly. All around me I heard screams and yells that seemed to be coming from all sides at once, and yet were weirdly muffled by the rain, so that they lost much of their energy and urgency. Everything had this weird, dislocated quality to it, like I was hearing it through a filter of wet wool jammed into my ears.

I couldn't focus on the fight in front of me.

Morven's head went down, under the water, with Dodds looking like a wild man, huge arcs of water like rainbows in the searchlights as he pushed her down and she slapped up at his face, then broke the surface gasping for air and tossed her head back.

Poppy surfaced half a dozen stokes away from where her mother fought for her life. She slapped at the black water, kicking up huge surges and splashes as the breath stuck in her throat for one seemingly endless second before she gave voice to a scream. It was as though she'd been choking on the air and panic had finally punched that knot from her throat and she found her voice.

Torches roved along the jetty.

More voices. Frantic cries. Shouts. Orders being barked. None of it made any sense to me.

I had to get to them.

The fronds lashed at my face as I struggled to get my feet under me, but even though I was well beyond the middle, the bottom was still tantalisingly out of reach as my legs kicked out, scrabbling for purchase. More and more of the heavy reeds slapped at my face as I tried to swim into the shore.

When I came up for air again, so much closer – but still too far away to do anything – I saw Poppy hurl herself at David Dodds's back, trying to claw his eyes out with her tiny fingers.

'Pops! No!' The two words barely registered as a ripple of noise and my heaving chest snatched away their strength.

Dodds wasn't giving up. Muscles corded along his arms as he gripped Morven's hair and forced her head under again.

Her hands slapped at the water, but each slap was weakening

and there was nothing I could do about it.

Not with Poppy on his back.

I needed her to get off.

I felt the ground under my feet. Barely.

I reached back for the gun in the waistband of my jeans, no idea if it would fire after the soaking it had had, even if I could pull the trigger and become a killer.

Morven's entire body shuddered.

Poppy hooked her fingers deep into David Dodds's eyes.

Dodds threw his head back and screamed out his pain.

But he didn't relinquish his murderous grip on Morven.

Another sudden surge of slaps churned up more frantic splashes around her, and then in the next moment the water was eerily calm.

'Get off him, Pops!' I howled, the gun in my hand aiming at his head.

I don't know how far away I was.

I've never shot a gun in my life.

Poppy clung onto his back; her arms wrapped around his head as he thrashed about in the shallow water. The boat drifted towards them. The searchlight finally found them, lighting the water around them like a super trouper.

'Get off him!'

Dodds lashed his head back and forth, trying to break her grip, and somehow got one of her hands in his mouth and bit down with such force I could have sworn I heard the bones snap.

Her screams were harrowing.

Behind her, I saw cops running along the jetty. I recognised Olivia, and the guy from the Protected Person's Unit who had turned up at my door. His name was gone. I don't know how they got here so quickly. Maybe they'd been in the helicopter. It didn't matter. Nothing mattered apart from that bastard Dodds and my girl on his back.

I heard voices screaming my name.

Dodds beat at her with the full force of his fists, fighting back.

I couldn't take my eyes from the horror of watching a full-grown man trying to beat the shit out of my daughter with her mother floating face down in the water a few feet away, and drifting. It was everything I'd ever feared, worst nightmare stuff, brought to life.

And then she fell.

'Poppy!'

My voice was nothing. Less than nothing. It broke before it managed that second syllable. And then there was only the sound of the rain.

And the gunshot.

FORTY-FIVE

I missed.

I have no idea where the bullet went. The recoil, without solid footing to brace against it, had the barrel whip upwards and sent the shot high and wide.

The others were throwing themselves into the water, trying to get to the crannog and David Dodds.

I didn't give them a second's thought. I pulled the trigger again, trying to visualise his head exploding in a bloody red rose, the flower blossoming in the middle of his forehead, but there was no gunshot, no recoil, nothing. The hammer fell on the head of the bullet and there was no detonation. I pulled the trigger again and again, harder and harder each time, and then I was shaking it and starting at it like the traitorous bastard was deliberately fucking with me. But it wouldn't fire again. For whatever reason the mechanism was jammed, and I'd wasted that one good shot.

I threw the gun away and plunged towards Dodds, ready to choke the life out of the bastard. I wanted him dead. God help me, in that moment, I wanted him dead, and I didn't need a gun to make that happen.

I splashed forward. I only had eyes for David Dodds. The reeds parted for me now that I had solid ground under my feet. I plunged on, my clothes weighing heavy on me. The rain ran down my face. There were no tears. Not yet. They would come. For now, the rain was the only way I showed my grief.

Every new step was a wide twisting lurch, my shoulders

dipping and rolling. My fists were clenched so tightly every muscle along the lengths of my forearms and biceps quivered, thrilling to the promise of violence.

I heard them shouting my name.

I didn't care.

I wasn't stopping.

Not now that he was within reach.

Dodds was on his knees in the water when I reached him. He looked up at me, a weird symmetry going on to the last time we'd laid eyes on each other through the window of his white panel van, only this time it was him looking up at me and me with all of the power to walk away.

'Alex! Stop! Don't! Alex!'

I had him. I grabbed Dodds by the throat and hauled him up, only to hit him so hard I thought I'd broken my fist.

Dodds went spinning and flailing, hitting the water hard, both hands out as though he thought he could somehow brace his fall. White spumes of froth capped with more of that weird algae splashed up around him as he went under.

I stood over him, waiting for him to try and come up again, damned sure he wasn't going to draw in another breath of air.

His hair breached the surface.

I was on his back, forcing it down.

My grip was iron.

I felt hands on me, trying to stop me, but nothing was breaking my vicelike hold.

I was going to kill him.

I put all my weight onto my arms, driving Dodd's head back under the water as he clawed at the surface trying to fight me.

And it wasn't enough for me.

I didn't just want him to drown. I wanted him to die a thousand different deaths, and that was only one of them. I reached around with my right arm, getting him in a chokehold. Dodds couldn't get any sort of purchase to fight back. The muddy ground slid out beneath his wildly kicking feet. The water took him.

I kept him under.

But the hands on my back wouldn't be refused. There was so much shouting. So much splashing and flailing at the water as they dragged me off of him, leaving me kicking uselessly at the water as two uniformed officers helped David Dodds out of the lake while others held me back.

'He's not worth throwing your life away over.' That last voice cut through the haze in my mind. Nora. Of everyone here, surely she had to know what I was suffering. She'd been Morven's surrogate mother in her new life, closer than blood. She was in the water, wading out towards where Morven lay face down, unmoving.

I saw Poppy looking at me.

And it hit me then, the reality of it all.

I looked from her to the shape of Morven floating face down in the water, back to Poppy, and knew where I needed to be. I couldn't help my wife. I couldn't fail Poppy. The moment really was as binary as that, coming down to the living and the dead.

I crawled through the water to my little girl and held her so tightly I thought I'd never be able to let go again.

I cradled her face into my chest, trying to take it all away, so she didn't have to see any of it, not David Dodds, not the madman I'd become, rising up out of the lake, soaked and covered in that weird algae, but most importantly, not her mother.

I felt her body shuddering against me and that just made me cling on tighter.

We weren't alone in the lake now. There were a dozen officers trying to get Morven out of the water, manhandling her onto the shore as they desperately tried to get the water out of her lungs and life back into them.

I clung onto Poppy as the searchlight left us to focus on Morven and the efforts to bring her back.

I couldn't watch and I couldn't turn away.

The little slope of beach was frenetic with activity. They'd turned her on her side. I could see the brackish water dribbling out of her mouth, but she wasn't taking that deep breath and suddenly coughing up half of the lake water.

'She's still out there,' I said, meaning Susan, on the other side of the lake. But what they heard was me pleading to keep trying to bring Morven back. Two figures huddled over her, one doing chest compressions, the other breathing into her mouth in a regular rhythm.

I just stood there, waist deep in the water.

I couldn't move and I wouldn't let anyone move me, even as they tried to bring me back in to the shore. As long as I didn't move nothing around me was real and I could make all sorts of deals with the universe.

Nora splashed up to my side and put her arms around my shoulders. 'Come on, Alex. Come with me.'

'She's still out there,' I said again, willing her to get it, so I didn't have to explain beyond a name. 'Susan.'

'Where is she?'

'On the other side of the lake, there's a farm track. She's parked in a field.'

Nora shouted orders back to the jetty that were met by more headlights and the sounds of engines as cars were dispatched to find Susan and bring her in.

And still, I didn't move.

It was Olivia who finally got me out of the water, leading me dumbly by the hand as I stumbled towards the lights. I have no idea how long I'd stood there. The ambulance had come, and the paramedics, but there were no heroic life-saving measures now, no cracking the chest or charging the defibrillators. They waited until they were able to take her body away, while the methodical jobs of police work happened around them, taping off the area, securing the crime scene and making sure nothing of forensic worth was lost – which, in the torrential rain was a thankless task.

I thought she was taking me back to our car, which was parked up across the way, but she wasn't about to let me drive in my state and I wasn't about to fight her. She promised me someone would bring the car as soon as they were done with it. I just nodded. It didn't matter.

As Olivia prised Poppy out of my arms and steered her with so much tenderness it hurt into the warmth of her car, she turned to me and said, 'I'm going to pretend I didn't hear that gunshot, Alex. And I most certainly didn't see you throw anything away.' Her words were pitched so softly only I could hear them, but even then, she wasn't taking any chances. She closed the car door. 'You've ignored pretty much every single piece of advice I've tried to give you thus far; I'm begging you to listen to me now, okay?' I nodded, more from shock than agreement. 'I don't want to know where you got a gun. You aren't going to mention it if Mason—' that was his name, Malcolm Mason. Christ, how could I have forgotten? It had only been a few days since he'd walked through the door with Nora and turned my life upside down. '—even if he says he heard something, you didn't, okay? There was no gun. I don't want to hear a word about trying to kill David Dodds, not now, not at the station when you're giving your statement. That's not what you were doing here, even if it was, alright? I need you to tell me you understand, Alex,' I nodded. 'I want to hear the words; I want to hear you say it. Tell me that you understand.'

'I understand,' I said, a million miles from here and struggling to focus on her words.

'I'm trusting you, Alex. Because if you do say something, if they find the gun, that gives Dodds a chance. It doesn't help anyone if we have to explain the gun away. Not you, not your little girl in there, and not Morven.'

I looked at her then, not seeing the uniform or any of that, just seeing the young woman beneath, who understood, who empathised, and knew there was a family hurting and trying to make sure we didn't hurt any more than we had to as the nightmare refused to end.

I nodded again.

Olivia opened the car door and put her hand on top of my head as she steered me into the seat beside Poppy.

Poppy cuddled in close to me.

She hadn't said a word since I'd found her in the water.

Olivia drove us away from there.

I didn't look back.

I couldn't.

FORTY-SIX

I see her ghost everywhere now.

It's in the reminders of a life lived together. Stupid stuff like the first time I walked into the bathroom and saw her expensive shampoos and conditioners, hair treatments and other stuff lined on the shower shelves, crowding out my one all-in-one bottle of shower gel. Then there was the thirty different skin creams and all the other things that filled the cabinet. All of the bottles and tubes that would never be emptied.

The worst of it, that first night, was her electric toothbrush in the little porcelain holder beside mine.

I never imagined a toothbrush would make me cry.

She was in every room in the house, and not just in the clothes still piled up in the washing basket or the food stacked up in the fridge. Everything was a choice we'd shared, from the cups we drank our coffees and teas from and the plates we ate off, to the cutlery we'd deliberated over for weeks trying to find something not too heavy, not too light, a real Goldilocks of the knife and fork world. Couch cushions – because let's be honest, before she came into my life I didn't have a clue about cushions, candles or light-fittings. So, every single one of them, wherever I turned, carried her spirit with them.

And on and on it went.

These little things haunted me now. Every time I walked through our house. I knew I couldn't bring myself to throw them away, but there would come a time when I would have to, or I wouldn't be living in a house anymore, I'd be like Susan Hall living in her mausoleum. It was the same with the thirty days of footage Dodds had stolen from our lives. Olivia had offered to give the files to me, and it was tempting, believe me it was tempting . . . the chance to relive those days, even as a voyeur, watching our happiness . . . the chance to more than remember that last time we'd made love . . . it was dangerously seductive, but I'd seen what it had done to the old woman, and I wasn't about to let that happen to me.

It wasn't just inside the house, either.

She was everywhere I went. The streets I walked down, that we'd walked down together. The school run, Maggs' little Jamaican cafe, the shops where she'd window-shopped regularly, and so many other places. I'd walk along, thinking I'd caught a glimpse of her out of the corner of my eye, but she'd never be there when I turned. But I didn't mind.

She was in the music, too. All the songs that we'd loved, or that I'd loved and she'd hated, or she'd loved and I thought were god-awful. She was in all the songs that had defined our lives together. I couldn't listen to them anymore, and for someone who had marked out every happening in their life by music that was hard, but listening to them would have been harder.

She was everywhere.

And she was nowhere.

That was the hardest part.

The carrying on.

It was in Poppy too. In the little things she did that subconsciously mimicked her mum. They were echoes of Morven and they were so hard to see. I'd bite my lip and Poppy would ask what was wrong and the best I could manage was a shrug and she'd say, 'I know.'

But I had Poppy to keep me grounded. She still needed all of the same necessities she'd needed last month and last year,

284

and that meant providing food, getting her to school, and somehow giving her something approaching a normal life. It was very much me and her against the world now. Sometimes I'd catch a glimpse of myself and find myself thinking God help the first boyfriend who comes knocking, then I'd smile and imagine Morven telling me not to be such a miserable git and let our little Popsicle grow up and the smile would hover for a few seconds longer as I thought about crying. Sometimes I would, other times it was enough to just remember. If I ever really needed to remember though, all I had to do was buy a packet of Fruit Pastilles.

There was one place I'd been putting off going back to until I was ready, and that was a small hole-in-the-wall bagel place down by the river.

With an appointment later, I'd decided today was the day.

I had my phone in my pocket. Not that it rang much these days. I carried it more out of habit; Mac was the only person who I talked with on any sort of regular basis. He was checking up on me, not that he could fix me. I was beyond fixing right now. I've lost everyone I've ever loved, with the exception of two people, and the thought of losing either one of them would prove beyond all reasonable doubt that Hell was a place on Earth and we were living in it every single day.

Mum was okay. Dodds had given her a scare. He'd hit her. She was an old woman. She'd fallen, screaming for help. But he was gone before anyone moved. And that was an indictment of London, too. An old woman getting beaten as she walked along the side of a road, and no one came to her rescue until it was too late and her attacker was gone. She'd had a black eye for a week, but the real bruising was to her confidence. No broken bones. She hardly left the house anymore. That would change, given time. I'd asked Poppy what she wanted to do this weekend and she'd already told me she wanted to take nan to the museum to see the mummies. For just a second there when she'd said it, I thought she'd said mummy.

It would be a long time before the traumas of the lake left her. Mum regularly said stuff like kids are resilient, trying to be helpful, and reminding me how I'd coped with losing my brother, but I'd been older and this was different. This was my little girl, and it was her mum. She was hurting and I couldn't help her.

But I wouldn't stop trying, because that's what dads do. It wouldn't matter if it took years of grief counselling and therapy, I'd hold her hand every step of the way, and let's be honest, she'd hold mine too, because neither of us were picking ourselves up, dusting ourselves off, and carrying on as if nothing had happened. I was just grateful I had Poppy and she had me.

After a couple of minutes in the street contemplating my reflection in the window, I went into the bagel place, ordered myself a hickory smoked chicken, and a second salmon one I had no intention of eating. I just wanted it on the other side of the table while I ate mine. I took up a seat by the window. I was nervous. Everything about this afternoon needed to go well. But the more I built it up in my head the more likely I was to fuck it up.

I put my phone on the table.

When they'd brought the car back, I'd found it on the seat. It had been plugged into the dashboard charger. There was a missed call. I hadn't recognised the number immediately, but I worked it out. It was Susan Hall's phone. In the hours after I'd found her in the herder's cottage when she'd been driving to face David Dodds and get our daughter back, Morven had called from the phone on the seat beside her and left me a message.

I hadn't been able to listen to it.

The thing is, these things don't last forever.

Thirty days.

Meaning it was today or never, and I couldn't imagine never hearing her voice again, so I'd come back here, to the one place I hadn't been able to return to, to share a bagel with her and listen to her final message.

I unwrapped the salmon bagel.

The poppy seeds on the top of a bagel just like this had given us more pleasure than a mouthful of bread ought to. I knew I was crying thinking about it. But these were happy tears. I was remembering when we'd first come here, trying for the life of us to work out what we were going to call the little girl growing in her womb, when Morven had got a poppy seed stuck between her tooth and gum and in that one bite we knew exactly what we were going to name our little girl.

I unwrapped my own bagel, but rather than eat it, I picked up the phone.

The bagel went cold while I stared at the screen, trying to bring myself to press that button to dial in to my messages.

I'll be honest with you, I thought about not listening to it because I knew how much it would hurt, but in the end I put the phone to my ear and listened to the past.

'*Hello you,*' she said in my ear, and I almost died. It was so good to hear those two words, '*I haven't got much to say. I just wanted to tell you that whatever happens I've loved our life together. You've made me happy every single day. Happier than I ever dared believe I deserved. I'm going to get our little Popsicle back. He's not going to win, Alex. Me for her. That's what he wants. My life for hers, back at the lake. He's going to drown me like I drowned them . . . that's what he says . . . it's that or he drowns Poppy so we understand the pain they all felt . . . I'm not going to let him hurt her, Alex. I know what that means for me. I can't see another way out of this . . . I accept it . . . I've had a happier life than I ever had any right to . . . you did that for me . . . You and our Poppy . . . Promise me something . . . promise me you won't let her forget me, Alex.*'

'I promise,' I said, tears streaming down my face.

I didn't care if people were looking at me.

'Okay, I thought I was done . . . but I'm not . . .' she laughed then, and it was the most glorious sound in the whole world and all I could think was I was never going to hear it again and it killed me. '*I need you to promise me something else . . . I need you to promise me you'll live . . . and not just live, Alex . . . live brilliantly. I love you.*'

And then she was gone.

FORTY-SEVEN

I was back in the same glass-walled office I'd been in a year ago, listening to the same people across the table tell me that I'd wasted months of my life on an idea that they just didn't love, for whatever reason. It didn't really matter what the reasons were, hell, they'd change with the weather. Sometimes an idea just didn't hit.

I was terrified they were going to say no.

This wasn't just an idea.

I'd invested everything I had in it emotionally. But more than anything it was a connection to Morven. If the three people in this room said yes then she'd be a huge part of my life for the next year, through the writing and the filming of her story.

'Thanks for coming in, Alex.'

I smiled. I knew my eyes were still red. No one asked, so I didn't tell.

'We're eager to hear what you've got. Why don't you talk us through it?'

'Children who kill,' I said, and could see the lights flickering out behind their eyes even as I said it. I didn't let it put me off my stride. I'd practiced this a hundred times. It was a killer pitch. Literally and figuratively. 'I'm not going to pretend you guys don't read the papers or watch the news, you know my life, you know what happened to my wife. I want to tell her story. She never denied she did what she did, but we're not talking some monster here, she killed two kids to protect the real monsters,' and slowly, bit by bit, I walked them through Morven's life after she stopped being Lucy, all the way through to the message I'd just listened to, with her choosing willingly to sacrifice herself to save our daughter. It was the end my pitch had needed and hadn't had. A parting gift.

The room was utterly silent through the entire thing.

No questions.

I had them in the palm of my hand.

'There are a thousand articles about Lucy Galvin painting her as our generation's Mary Bell, but every single one of them is fundamentally wrong. I want to tell her story. I want everyone to know her truth, because it's so much more than just a thirteen-year-old girl drowning two school friends.'

I looked from face to face, waiting for someone to say something.

'It feels like it should be a movie,' the only woman in the room said. 'And I don't mean that in a bad way . . . I'm just not sure a documentary is the best way to tell this.'

'Oh, I'm not sure, Andrea, there's real power to the truth,' the man to her left said. 'And Alex is right, this is far more than just another five-minute segment about kids doing horrible things we can't or don't want to imagine.' He was nodding along, convincing himself this was the right thing to do.

'I want to ask you a question, Alex,' the third man said.

I nodded. 'I'll answer it if I can.'

'That's the best we can ask for at this stage. Okay, think carefully before you say yes or no, because once we commit this becomes your life for the foreseeable. Are you sure you can handle this? I saw the stories on the news last month. It's got to be so raw . . . most people in your place would be a wreck. But to willingly throw yourself into something that is going to mean you're re-treading every single step of her way, from the killings by the lake to her dying in the lake in the place of her daughter, that's going to be *hard*.'

'I can handle it,' I assured him.

'Then I don't know what else needs to be said.' He looked around the table. There were nods. 'You want to add anything? Andrea? Mike?' That one was greeted by the slightest shake of the heads and followed by the sound of chairs being pushed back as he rose and the other two stood half a second behind him.

He held out a hand.

'Then let's make this happen.'

Acknowledgements

There's no getting away from the fact that we are the sum of our parts. For that reason, when I went in search of where this harrowing school trip had taken place, I found myself going back to a week in the very early 80s, where, as a new kid at Stamford Green Primary School – and the only one with an 'accent' because I'd come down from The North – I'd finally felt like I belonged. Along with Miss Bennett, Mr Mendes, and Mr Rees, we'd ventured into the wilds of Wales, doing the Brecon Beacons (where I'd nearly been knocked off my feet by a jet fighter barrelling down a valley . . . my perch meant I was higher than the fighter plane – it's the kind of memory seared in now, never to go away), the Wye Valley, Ross, Chepstow, and of course, St Brievels, where we stayed in the old Keep.

I'm not one of those people who remembers loads about their childhood. There are snatches, sure, but most of it is a big vague blank of *yeah, we played football and messed about, made a nuisance of ourselves,* and is otherwise nebulous. But this trip I remember, and the kids on it with me. A couple of them, over forty years on, are still friends now. A couple are no longer with us, both lost to suicide. When I look at those grainy old photos, though, everyone is still very much alive and always will be inside my head.

This book is for them, like I said at the beginning.

And it's for Miss Bennett, Mr Mendes and Mr Rees.

They shaped me in ways they could never have expected. Miss Bennett had faith that this scrawny kid from Up North would be

293

a perfect lead in her production of *A Christmas Carol*. Mr Mendes read *Elidor* and *The Hobbit* to us, last lesson, every day. Mr Rees encouraged me to draw and write – even if one of those stories ended up having the school call my parents in, suggesting grief counseling because I obviously wasn't coping with their divorce.

It's for Elaine and Ella, who both survived that trip and are still in my life today.

But that was then, so much of *I Know Who You Were* is down to today, and was written in the wake of a professional 'break-up' that saw me unagented for the first time in over thirty years, before – thanks to Samantha Lee Howe – I found Camilla Shestopal, and a new home at The Shesto Agency. I owe both of these ladies buckets and buckets of love and thanks. This book wouldn't be in your hands without them. When you find good people, you cherish them. Simple as that.

Then there's my editor, Krystyna Green, with deep appreciation for the risk she's taken in me and my stories, and the wry smile that knowing her son went to my old school brings with it. Plus she shares the cutest dog pictures, even if he's a terror, and puts up with hearing about Buster's adventures in return. I can't emphasize enough, how after years bouncing around the industry, it feels so good to have found a home where people just 'get' me.

And those people include copy-editor Karyn Burnham and proofreader Rebecca Lee, who went above and beyond to make me look better than I am, and Amanda Keats, who caught one telling detail that I'd managed to miss a thousand times, and was there to make sure every single line was exactly as we wanted it to be, right to the very end. Grateful thanks go to Sean Garrehy who designed everything about what you're holding in your hands right now. Then there's Jess Gulliver who has done everything humanly possible to make sure you heard about this book, and convinced you that you just had to pick it up and take it home with you. And, if you're lucky enough to be reading this in anything other than

English, well, then, that's down to the brilliant rights team at Little, Brown who worked tirelessly to make it possible for that to happen.

Nothing can survive in a vacuum.

It takes a village.

Me? I'm a vacuum-breathing villager, and I love it.

Seriously.

Thank you.